THE ACADEMY

THE ACADEMY

KATIE SISE

BALZER + BRAY
An Imprint of HarperCollins*Publishers*

ISBN 978-0-06-240414-5

Typography by Aurora Parlagreco
18 19 20 21 22   XXXXXX   10 9 8 7 6 5 4 3 2 1
❖
First Edition

*For my family members who bravely served in the United
States military, including my grandfathers, Robert Sise
and Raymond Ebert, my uncles Michael, Bob,
and Bernie Sise, and my cousins Bob and Alex Sise—
you make me proud every day.*

*For the brave hearts in my life,
especially Meghan, Brian, Luke, and William*

ONE

I'M READING *VOGUE* ONE NIGHT in my bedroom when there's a knock on the door, four hard ones in rapid succession: the code knock that means *Emergency!OpenThisDoorRightNow!*

I shut my magazine. It was upsetting me, anyway. I can't get on board with this whole new trend of wearing athletic sneakers with dresses, and I'm speaking not only as a fashion person but as a human. The *Vogue* editors almost never lead me astray, but right there in a glossy spread was a bazillion-dollar Givenchy tee and skirt paired with Nike Jordan high-tops. Who wants to look like a tourist? Or a mom?

I can't even.

I open the door to see my little sister, Ella. She's super lovable, and almost five years younger than me, so there's no weird competition between us, and only the rare fight.

"They *know*," she says.

Know what?

I'm keeping three (and a half) huge secrets, and if my parents find out any of them, I'm totally dead.

Secret Number One: I threw a parent-free rustic-glam mega party on New Year's Eve in our barn while my mom, dad, and little sister were visiting our relatives in Vail.

Most of my intentions were so pure: Help my high school ring in the new year! Inspire style and optimism among my peers! But my parents are vehemently against parentless parties. And though I didn't technically serve any alcohol, people totally brought booze in water bottles. (Celiac Gary Rapazzo brought gluten-free vodka in a squirt gun.) And that is *très* against my parents' rules.

Secret Number One Point Five: At said party, I kissed the love of my life, Josh Archester, while his girlfriend (not me!) was ten yards away drinking Diet Coke.

Kissing him was totally wrong, I know that, but I've been in love with Josh ever since he transferred into our school as a freshman last year. He made everybody laugh and feel good, and nothing ever seemed to make him nervous. I couldn't stop trying to catch his glance at school, but I'd always break away as soon as he looked back, knowing my cheeks were flushed and giving me away.

Two months ago Josh started dating Lia Powers—the

most vile girl in my entire school! Lia's as beautiful as she is cruel, so beautiful that it doesn't seem to bother anyone that she frequently wears denim jackets with corduroys. (Denim on top is meant to evoke a mood, not a lifestyle.) But beauty outweighs style and kindness for too many teenagers—maybe even for adults. Not for me. Style + kindness is beauty. But of course no one gets that here, which is why I committed Secreto Número Dos.

Secret Number Two: I applied to the American Fashion Academy in New York City, even though my parents explicitly told me not to.

AFA is like a prep school for fashionistas. It's basically my dream. I could finish all the credits I'd need for a regular dull high school diploma, but with hours of extra classes for fashion writing, design, and history—all the stuff I really care about. Plus there'd be tons of potential fashion mentors who could help me achieve my goals:

★ Become a great fashion blogger while still in my teens!
★ Parlay that into a fashion assistant job in my early twenties!
★ Emerge as a notable fashion editor by my midtwenties!
★ Be a fashion director at a major magazine by age thirty!

My AFA application included fashion essays and clips from my style blog, *FreshFrankie* (thirty thousand unique page views per month, thank you very much). Unfortunately the application also included my transcript, and my grades have been super crappy this year.

Still. AFA is looking for talent, a discerning eye, and discipline. I have those things in spades, I really do. And the thing is, I keep messing up here in Mount Pleasant— my teachers have been calling my parents and complaining that I'm *distractible* and *prone to daydreaming*. But maybe I wouldn't be so distracted by fashion magazines and blogs if I actually studied fashion at school.

My parents don't even know the worst of everything I've done, and trust me, they would kill me if they found out my final secret (*Secret Number Three: I don't even want to talk about it!*), because they've told me again and again that I'm on thin ice and last straws and all that. The end for me is so totally near—I can feel it in my bones—and now I'm staring at my little sister standing in my doorway and wondering just how bad my current parent-child situation is.

"*Frankie*," my little sister says, "Mom and Dad know you applied to AFA."

I gasp. My parents know about secret number two! My heart skips at least four beats—almost enough to kill me.

"My AFA letter came?" I blurt, my mind racing. *Please, God of Fashion and All Things Right: let me be accepted! And please, God of Parents: let them allow me to go!*

I fly past Ella and tear down our steep, creaking stairs.

We live in an old farmhouse in Westchester County just outside of New York City. Everything in it creaks, but sort of on purpose, like for the sake of charm. We live what my parents call *the high life*, and it *is* beautiful here with the stone walls and rolling acres of green grass—even if the ducks in our pond are *so mean*. Don't even try to give them bread unless it's organic, or you like being bitten by mean ducks. But just because I get to spend my formative childhood years in the idyllic countryside doesn't mean I can't make different plans for my future (fashion academy! New York City!).

Pardon me while I repeat what my personal hero, Diana Vreeland, said about that:

There's only one very good life and that's the life you know you want and you make it yourself!

D.V. believed you could make your life as incredible as your wildest dreams. I really think she's right. I could make my life all about fashion and New York City starting *now*—no matter what my parents want.

I'm reminding myself of all of this when I get to the kitchen with Ella hot on my high heels. She nearly crashes into me when I stop dead in front of my father. He's standing in the middle of the kitchen, his eyes roving over the letter. The logo looks a little different from what I remember—almost like a gross green and brown combination rather than the pop of magenta I could've sworn I saw on their website.

My mother looks from my father to me. It's her turn to make dinner, so she's chopping tomatoes we grew in our garden. It's très *Little House on the Prairie* for wealthy people out here. We don't even own a microwave!

I know I've got to make my case to them now; they have to know how important going to AFA is for me. "I need a change; I need to be better," I start, trying to imagine what Tavi Gevinson and my other fashion role models would say to their parents. "My creativity is getting stilted here: the purple flowers; the white churches; the grain-free granola bars."

My parents are staring at me like they have no idea what I'm talking about, per usual. I shut my eyes so I don't roll them. Originality is everything, so eye rolling is out until I turn thirty.

"An elite fashion program in an urban setting will broaden my horizons," I say, as steadily as I can. I'm nervous about leaving them to go to AFA, but this is how it has to be. "And it will teach me discipline, which you always say I need. And I already checked with school; my credits can count for the rest of sophomore year and I can transfer back any time you guys want."

My mom pops a raw green bean into her mouth. A wisp of her dirty-blonde hair falls from her ponytail. Ella and I have my dad's dark blue eyes, but we're white-blonde just like my mom was when she was younger. My hair is cut into a super-chic lob right now. (Lob = long bob. Google it.) I *was* working a temporary gold stain at the ends, but my parents made me wash it out for our Christmas pictures. Which made no sense, because the gold was so festive.

"Sweetie, what are you talking about?" my mom asks.

She slow-motion chews her green bean like an ad for mindfulness. She's so Zen sometimes it's infuriating—it's all the yoga she does, and probably the probiotic smoothies, too. My dad's scratching his bald head, and he's definitely not smiling.

"I got into American Fashion Academy," I say. I try to get a closer look at the brochure my dad's holding. "Isn't that what we're talking about?" My parents glance at each other, exchanging a look that never means anything good. My dad passes the paperwork he's holding into my hand, and I realize the AFA logo I thought I saw actually reads *AMA*. This isn't an acceptance letter for American Fashion Academy, it's enrollment information for Albany Military Academy.

"Wait, *what*? Grandpa Frank's old school?" I ask, my eyes darting from my mom to my dad. Grandpa Francis is who I'm named after, and Albany Military Academy is the elite military high school he went to eight thousand years ago. The Academy is the whole reason my family lives in New York State. Grandpa Frank was raised on a farm in Nebraska but moved across the country to Albany to attend the Academy, and then went on to West Point, and then went on to be some VIP military person I never met because he dropped dead of a heart attack the day after my parents' wedding. They had to cancel their honeymoon and everything.

"Sweetheart," my dad says, "we've enrolled you in Albany Military Academy for this semester. You leave Monday."

White-hot panic surges through me. "What?!" I yelp. Monday is in two days, and I wasn't planning on going anywhere except maybe to the Jonathan Adler store because they're having a sale on lacquered tissue box covers. "You can't be serious," I say.

"We're lucky enough that the Academy has waived the interview process and allowed you to transfer in midyear, all because of Grandpa Frank's legacy," my mom says.

"Lucky?" I repeat. "Is this some kind of sick joke? Like how you used to make us wear matching outfits?"

I turn to my sister, like maybe she can save me, but she's staring at her skinny feet. I look back to my parents. This has to be a fake-out. Like an act to make me realize how serious they are. My mother takes a breath, and I see it in her eyes—her Zen exterior is about to crack. She's about to cry and take it all back.

"We know about the party you threw," she says instead. "Without parents, and with alcohol, Frankie."

My father makes a grunting noise that sounds like an irritated pig. "You begged us to stay home, and we let you because we made the mistake of trusting you! Do you have any idea what could have happened here with that many kids drinking? You could have ruined your life! Not to mention ours!" He's a softy, my father. But not right now.

My grip tightens on the Albany Military Academy paperwork. This is all starting to feel like an after-school TV special about wayward teens. But my parents can't seriously be sending me to military school. They don't even like weapons.

8

My dad clears his throat, and that's the moment I realize he found out *Secret Number Three*, the worst one, the one I would take back if I could. If there's one thing my parents want me to be, it's a good person, and trust me, I wasn't that when I did this.

"Dr. Benson called," he says.

I swallow.

"He's accusing you of cheating on a test," my father says. He pauses a beat and my heart cracks open. "Did you do it, Frankie?"

It was so, so stupid and wrong, and it made me feel sick, like a faker and a liar, two things I really, *really* don't want to be. Things just got out of control so fast. One minute I was on top of my AP Chem homework and the next minute I was blogging about the Row's fall line, and the minute after that I was so far behind, it was like I missed some vital chemical concept and couldn't understand anything that followed. And all of the after-school help periods fell right during the live-streaming of New York Fashion Week, so of course I couldn't go. Then one thing led to another and Mark Hadwell's test was right there on his desk. He even slid it over closer to me and gave me this sly smile like he knew I'd cheat. And I did.

I nod, my tears coming faster, and then I make myself say the words. "I did it, I cheated in chem." I sink even lower when I hear my sister's sharp intake of breath. "I swear to God I won't ever do it again, because I know it's wrong, and please, please don't send me away!"

Tears spill over my lashes. I watch my parents' faces go

slack, almost like they're more sad than mad. I've told them so many lies this year, and maybe I deserve all of this, but it still feels terrible that they want me gone.

"This isn't a punishment," my mother says, and that's when I realize she's crying, too, and then she cries a little harder and can't finish what she's trying to tell me.

"You have big dreams," my dad says, "and you're whip smart: you got into the AP classes in the first place. And I know you think you don't need good grades because you want to work in fashion, but the truth is, your grades open doors for your future whether that's in fashion or somewhere else, and we aren't going to let you throw that away. The Academy isn't a reform school; it's a top-notch military academy. It's a chance to start over and learn the discipline you'll need to accomplish all the things you want to do with your life."

"But I could learn that at AFA, I could—"

My dad turns and grabs a manila envelope I didn't notice was sitting next to the cutting board. "You got in to your fashion school," he says, and my heart starts beating so fast I can hardly speak.

"I did?" I manage. If he's trying to break my heart twice, it's working.

"I'm sorry to disappoint you," he says, "but you're not going. You're going to the military academy." He shakes his head back and forth like a Ping-Pong ball. "And that's final."

TWO

THE NEXT MORNING, SUNLIGHT SPLASHES across the Albany Military Academy brochure on my bed. Uniformed students stare up at me with big smiles on their faces. I swallow back tears. Who could be happy wearing the same thing as everybody else?

My parents are dropping me off tomorrow. My eyes are bleary as I pack my suitcase because I cried and begged for hours last night while Ella comfort-ate caramels. It just doesn't seem real. My parents aren't perfect, but as far as parents go, I usually feel like I won the lottery. (Though I don't plan on telling them that until I'm at least thirty-five and caring for my first child, whom I already know will be a blonde little girl named Gwyneth.)

I thought my parents would protest when I asked to go away to New York City for fashion school; I thought they

11

wouldn't want me gone. I *never* thought they'd send me away.

I unzip the waterproof section of my suitcase and slip in nail polish remover and my favorite antiaging eye cream (not-so-secret ingredient: caviar). My phone is going nuts with texts. Everyone already knows I'm being sent away to military school tomorrow, partly because I blogged about it, but also because my high school is a grapevine, especially when it comes to scandal or bad news. And I'm pretty sure this is both.

One of Lia Powers's awful friends wrote on my Instagram announcement: *Good luck with that, Frankie!* So I posted a photo of myself wearing a black silk jumpsuit with military-inspired aviator sunglasses, and captioned it: *Proud to be an American.* Because even mean girls don't have comebacks for patriotism. It's like this big, mighty thing we all feel even if we can't totally describe it right, like peace and faith.

My suitcase is overflowing with fashion. Dance clothes are very in right now—just ask Alexander Wang—so I'm working on a few outfits that incorporate leotards. I've already stuffed four cashmere scarves into my suitcase and a cutout dress for my evening option. I'd really like to bring my delicate rose-gold peace sign necklace because it's so wartime chic. But will anyone at Albany Military Academy appreciate that I'm a pacifist?

Unlikely.

Plus, my brochure says uniforms are mandatory during physical training, meals, and classes—basically all day every day except weekends—which brings up another big problem: *physical training?* That just doesn't sound like something I do. How am I supposed to leave home, where I'm already messing up, and head somewhere even tougher?

I zip my suitcase and make my way downstairs. It's eerily balmy outside for January. Probably global warming. My boots scuff the gravel as I head toward the pond. The ducks glare at me and swim in the other direction.

I sit on a soft patch of grass. My best friends, Andrea and Julia, scheduled our special good-bye for this morning, and I wait to see Andrea's car for what feels like forever. (Andrea and Julia turned sixteen in the fall, but Julia refuses to practice driving now that it's officially winter, because even when it isn't snowing, it could always start. Andrea, on the other hand, drives everywhere with her older sister, Dani, in the car to supervise, because Dani goes to community college locally and her parents make her. Dani is extremely mean and also, she hates us.) When they finally pull into our long, winding driveway, Andrea and Julia stare at me through the windshield with concerned-therapist looks on their faces. Dani glares from the back seat. Andrea gets out of the car first, and Julia follows, clutching her phone. Dani yells, "Ten minutes max!" before Andrea slams the car door.

"Are your parents here?" Julia asks, gesturing toward the house. Her black leggings are tucked into Uggs, and her hunter-green vest is zipped over a cream-colored henley. She always looks pristine even when she's dressed down.

"They went to church. They let me stay home so I could

have some space," I say in the placating tone my mom and dad used when they rushed off with a still-devastated Ella.

Andrea sits next to me on a flat rock near the pond. Julia is afraid of lots of things, including ducks and moss, so she just stands there looking at us.

"They're serious this time, Frankie," Andrea says. She doesn't say it like a question; she says it like she knows it's the truth. Andrea, Julia, and I have been best friends since second grade. They know my parents almost as well as I do.

"They really are," I say. My parents have threatened me with lots of things this past year, taking away things I love, like *Nylon* magazine, and adding things I don't love, like father-daughter Pilates. They also tried to make me rejoin the school band and play my horrible clarinet because they thought I needed more extracurriculars, which I flat-out refused to do. It's one thing to be a first chair violinist and wear long flowing skirts and rock your solos, but it's another thing to play clarinet in the third row and suck. It's just not inspired.

"They think I'm ruining my life," I say, brushing my fingers across the brownish-green grass. (Obviously my parents don't believe in fertilizer.) "They told me I won't get into college based only on the merits of my blog."

I can't bring myself to tell Julia and Andrea the other reasons my parents are sending me to Albany Military Academy, and I can't admit I kissed Josh. They know about my feelings for him, of course, but Andrea would think kissing a guy with a girlfriend was terrible, because she was just the girlfriend in that scenario last year. Julia would

14

think cheating on the test was even worse. They're my best friends in the world, but I don't want to disappoint them.

"You know your blog is killer, right?" Julia says.

"Yesterday's post on how to wear red with pink was sensational," Andrea says, dark eyes blinking.

"*Lean into it with bold shades, darling! Only wallflowers tiptoe,*" Julia quotes from my post. She's a stone-cold genius with a photographic memory. She's planning on becoming a neuroscientist and studying the way the brain processes fear on an electrical level.

We're all quiet for a minute, and then Julia says, "*Military school.*"

I know how bad it sounds.

"Can we visit you?" Andrea asks.

"It's only two hours north," Julia says.

I shake my head. "Their site says only approved family members can get on campus, and only one weekend day per month. Plus I'm in classes till, like, five o'clock every day, and the classes have names like *Military Strategy* and *Corps Leadership*, which obviously I don't belong in, because . . ."

My voice trails off. I feel itchy all over. This is *not* good. I have what is potentially a huge problem with authority and rules, and the last thing I need is to be stuffed inside a military uniform, forced to do stuff against my will.

"I'll have internet at least," I say, trying to coax away the lump in my throat, "and phones are allowed, just not video games. It's not like reform school or anything." I'm trying to sound positive. "Just military academy."

15

Andrea looks dubious.

"Maybe there will be cute boys there," Julia says. She tries very hard to remain undistracted from school and grades, but she secretly loves cute boys more than anyone I know, even me. Andrea has had seven and a half boyfriends (one guy transferred schools without telling her, so we only barely count him), but Julia and I have both had only one boyfriend each, which means we spend more time fantasizing about the idea of boys than actually living the romantic high life.

"I guess I still can't believe it," I say, and I'm about to cry a little when I hear a scuffle on our driveway and glance up to see a blur of bike and boy. My breath catches.

No way. It can't be him. It just cannot.

"What the—" Andrea says.

It's totally freaking him. Josh Archester bikes closer and stops short, about twenty-five yards away from us. He's gets off his bike, puts his helmet on the handlebars, and takes his beat-up Mets baseball cap out of his jacket pocket and puts it on.

My pulse goes nuts. What is he doing here?

Julia says, "Frankie?" and Andrea takes a big gulp of air.

Josh is staring at me, but it's like his feet are rooted to the driveway. Is he going to walk over to us? Are we supposed to go to him?

He's standing a little bowlegged like a cowboy, and he's not far from the woodpile behind the barn, where everything happened at the party. Does he see it? Does it remind him of what we did? Does it make him feel *like this*?

It can't. Because there's no way he'd be able to stay so cool.

When Josh starts walking toward us, I turn to catch Julia and Andrea staring, wide-eyed. The three of us aren't huge losers or anything, but we're not exactly super popular, either. On a scale of denim overalls to black-tie evening gowns, we're knee-length cocktail dresses. Sometimes, we do enviable, almost-popular things, like win tennis matches (Andrea), or get perfect scores on our PSATs (Julia), or throw super-glamorous parties on New Year's (me). But mostly we do quirky, semiawkward things, which I'm totally fine with because everyone knows it's those kinds of people who eventually lead inspired grown-up lives. I'm just saying that it's highly unusual for a demigod like Josh to be standing on one of our driveways in stark daylight.

A stab of vulnerability hits my stomach as I watch him come closer. Someone needs to say something, but no one does. Julia looks at me and mouths, *What is he doing here?!* Andrea makes a funny gurgling noise, but then she pulls it together when he arrives at our little spot near the pond. "Hi, Josh," she says, almost confidently. Competitive tennis has done wonders for her composure. She climbs to her feet and stands next to Julia, and then I stand, too.

Josh's dark hair flicks out in little wings beneath his hat, and his green eyes are bright. His nose is big, but in a manly way. And he has this great scar on his jawline, which Andrea told me she heard was because he had a mole removed, but which I also heard was from a shark bite he got surfing off the coast of Mexico. I choose to believe the

17

shark attack rumor because of course it's so much sexier than a dermatological procedure.

I try not to stare at him. What's he going to say? What am I going to say?

Am I imagining all this?

"I have practice," Andrea says suddenly, and of course I know she's trying to give me space with Josh, and normally I *would* want to be alone with him, but now I'm just so nervous!

"Tennis?" Josh says, which is like the stupidest comment anyone has ever made, because everyone existing within a thirty-mile radius of Andrea Summerville knows that she's the best tennis player in Westchester County.

"Yeah, tennis," Andrea says, and Julia rolls her eyes because she has no time for stupidity, even from a demigod.

Don't leave me! I beg them with my eyes.

"How about we pick you up that coffee you wanted and then we'll be back here in like a half-hour? 'Kay?" Andrea asks. "It'll be better if we're caffeinated when we do our good-bye, anyway. We might cry less."

"Um, okay, *almond milk*, please," I say, not daring to look at Josh. Julia and Andrea pile into Andrea's car. They stare at me through the windshield and wave excitedly as they drive off, like something super special might be happening. Dani is still glaring at me like it's my fault her parents prefer Andrea.

When they're past the gate at the end of my driveway I turn to Josh. And all I can think is:

Now what?!

Josh Archester has driven to my house, on the day before I leave for military academy. Does he want to say good-bye? Did he break up with Lia?

I exhale. It comes out like a big puff, way louder than I meant it to. Josh says, "Hi, Frances."

Almost no one calls me Frances, except for my grandma Lillian, who wears satin robes and dark red lipstick to bed.

"Hello, Joshua," I say back, making my voice formal, and he smiles a little. I love his smile. It strikes me that I don't really see it that often at school, maybe because he's usually the one getting everyone else to laugh. I wonder if he's secretly sad. Or maybe I'm just being dramatic. I don't know him like I want to.

Josh comes closer and I breathe in cologne that smells like the mall. My eyes go to his mouth, and all I can think about is our kiss, and how much I want him to kiss me again.

"I came here to talk to you," he says, his voice gentle, "before you leave, I guess. I saw your posts and stuff." I can feel my pulse in my ears as he speaks. He leans so close I swear he's about to kiss me. I swear it's what I see on his face—that he wants to. But then his dark brows furrow and he looks sad again. "I shouldn't have done what I did at the party," he says.

My stomach tightens. *No.* Please don't be saying this to me.

He keeps going. "I shouldn't have kissed you. It was me, not you, and I shouldn't have done it."

Didn't you feel me kiss you back?

19

He's still so close to me. Why is he standing this close, saying these terrible things? I want to tell him to *go*, but I can't open my mouth, and then it gets worse, because he gestures in the direction that Julia and Andrea drove. "Do they know?" he asks.

Why can't I speak?

Josh's face is flushed. Probably because he's wearing a black North Face jacket that's as thick as a sleeping bag and it's fifty degrees outside. Or maybe because this is the most horrible, awkward moment anyone has ever lived.

"They don't know," I finally say. My throat has gone dry, and the words hardly make it out. I want him to stay and leave so badly I can barely keep myself from saying it.

"Good," he says, and I flush with embarrassment. It feels so terrible to hear him say it like that, like I'm some dope he doesn't want anyone to know he kissed.

Please, Josh.

He smiles at me, the kind of smile you have to force yourself to make. "I don't think we should tell anyone," he says. The look on his face tells me he hates himself for saying it, but that's not enough to make it better—not even close. This probably sounds so stupid, but I honestly thought he liked me a little—I even thought he might break up with Lia for me. And I know that's terrible—I know I'm not supposed to want to break up couples! But it felt so good that night we kissed, when I thought the guy that I'd liked for so long liked me back.

"But you said you think about me," I say, my voice

barely a whisper. "And you kissed me, and now I can't forget it."

My heart thuds. This is too dangerous. I can hardly breathe as he looks at me. He moves closer. Is there any way—is he going to kiss me again?

"I messed up," he says again, and it makes me feel so small, like I could melt into the cracks in our driveway.

"*We* messed up," I say. I need him to remember that I was there, that I was a part of this. I want to remind him that I was the girl he was kissing, and that it's not all about him.

"I'm with Lia," he says, and he steps back an inch that may as well be a mile.

"I know that!" I blurt, my cheeks hot. "So you're not going to break up or anything at all? You're not even going to tell her?"

"Um, no, I wasn't planning on it," he says.

What a jerk! And maybe I am, too, for doing this to Lia. And why is Josh just standing there, like this can be solved so neatly if I comply? "So let me get this straight," I say, my voice shaking a little. "My whole life falls apart, but you just cheat on your girlfriend and keep it a secret like no problem?"

Josh's eyes widen, like he's surprised I'm not just taking it and shutting up. He must not know me very well. My mother says I'm very mouthy.

"I want to be with Lia," Josh says. It's like a dagger, and I'm going to cry and I really don't want him to see it.

"Please just go," I say, staring down at my shaking hands. *"Please.* Leave." And I really mean it, I do, and I know he knows, because he doesn't even wait a beat to make sure I'm okay. He turns and walks away, and I'm left standing there, wanting to kick myself for getting my hopes so high thinking he actually liked me when he obviously doesn't, and thinking maybe I knew him—and I totally don't.

Tears start, and I try to fight them with everything I have. I watch as he rides away, wishing that anything— *everything*—were different.

THREE

MY PARENTS ARE TRYING TO act like this is all so completely normal.

"I'm sure the leaves will be gorgeous in the fall," my mom says as we speed along I-87 the next day. Sometimes she's so obvious.

"I won't be there for the fall semester," I remind them. "One semester at Albany Military Academy and then I'm back home, right?"

"*Right?*" Ella repeats from the seat next to me, her voice shrill.

"If you behave yourself and get good grades, Frankie," my dad says, "and if we *truly* feel as though you've learned discipline at the Academy, we'll consider having you return to Mount Pleasant High for your junior year."

I don't push back because of course I can behave and

get good grades if it's just for one semester. I mean, I think I can.

My dad fiddles with the AM radio stations for traffic reports, and my mom keeps trying to catch my glance in the mirror. When we do meet eyes, she smiles, but it's a nervous one.

We pull off at exit 23 for Albany. I've only been to the capital once, on a field trip in sixth grade to see performance art inside a sculpturelike building called the Egg. The performance art was only so-so (unless you like exaggerated displays of love and war via dance, which I don't), but what caught my attention on our drive through Albany was the picturesque park, the historic-looking brownstones that lined Lark Street, and the stoic capital building, where people were probably making important government decisions about things like school dress codes. (No one was happier than I was when they banned half-shirts at Mount Pleasant High School.)

We pass by the gleaming city and continue up a ramp that takes us beyond the city borders. Bucolic houses line the street for a few miles, followed by an explosion of minimalls featuring Verizon stores alongside day spas. There's a bookstore called Book House, a Whole Foods, a run-down pet mart, and an upscale-looking salon called Rumors. A gold dome arcs high above a beautiful college campus farther along Route 9, and houses line neighborhoods with evenly spaced yards much smaller than the two- and four-acre plots I'm used to. There are no ponds, no ducks, no moss; it's very pretty, but it's way more suburban than Mount Pleasant.

I chew my lower lip as we fly past a Dunkin' Donuts where teenagers are smoking in the parking lot, plus they're wearing leather jackets, and not in the way they style them in *Teen Vogue* over flowing floral skirts.

"She'll be okay, Marie," my dad whispers to my mom. "The students aren't even allowed off campus."

Ella clutches her bear. "Just like prison," she whispers.

"Military academy," my dad corrects her.

Every inch of me prickles. "If we turn back now, I will never ever do anything wrong again," I say, my palms sweating against my faux-leather leggings.

My dad turns down a skinny road marked Academy Way and drives toward a security gate. Behind a pane of plastic stands a security guard wearing army fatigues. Panic rises in my chest just like when I see army guys at the airports holding (real!) weapons.

"She's going to hate it here," Ella says to her bear.

The army guard stares at us. "Identification," she says, and my dad passes his license into the slat beneath her window. She compares his picture to his smiling face, and gives him a suspicious look, which for whatever reason unsettles me. How *military* is this all going to be? Am I going to have to worry about intruders breaking on to campus to steal government secrets? Will I be *learning* government secrets and/or how to fight in a war? Have my parents thought this through?!

Just then a tall, built guy rounds the corner of a brick building. His skin is smooth and olive, and his gaze is fixed on an oversized, vintage-looking book. The security guard is saying something to us, but I can't pay attention. This guy is *cute*, even in a bulky flannel shirt that makes him look like a woodcutter or a person who enjoys hiking. (Has anyone noticed that hiking is basically walking, but with ticks and less comfortable footwear?) He comes closer and I see that what he's reading isn't a book. It looks like newspapers tucked inside a folder. I watch as he disappears into a thick cover of trees.

"Um, we need to leave you here," my dad says.

I snap my head around to look at him. "What?"

He gives a nervous laugh. "Apparently we can't take you on campus, because we're not approved visitors, according to this nice woman." He gestures to the guard, who does not look like a nice woman at all. She stares at us as my dad unloads my suitcases. I feel numb with nerves—I'm seriously supposed to walk across campus with my heavy suitcases?

We all get out of the car. "Shouldn't there be some kind of concierge service for incoming students?" I ask the guard. I sound snotty even to myself. The guard glares at me, and I look away, embarrassed.

"Frankie, please," my mother says. I turn to see her crying, and then Ella bursts into tears, too.

"Mom," I say, my voice choked, and suddenly we're saying our good-byes at the curb. I throw my arms around my mom and Ella. Even my dad looks like he's on the verge of crying. He arranges my suitcases carefully on the sidewalk and joins our hug, kissing the top of my head. It doesn't matter how mad I am at them—the moment I watch them pile into their car and drive away from me breaks my heart. Why did they do this to me? Why did I do this to myself?

The guard is watching me sob and it pisses me right off. I glare at her, determined not to be scared just because she's wearing army fatigues and could definitely kill me in hand-to-hand combat. I swipe away my tears and glance down at the map my dad gave me. I grip my suitcases in each hand and set off down the skinny road.

The first thing I see as I near the campus is a sprawling field where students decked in serious-looking military uniforms are playing a game of Capture the Flag with wayyyyy too much enthusiasm. Nearly all the students appear to be athletic, like a bunch of Andreas running around. Worse, they look like they're actually enjoying themselves.

Here's the thing: I hate athletics and also, I suck at them. The extent of my normal physical exertion is slugging through the American Heart Association's recommended thirty minutes of daily cardio on my mother's elliptical machine, while wearing coordinating Lululemon workout clothing. (People who use exercise, yard work, and/or pregnancy as a means to dress sloppily need a reality check.) I do not participate in activities such as but not limited to:

field hockey
lacrosse
soccer
basketball.

Don't even get me started on basketball! The ball is too heavy; the net is too far away. How is that a good time?!

I watch as a tall blonde girl chases a hardy guy with flushed cheeks who looks like he eats red meat for every meal. I scan the players one by one, my anxiety rising with each moment. Where are the artistic and/or fashion-forward students? Classes this semester don't officially start until tomorrow according to the Academy's calendar, which apparently means today is uniform optional. Shouldn't at least some of the kids be expressing their inner fashionistas?

Posted to the chain-link fence surrounding the game is a handwritten sign—WAR GAMES PREP!—and what looks like a sign-up sheet with at least fifty names. Are all of these students playing this War Games thing voluntarily? Like for fun?

Ugh.

I turn onto a winding road that leads me past a few serious-looking brick buildings, and then the campus opens onto another quad about the size of three of Andrea's beloved tennis courts. A rectangle of 1970s-style buildings surrounds the quad. Why is it that 1970s fashion went wild but the architecture stayed so functional and blah?

I crunch through the snow and try to tell myself maybe my roommate will be awesome. Maybe she'll be a blogger, too. Like a military one who writes passionately about serious issues like wartime economy.

I get a little nervous thinking about how I don't know that much about the military. I know there's the army, the navy, and the marines. I know that soldiers and military personnel put their lives on the line to protect us, and that they sometimes have to be separated from their families for a very long time, because, duh, everyone knows that. And I'm also pretty sure they must be eight million times braver than I am, because I get scared watching *Homeland*, and I know that's fake.

But that's it: that's what I know, and it never struck me to be embarrassed about that until right now. We barely even talk about the military in my family, except tangentially, with my parents saying they're praying for the troops to be able to return to their families soon, and of course the legendary war stories about Grandpa Frank. But I mostly forget to listen when my parents start talking about dead relatives, even really brave ones. The closer I get to the dorm, the more I realize how incredibly unprepared I am for all of this. This isn't a life I know.

I carefully wheel my suitcases around the patches of snow and watch as two short guys dressed in uniform, carrying instrument cases, cut across the quad. I have to admit, they *do* look good in their uniforms. But the whole concept gives me such anxiety. I'm not suited for a uniformed life. This spring is all about silhouettes with movement, and now I have to contain myself in a stiff uniform? It makes me shudder. Last night I had to give my measurements for the thing, which consisted of my mom trying to measure my bust, and Ella laughing like she did when I had to get fitted for a bra at Victoria's Secret.

I round the corner of another blah, brown-brick building

and check out the sign: LYONS DORMITORY, 1979. I push open the door to a lobby covered in industrial carpet that makes me feel itchy just seeing it. Uncomfortable-looking couches surround a wooden coffee table. There's no art on the gray walls, only framed photos of uniformed students in formations that look meticulous and practiced. Where am I supposed to go? Why didn't they let my parents help me with this part?

"Private Brooks," says a woman. I turn to see a severe fortysomething woman in a navy military uniform with a stiff jacket covered in pins and medals sitting behind a desk. Did she just call me by name? Or maybe I misheard her? I try to smile at her, but she's giving me a once-over, and she's obviously displeased with what she sees. Is it my hot-pink cashmere scarf? My faux-fur Eskimo trapper's hat? It's not like I understand her look, either, so I can empathize. She's all uniform; no accessories or makeup. (Reference *FreshFrankie* post #456: "Would It Kill You to Swipe on a Little Lip Gloss?") And I don't think her hairstyle is a fashionable pixie cut gone wrong. The possibility is terrifying, but I think she may have purposely cut her hair to look like a man's buzz cut.

Yikes. Now we're staring each other down. Not good.

I walk toward her. "Hi, I'm Frankie Brooks," I say, extending my hand. She takes it with a surprisingly warm grip.

"Lieutenant Sturtevant," she says, still choosing not to smile or express any act of welcome, which is just rude. Warmth and kindness are always in fashion.

"I'm a new student this semester," I add.

"I know exactly who you are," Lt. Sturtevant says. "I know all of my cadets." Maybe she thinks I don't believe her, because she says, "Frances Abernathy Brooks."

"Yes," I say, nodding eagerly to convey my enthusiasm. "My initials spell *FAB*."

The look on her face tells me she didn't bother noticing this awesomeness.

"Fifteen years of age," she goes on. "Formerly a sophomore at Mount Pleasant High School."

She's still holding eye contact. If she's trying to freak me out, it's working. I don't want to avert my eyes—I don't want to show weakness. But then she lowers her voice to say: "GPA two point nine."

I finally break. I glance down at my hands. "That's me," I muster, exposed.

"You'll need to keep your GPA at or above three point five to remain at the Academy," she says.

"*What?!*" I blurt. Three point five?! I've never had a GPA that high, even at my normal school!

"Will that be a problem?" Lt. Sturtevant asks.

"Um," I say.

"Good," Lt. Sturtevant says, mistakenly taking my *um* for a *no*.

Lt. Sturtevant scans the paper in front of her and makes an illegible note next to my name. Then she looks at me again. There's something so unnerving about her stare!

"Your schedule," she says, passing me a piece of paper that makes me throw up a tiny bit as I read it over.

31

BROOKS, FRANCES ABERNATHY

0500: Reveille

0515–0520: First formation and accountability

0530–0620: Physical training

0630–0720: Mess I formation

0730–0740: School formation and announcements

0750–0840: Block I Class: Military Strategy

0850–0940: Block II Class: Trigonometry

0950–1040: Block III Class: English Honors

1050–1140: Mess II formation

1140–1200: Personal time

1200–1250: Block IV Class: Spanish 201

1300–1350: Block V Class: Chemistry

1400–1450: Block VI Class: Pottery

1500–1550: Computer Science

1600–1650: Athletics: TBA

1700–1800: Personal time

1800–1900: Mess III formation

1910–1950: Study Hall Block I

2000–2050: Study Hall Block II

2100–2130: Personal time

2130: Lights-out

My schedule hasn't been this rigidly organized since I was a toddler and my mom was in charge!

"Sometime this week you'll be assigned to a tactical officer and be enrolled in a leadership seminar," Sturtevant says. "You'll begin planning your leadership project under the supervision of said TAC. You will also be entered into the Academy's annual War Games, an elite competition recognizing the top fifty percent of cadets as determined by their physical performance, leadership qualities, and strategic thinking abilities. All ranking is at the discretion of your tactical officers. The scores are updated daily."

Is she serious? I get that this is supposed to be harder than regular school, but GPA over 3.5 plus sports and leadership projects? There's no way I'm going to be able to make this work!

"All of this information will be sent to you tonight via email, and you may check your War Games ranking at any given point on this link," she says, handing me a small square of paper, as if I'm really gonna want to see where I stuck up against kids who actually already know how to do military stuff.

She passes me a key. "Room 321," she says, and then hands me a laminated student ID card with a photo (not my best) that my parents must have submitted. It makes me queasy thinking about my mom and dad getting all this ready behind my back. "This serves as both your identification and meal card," she says. She reaches into a drawer and retrieves a bound handbook. *Albany Military Academy* is emblazoned on the front in gold letters. It's the first flashy thing I've seen since I've been here. Lt. Sturtevant sees me looking at it, and frowns. "Uniform policies and behavior codes are not taken lightly here at the Academy; nor are matters of ethics," she says, "which I recall may have been a problem for you at your last school."

My face gets hot. My parents told her about the cheating?

33

"Your uniform is waiting in your closet," she says. "Please change immediately and wear it to the dining hall tonight for dinner so we can be sure it fits properly."

"Um, no," I say, because I really don't think that's going to work for me. "Aren't I allowed to wear my own outfits on days when classes aren't in session?" I'm not going to let this woman boss me around. She can kick me right back out of here for all I care. What are my parents going to do? Make me go somewhere else?

Wait. *Would* they do that?

"The thing is," I say, a little more carefully, "I've already planned my outfit for tonight, and you'll probably be happy to know that I incorporated a chic military-inspired bomber jacket while still staying true to my romantic and feminine personal style."

"From now on you'll do exactly as I say without question," Lt. Sturtevant says, and then she transfers the handbook into my shaking hands. Ugh! I hate when my hands shake! So much for confidence. "You're dismissed."

I sashay over to the elevator and try to regain my attitude. I board the elevator and flash Sturtevant my best smile. She glares back. I ride the elevator to the third floor, and when the doors open, I see that my father was being generous by calling my new home a *dorm*. This isn't a dorm—it's military barracks; the white-brick walls and cold tile beneath my feet make me sure of it. There are no decorations on the walls, and no jazzing up of the dorm room doors with selfies or inspiration boards culled from

Pinterest. There must be rules against making this place look nice, and they're probably somewhere in this horrible handbook. I pass a garbage chute and suppress the urge to throw the book down it.

I stop outside room 321. A hard plastic label marks MURPHY, and my last name hangs below it. BROOKS has never looked so severe. I fumble with my key and open the door. The two beds lining the walls are covered with monochromatic green bedspreads. The fabric is mildly offensive: it looks like a poly-wool blend, and it's the kind of green that should only be glimpsed when gazing into a bowl of split pea soup.

There's a sink to my right, and—thank God—a mirror above the sink with lighting strong enough to apply evening makeup without going overboard. A crucifix hangs above one of the beds, but otherwise, it's hard to tell which bed is taken. Both beds are made tightly enough to make me realize military-style beds are not just a product of Hollywood movies. And except for the crucifix, there's nothing on the ivory walls.

A closed laptop and two framed photos sit on one of the two wooden desks. I move to the empty desk and gingerly open the top drawer. It's bare besides a small velvet-covered book. I open it without thinking and see a note inscribed on the first page:

Rachel,
Happy birthday. I know a diary is a lame present, but it's

supposed to remind you of all the good things your future holds.

JW

I shut it quickly, vowing not to read any of the entries. Maybe I could try to track the girl down and let her know her secrets are safe with me. Maybe she'd want to come get the diary.

I put the diary back and close the drawer slowly. I feel like I'm moving underwater. I can't believe this is where I'm going to spend the next five months. I step toward the other desk and check out the framed photo. The picture is of a strawberry-blonde girl standing next to a tall, gray-haired man dressed in uniform and a woman in a cocktail dress. I'm about to touch the frame for some stupid reason when the door swings open.

"H-hi," I stammer. My hand still hovers above her picture frame.

The girl in the doorway stares at me. She's short like me, and her makeup-free face is pretty, with high cheekbones and big, deep-set blue eyes framed by stick-straight strawberry-blonde hair. Freckles mark every inch of her skin, making her look sun-kissed and a little younger than she probably is. She's wearing the Academy's military uniform—the same one I saw on all the kids in the brochure: a light blue button-down shirt, gray-blue pants with a black stripe running down the side, and a matching gray-blue hat that looks like an upside-down boat. I'm not sure if it's the uniform or what, but she looks quite serious.

"Hi," I say again, hoping to jog her memory about how you're supposed to say hello to new people standing in your room.

"Hi. I'm Joni Maguire Murphy," she says, still standing in the doorway. "My last roommate was kicked out."

Okay.

"I'm Frankie. It's nice to meet you," I say, because I have no idea what else to say to that piece of information.

Joni smiles, and then tucks a lock of strawberry-blonde hair behind her ear, but she doesn't look like she agrees. She moves to the bed and sits with her slouchy duffel bag still slung over her shoulder like she's not sure if she's going to stay.

"Mess III formations start in five minutes," she says. "You can't be late here."

"Mess what formation?" I ask.

She rolls her eyes. *"Dinner,"* she says, like I'm just so dumb.

We stare at each other. There's nothing I want more than to be alone, but I'm starving, and plus I need to get the lay of the land here and see what I'm up against. Maybe there's a way to politely get myself sent back to Mount Pleasant. Not get expelled or anything, just returned, like a too-tight dress from Nordstrom.

"Look, can I come with you?" I ask. "I just need to . . ." I dig through the precious junk in my handbag. "This is the food card, right?" I ask, flashing the plastic square at her. My cheekbone highlighter must have leaked out of its

37

compact inside my bag. I try to brush off the dusting of gold sparkly powder that covers my picture on the meal card, but I can't seem to get it off completely.

Joni nods warily.

"Can I go to dinner—the mess formation thing—with you?" I ask her again. "Maybe I could meet your friends?" This is getting embarrassing; I'm practically begging. "I just need to change into my uniform because that scary woman downstairs said so."

"Yeah, you definitely can't wear *that*," Joni says, pointing to my Eskimo hat, which looks like a wild animal perched on the desk.

"I *know*," I say, and then I march confidently toward my closet like I'm not inwardly freaking out. I open the door and that's when I see it—my uniform. It's hanging inside plastic and my name is right there on the lapel:

PRIVATE FRANCES BROOKS

I let out a little gasp, which is obviously mortifying. But it's just so official. There's the same blue button-down shirt and gray-blue pants with a navy stripe running down them that Joni's wearing, and flat, shiny shoes that look like the kind my dad wears to work. Behind the whole ensemble is a black parka with *Albany Military Academy* stitched over the chest in red letters. And then, the pièce de résistance: the upside-down boat hat.

"I'll wait for you in the hall," Joni says. She stands up and leaves our room, shutting the door behind her. I get to work, telling myself it's only a uniform, and lots of girls wear uniforms: like private school girls and field hockey

38

players. I'll just pretend I'm in the dressing room at Saks and the saleslady has brought me something terrific.

I take the pants off the hanger and shimmy into them. They feel trouser-y and comfortable. I put my arms in the shirt, which feels tight like a straitjacket. I can hardly breathe in it! It feels like the time I borrowed one of Andrea's tube tops against my better fashion judgment and kept feeling like I couldn't take a full breath all night. It was like living on the edge of a panic attack, and I kind of feel like that now.

I try buttoning the buttons but keep messing up the alignment. My fingers are sweating. I finally get the buttons right, and then try to tuck the shirt as neatly as possible into my pants. Then I put on the belt. I wish it were like a neon-colored faux-lizard skin, but it's not. It's just black. Which is functional and everything, it's just the whole thing is so monochromatic and really I need a pop of color.

I duck to put on my shiny shoes. I'm usually a size six, but these feel tight. Ugh. They're definitely pinching.

I lace the shoes and check myself out in the mirror. *Whoa.* I look really different, but actually sort of cool: very military and maybe even kind of brave. Shoot—the *hat.* Ugh. No way am I looking cool in this thing. I'll just accidentally forget it. The *tactical officers* should probably know that I'm going to do my own thing here. I'm not going to go against my fashion beliefs just for the sake of the US military. That would be crazy!

I check myself out one more time, then swing open the door and grin at Joni like *hey, isn't this fun?*

Joni does not seem moved by my change of clothes. Instead, she manages to roll her eyes for about the eighth time since she's met me. She locks our door, and then slips on dark brown leather gloves way too masculine for her delicate hands. They make her look like she's about to commit a crime.

"Did you not get a hat?" she asks me.

"I did," I say. "It's not my style." Joni raises her eyebrows, but doesn't say anything. We start down the hall. "So are you from Albany?" I ask.

"Phoenix," she says.

"Hot," I say. "And so drying for the skin. Do you moisturize?"

She looks at me funny as we board the elevator. I don't think she's going to answer, but then she does. "I wear sunblock. Does that count?"

"Some products work better than others," I say. "I can get you some samples. I have a lifestyle blog, so sometimes the companies I profile send samples for my consideration."

Joni smirks. "A lifestyle blog?"

"Yes. It's called *FreshFrankie*. Have you heard of it?"

She gives me a look like: *Of course I haven't heard of your stupid blog*, and jabs the button for the lobby.

"It's a blog about how to live your most extraordinary life," I say, maybe a little too defensively.

The elevator opens and I scan for scary Lt. Sturtevant, but she's nowhere to be found, thank God. Out on the quad, Joni starts sprint-walking. I'm not sure if she's trying to get away from me, or if this is just how she walks.

I can barely keep up without jogging a few steps. My feet are already killing in the shoes—they're way too snug. We whiz by packs of students as we zoom toward a brick building, and when we get there Joni holds the door open for me.

The cafeteria smells vaguely like Applebee's, which is where my one-and-only official boyfriend ever, Carl Jensen, used to take me for dates. (With his parents, who would sit a few tables away and drink root beer floats and stare at us. #WelcomeToMyLife.) A meandering line of students has formed inside the lobby. Each student passes his or her meal card to an old lady who swipes the card and says things like, "Go on in, Jonathan." Or, "Have a nice meal, Victoria."

My eyes keep scanning the lunch line. Almost everyone's wearing his or her uniform, and most of the kids look a little more conservative and clean-cut than I'm used to, but overall they seem pretty normal. They look kind of nice, actually. The majority of the guys have buzz cuts, but there are a few with shaggier hair, like the dark-haired guy I saw walking on the quad reading newspapers. None of the boys have hair past their ears, because it isn't allowed, apparently.

"Enjoy your dinner, Frances," the lunch lady tells me.

I follow Joni into a massive dining hall filled with at least twenty tables holding about ten students each. We get our trays and drinks, and when Joni heads to the salad bar, I follow—I don't want to lose track of her. We pile chicken and pistachios on top of spinach leaves (the food is fancy-looking, actually), and just as I'm choosing my dressing (French—so underrated), Joni takes off. It's almost like she's trying to lose me! I have to tear after her, and I don't catch her until she puts her tray down in the middle of an empty table.

"Are you meeting your friends here?" I ask as I sit across from her. Most of the students are sitting in clumps of threes and fours.

"No," she says matter-of-factly. But she doesn't meet my eyes.

We start eating, and Joni still won't really look at me. What if she doesn't have any friends at all? I try to push away the thought. "So do you like going to school here?" I ask. I poke at my salad, annoyed at the crouton that somehow slipped in with my spinach leaves, because I just don't think gluten is necessary or beneficial. I also feel that way about perfume.

"I love being at military school," Joni says softly. "My dad and his two brothers were in the military, and so are a few of my cousins. My whole family, really."

"Your mom, too?" I ask.

She jabs at the ice in her Coke. She reminds me of a little bird with quick, unpredictable movements. "No," she says, and the way she says it makes me think I shouldn't ask anything else about her mom.

"So do you want to be in the military?" I ask instead.

"*Yeah*," she says. "That's the plan."

I fall quiet. The silence clearly doesn't bother Joni. She picks at her salad and keeps checking her watch. The watch looks like it could survive a deep-sea fishing expedition or, more likely, a war. It's a huge black rubber thing with teeny buttons and flashing lights.

At the table diagonal from us, two girls erupt in riotous laugher. I look at Joni and find her staring at them. The girls are shouting over each other, laughing so hard their shoulders are shaking.

"Do you know those girls?" I ask.

One has smooth deep brown skin and a side bun peeking out beneath her hat, and the other is a curvy blonde. I can see how big the blonde's boobs are, even beneath her athletic Albany Military Academy windbreaker. (There's a special place in fashion purgatory reserved for garments constructed to protect against specific weather conditions.)

"I do know those girls," Joni says, munching her lettuce with tiny but rapid jaw movements. Then she locks eyes with the girl wearing the side bun, and she flushes pink in that pretty, understated way that freckled strawberry blondes blush (think: Ralph Lauren ad). Joni looks away quickly, and so does the girl.

I try to force down a few more bites of my salad. I'm getting nowhere with Joni, and the idea of meeting a whole group of new students and trying to figure out military school sounds exhausting. I'm about to make an excuse to leave early and head back to our room when I see the dark-haired boy from the quad. This time he's in his military uniform, which looks so handsome and natural on him, like he was meant to be wearing it. He's heading in our direction, his eyes on Joni. He says her name, and his voice is deep, and I know it's so romance novel to be turned on by that, but I am.

He's cute. Really, *really* cute. His skin is olive, and his dark eyes are the color of coffee. And he's tall—so wonderfully tall—maybe six four or so. He arrives at our table and towers over us, noticing me for the first time. He doesn't say anything. He just looks at me.

"Hi," I say.

"Hi," he says back. I can see tiny, clear tubes snaking over his ears into his mussed hair. I'm pretty sure they're cochlear implants because there's a drummer in a band I love who has them and they look the same. His cheekbones are so chiseled that looking at him is like staring at a hot lead in a movie. He's close enough that I can smell cinnamon gum and fresh air and *boy*. He smiles a little. It's crooked, just the way I like.

For a second I flash back to Josh Archester, and then feel guilty remembering what I did.

Joni's watching us. "This is my new roommate, Frankie," she says. "Frankie, this is—"

"Jack Wattson," he says.

JW—just like in the journal in my new desk. My heart picks up, and I turn to Joni. "Joni's been showing me around," I say, and Joni smiles like she's having the time of her life doing so, which is obviously the opposite of reality.

"How nice of her," Jack says, but he's still looking at me. He finally turns to Joni, who now looks a little pissed. "Maybe we should show your new roommate the Tombs," he says, his words low and even.

"Um . . . ," Joni stalls.

"Unless you're afraid of spiders," Jack says to me.

"We don't have written permission to leave campus, *Jack*," Joni says.

I take a sip of my seltzer, the carbonation tickling my throat. I wonder how much trouble you get in if you sneak off campus.

"Actually, I love spiders," I say to Jack, unable to stop myself. "And tombs."

"Really?" Jack asks, dark eyes shining.

It was a dorky thing for me to say, but he didn't seem to think so, so I keep going. "Oh, totally," I say. "Ever since I saw *Raiders of the Lost Ark*. Iconic costume designer Deborah Nadoolman combined leather and linen for a lasting effect on men's fashion."

Jack raises a dark eyebrow, and then he laughs a deep, rumbling laugh, and I smile back at him. He's so cute!

"I haven't seen that movie," Joni says flatly. Her words hang in the air between the three of us.

"We could see it together," I say to Joni. Isn't that what being away at a boarding school is supposed to be like? Staying up late and watching movies with your friends while eating snacks your parents would never allow? Visions of non-artisanal chocolate and butter-drenched popcorn float through my mind. I push away my salad. "We could make popcorn and watch it one night."

"We don't have a TV or microwave in our room," Joni says.

45

"We have laptops," I say, because it seems like such a 1990s suggestion to let that stop us. What's up with this girl? I can't tell if she's a little socially awkward or just doesn't like me.

"The classes are really hard here unless you're a genius or something," Joni says. "So you might want to use that time to study."

I remember the 3.5 GPA Lt. Sturtevant told me I need to get (and keep!) in order to stay here. I obviously *don't* want to stay here, but I also don't want to get kicked out based on grades, either, because that would be so embarrassing. Everyone back home would find out!

I used to get good grades in junior high and some of freshman year. It wasn't like I was the smartest kid in Mount Pleasant, but I used to genuinely like studying and getting good grades and showing my parents my test scores. And then I just got so distracted being online for fashion stuff, blogging and social media, too, and then I couldn't keep up, and then the cheating . . .

"Guys aren't allowed in the girls' dorms after seven p.m.," Jack says. His voice sounds serious, but I swear he's trying not to smile.

I look at Joni. Visions of chocolate are replaced by thoughts of endless nights studying with her in our minuscule, monochromatic room. Could I even do that? I feel like Instagram has taken up the part of my brain that used to be able to focus on schoolwork.

"Plus, we have mandatory lights-out at nine-thirty," Joni says.

"I blog at least until midnight," I say. I guess I could do it in the dark.

"Not anymore you don't," Joni says. "Guards patrol the campus. If they see the glow of screens through our windows, we get written up. Plus, all the tactical officers have the keys to our rooms. They're allowed to enter at any time if they suspect we're doing something we're not supposed to."

I sense a small prick of joy while she recounts this awfulness.

"The Academy isn't exactly Fun City," Jack says.

Right then the girls at the next table burst out laughing again. They get going even louder this time, until the cafeteria feels full with the sound of their giggling. They look fun—maybe I should try to make friends with them? "Those girls seem to feel differently," I say, and as I turn to look at them, I notice the blonde windbreaker wearer stealing a glance at Jack. She's sipping a soda, her eyes carefully lifted like she doesn't want to get caught staring.

"You may want to steer clear of Amanda, actually," Jack says. "The blonde one." It catches me off guard, and I glance up to see his features darken. When he sees me eyeing him, he forces a smile, and then he mumbles something beneath his breath and leaves us just like that, midconversation. I watch him head toward a door that leads to the quad.

Weird.

An awkward moment passes between Joni and me. I busy myself arranging my salad into a triangle on my plate, my appetite gone.

"We usually eat together," Joni says numbly to her dinner.

Because you're boyfriend and girlfriend? Is that what's going on?

I take a sip of my seltzer. "Are you guys together?" I ask, unable to stop myself.

Joni doesn't look at me. I know she's going to tell me they aren't even before she says it.

"We're not," she says. She straightens like she has something to defend. "But we're *really* close."

What's that supposed to mean? Is he off-limits? Not like I'm assuming he would like me, I'm just wondering . . .

"So, tomorrow," I say, changing the subject to my immediate survival. I shouldn't get distracted by boys, anyway, because I need to do well here or God only knows what will happen to me. "We have physical training, right? PT? That's how the day starts?" I'm so nervous I can barely get the questions out. What if I can't do the military training stuff *at all* and they just kick me out based on that? That would be mortifying!

"Yeah, PT," Joni says, slicing a tomato in half. "We have War Games prep for the next few months, so just try not to suck too much."

My body zings with nerves. "That lady lieutenant mentioned the War Games thing," I say.

"They're a big deal here," Joni says, sprinkling salt on her tomato. She pops it into her mouth. "They select the best cadets and we compete in all kinds of events against

48

other military schools. You have to be in the top fifty percent to get in."

"Top fifty percent of *what*?" I ask. I didn't totally get what the lieutenant meant when she told me this back in the dorm, either. But if it's at all based on confidence or personal style, I could make it.

"*Physical training*," Joni says, like *duh*, "and you know, more nebulous things like strategic thinking and leadership." She takes a bite of salad. "It's all based on our TACs' discretion."

"TACs?"

Joni gives me this look like *oh my God you seriously know nothing*. "Tactical officers," she says. "And Lt. Sturtevant— or *that lady lieutenant*, as you called her is our head TAC."

My cheeks burn. "Right," I say, trying to act like I couldn't care less. I'm not going to act like War Games are the coolest thing I've ever heard of when they're obviously not; and I'm not going to get my hopes up about something there's no way I can do. "Your little *War Games* don't exactly sound like my kind of thing," I say. Joni flinches a little, and I instantly regret how insulting it came out. My cheeks go hot and I fumble to explain. "What I mean is, I just have to survive this place and get back home where I *belong*."

"Suit yourself," Joni says.

"I always do," I say, because it's true. And I don't plan on changing now. Why would I?

FOUR

BEEP! BEEP! BEEP!

My eyes open the next morning and the first thing I see is Joni's face. She's staring at me like she's been waiting for me to wake up, which—even though I'm half asleep—strikes me as incredibly weird.

Beep! Beep! Beep!

"What the *heck*?" I say, flinging my arm out from beneath the covers. I try to find my phone on the floor and knock over my mug. Cold hibiscus tea sloshes across the cover of *W Magazine*. What time is it? It can't be five a.m. already.

A crazy-loud trumpeting noise sounds in the distance, overpowering even my alarm.

"What is that?!" I ask, hysteria creeping into my voice.

"Reveille, obviously," Joni says. "Haven't you seen any military movies?"

50

I barely slept last night because I was so nervous about today, and my bones feel full of sand as I rummage for my phone and press snooze. The bugle trumpets along with a snare drum in a feisty rhythm that *almost* makes me want to wake up and protect my country. I close my eyes and try to go back to sleep for just five seconds, but the music is actually kind of moving, which is really saying something because I'm the last person on Earth who wants to be literally or figuratively moved right now.

Joni flicks on the overhead light and sears my retinas. She's fully dressed in her uniform. How did she do that in the dark? "Wake up!" she yells.

I yank my covers over my eyes. Waking up gracefully has never been my strong suit. Chanel Iman said that a good night's sleep is always the best way to wake up and go to work, but the people in charge of school wake-up times never seem to get that. "I'm just going to snooze for a few more—"

"Frankie, I can't wait for you. I can't miss formation and inspection," she huffs. "And don't forget to make your rack before you leave."

The door slams. My rack?

I pull the covers off my face. Did she seriously just leave? I swing my legs over the side of the bed.

Ugh. I was kind of counting on her to show me where the gymnasium was for morning PT. I glance at my schedule. It has something called *First formation and accountability* listed for 0515, right before *Physical training*, which starts at 0530. Maybe that's what she meant. Shoot! Why didn't I clarify this with her last night?!

I pull on a heavy-duty sports bra that isn't necessary for my lack of cleavage, but it makes me feel nice and sporty so I go with it. I open my closet door and see my uniform. Here I go again . . .

I put on my uniform, and then I stare down my hat. I think I need to wear it—I don't want to get yelled at in front of everyone. My phone says it's thirty-two degrees outside, but there's no way Sturtevant is going to let me get away with my faux-fur trapper hat. I put on the hat and check myself out in my mirror. The problem is my body is skinny but my head is quite large because big heads run in my family. So the tiny hat is drawing attention to my big-ass head, and now I look even more like a lollipop than usual. Whatever. *Ugh!* I slip into my shoes and no, just no, *no freaking way.* I absolutely cannot wear these shoes again. I already feel them ripping open the blisters they made on my feet yesterday.

I glance over to my running sneakers beneath our sink. I wonder if I could just wear them until I can reorder shoes that fit? That seems reasonable—the tactical officers (*TACs*, as Joni said) can't possibly expect me to wear shoes that pinch. I make my way toward them. They're barely scuffed, because a person who seeks a fashionable life should not wear serious running shoes with gel cushions except for the following reasons:

exercise

athletic shoe modeling

working at Foot Locker

orthopedic problems.

I slip them on and tie the neon-yellow laces—at least now my uniform will have that pop of color I wanted. I try to tie my hair into a side pony so it looks cuter in the hat, but it doesn't quite fit because my new lob is so short: white-blonde pieces spike everywhere! I clip the pieces back with barrettes, which makes me look like a weird science experiment.

I check my watch and realize I need to seriously hurry. I'm zipping my meal card and my phone into my jacket pocket when the bugle sounds again. Reveille, as Joni called it. This time it sounds even closer. I move to our window and glance out to the quad, where two hundred uniformed cadets are standing in the dark in a neatly arranged formation. I squint to see an older man in uniform pass a folded flag to a boy who's maybe fourteen. He's so scrawny he looks like he might crumble beneath the weight of the flag, but I can't stop staring at his face, illuminated beneath a streetlamp. A look of sheer reverence transforms his features as he holds the flag and carries it to two other cadets, who attach it to the flagpole. I crack the window and hear someone shout:

"Set, huh! Accompanied by sergeants Sturtevant and O'Neil!"

Shoot. This is definitely the formation part because they're certainly forming something: all two hundred uniformed cadets salute as the flag is being raised with a snare drum firing and the bugle sounding behind them. I bite back tears. This is so foreign to me, but it also feels oddly familiar, like the swell of patriotism and camaraderie I sometimes feel during the Pledge of Allegiance or whenever I hear the national anthem at Mets games. I love my country, too, darn it!

I race out the door, determined to join the other cadets, but as soon as I get in the elevator, it stalls. I jam a few buttons and sweat breaks out on the back of my neck. Am I trapped in this thing? I crush the *open door* button a dozen times. I take out my phone to call someone—who, though?—for help, but I don't have any service inside the elevator. I'm one second away from pressing the alarm button when the thing jolts to life, descending to the lobby. The doors open and I speed across the carpet, passing a poster taped to the wall about an upcoming dance. Then there's a list that says: CONGRATULATIONS TO OUR TOP TEN PERCENT! War Games again, I guess. The top name jumps out at me: *Private Jack Wattson*.

I push through the doors, but by the time I race onto the quad, all of the cadets are gone. It's like a ghost town. The whipping American flag is the only sign that someone was just here. I'm standing there on the rocky gravel, frozen, when my phone beeps with a text from Ella.

I know you're probably already running five minutes late for PT, so you'll need to hurry. Cross the parking lot in front of your dorm, then take a right. Follow the sidewalk—there's a shortcut past Sorin Dorm that will put you onto South Quad. The PT gymnasium is directly across South Quad smack in the middle of a bunch of dorms. It's marked Rockne Hall. Good luck!

Homesickness washes over me. I text back: **Best sister ever. I love you.**

I start running. The sun isn't up and the air is bitingly cold, but the Academy's campus is beautiful, filled mostly with older, gray and white-brick buildings that are much lovelier than the 70s-style barracks I'm inhabiting with Joni.

I sprint across South Quad, and, just like whenever I sprint, I'm struck by the fact that my halfhearted flirtation with my elliptical machine isn't working out so well for me. Maybe this new daily PT routine will be a good thing. My endorphins kick in as I tear over the grass and sidestep the patches of snow like an action-movie heroine, and suddenly I start feeling hopeful about things.

Military school could be a new beginning for me, a way to shake off everything that happened at home. Maybe I could try to make it work for me here. I don't need to do the whole War Games thing, but I could definitely use a regular workout to get some more muscle tone in my arms to make my sleeveless tops look better. I'm smiling just thinking about it as I push through heavy glass doors into the building marked Rockne Hall. I step inside and see closed double doors right in front of me, and I can hear a woman's voice coming from behind them, in what must be the gymnasium. I inch open the doors, figuring I'll just slip inside and take my place among the students, but the door is heavier than I imagined, and I need to shoulder the thing.

Crack!

The hinges moan as the door swings wide. I freeze. Every single cadet is there, staring at me. I've somehow picked the door that opens to Lt. Sturtevant's backside as she lectures to what appears to be the entire student body. Hundreds of eyes go huge as Lt. Sturtevant stops midsentence and pivots on her heel to face me. She looks shocked, but her features quickly morph into disgust, then acceptance, and then—most terrifying of all—*pleasure*. She's staring at me like she's been waiting for this moment her entire life. A smile twists her lips.

"Brooks," she says, her voice slick. "You've missed formation and inspection, you're tardy, and you're wearing *sneakers*."

She says *sneakers* the way most people say *fungus*.

"Right," I say, "because my shiny uniform shoes don't fit, and . . ."

My cell phone rings. *Oh my God*. How did I not silence it? I dig into my pocket with shaking hands, knowing it's Andrea even before I see her name because she's the only other person besides my sister I know who's awake at this ungodly hour, doggedly hitting balls at indoor tennis practice. Lt. Sturtevant looks like she's actually going to end me. The cadets are all staring, and Sturtevant is now grinning with pointy canines that look like fangs.

"Would you like to answer that?" she asks.

Ring! Ring!

I make out Jack standing in the first row of cadets, seeming even bigger than he did in the cafeteria last night. His clear dark eyes hold mine, and he shakes his head just slightly, like he's trying to warn me.

"*Do you want to answer that?!*" Lt. Sturtevant shouts, so rudely that I flinch.

"I *do*," I say, because I really don't appreciate her speaking to me like that. In Mount Pleasant the teachers all take a course taught by a local expert called Why Yelling Ruins a Teachable Moment.

Sturtevant stares at me, and it's right when she bares her teeth that an eerily calm feeling comes over me. Because if there's one thing I've never been, it's a rule follower. I take a breath, and then swipe my finger over my phone's screen. "Hey, Andrea," I say, as casually as I can.

Students are gaping at me, their mouth slack. A few kids audibly gasp, and one girl says "*No way*" loud enough that I just make it out above the low hum of the radiator. The entire student body is hooked on my every word, my every movement, and as calm as I'm trying to stay, my hands are sweating all over my phone. It's so slippery I can barely hold it against my ear.

"Why didn't you call me back last night?" Andrea asks me.

My heart is racing for so many reasons I can hardly breathe.

"Um, now's actually not a great time," I finally sputter. "Morning PT."

Andrea tells me to *oh my God fine* call her back whenever, and then Lt. Sturtevant shrieks: "Frances Abernathy Brooks!" so loudly the entire gymnasium shakes. Her shoulders are squared and her body is so rigid it looks

57

painful, but her voice gives away how furious she is. *"You have officially received one demerit, which is extremely generous for every way you've disobeyed code today,"* she says through gritted teeth. I can hear the effort it takes her to keep her words steady. "Two more and you're out of Albany Military Academy!"

That wouldn't be the worst thing for either of us! I want to say as Sturtevant gestures with a straight arm. "Take your place next to Ciara Washington," she says. She's pointing at a girl standing three spots down from Joni. I recognize her as one of the two girls who couldn't stop laughing in the cafeteria last night—the side-bun girl. And the other girl, the blonde windbreaker wearer named Amanda who Jack warned me about, is right next to her.

I catch the look on Joni's face as I start toward Ciara. She's staring straight ahead with lips pursed, not daring to look at me. And neither is Jack. Ciara, unlike Jack and Joni, is staring directly at me with an incredulous look on her face. She looks like she wants to throw her arms around me, and she actually grins as I scoot next to her. I'm almost worried she's going to put her hand out to high-five me, but she doesn't. Amanda just stares.

"As I was saying," Lt. Sturtevant starts. Now she's glaring at both Ciara and me. "I expect you to push yourselves to the top of your game not only because of War Games selection, but because Albany Military Academy demands this of you each and every day. You *will* be the best you, or you will be removed from the Academy." Her gaze narrows on me. *"Is that clear?"*

I nod. It's clear.

The gym is quiet as Sturtevant goes on, "We train our minds and our bodies daily at the Academy because a sound mind and body take us where we want to go, whether as a civilian or as a member of the United States military." She starts pacing, and I sense the portion of her speech meant specifically for me is over. "You'll be working in groups of threes for drills this morning. Your scores will be tallied for War Games based on how well you do as a group, so choose your partners wisely."

Okay, so, *wisely* probably means I should try to stick with Joni. I glance down the line at her, thinking maybe she'll want to be my partner, which I realize might sound deluded, but we *are* roommates. She doesn't. She grabs Jack's arm, and says, "Partners?"

I can't see his face. But it's obvious he's not saying no. I stand there feeling vulnerable and exposed, thinking they're not going to ask me to be a part of their group. Then Jack turns to me and says, "Do you—" but Ciara's arm is already around my waist.

"You. Me. Us," she says, pointing to Amanda. The girl's green eyes are on me for a beat too long before she breaks into what looks like a forced half smile. "Amanda," she says. Ciara glances at Joni, who quickly turns away, looking flustered.

"Frankie," I say.

"Partners?" she asks.

I turn to look at Jack. "I'm just going to . . ."

"Perfect," Amanda says, grabbing my hand and giving it

59

a squeeze. Her fingers are freezing.

I try to smile at Amanda and Ciara, but I'm uneasy. I'd rather be the one to make the decision, not Amanda.

"You ready to be top-notch military school material?" Ciara asks me.

"Good luck, Frankie," Joni says quietly.

"We don't need luck, remember?" Amanda says. Something dark passes between them, and Joni opens her mouth like she's going to say something, but then Ciara gives Joni a pleading look, almost like she's asking her to just be quiet and leave it alone. There's definitely something up between the three of them.

Jack puts his big hands on Joni's arms, turning her toward him. "Let's find a partner," he says, his voice smooth and reassuring. He guides her into the fray and I try not to watch his broad shoulders move through the crowd.

"So, Frankie, you're new," Amanda says matter-of-factly. She kicks her leg back and stretches her hamstring.

I nod. Other students are settling into their groups of threes, and there's a sense of chaos in a place that felt so still a few minutes ago.

"When did you get here?" Ciara asks. Her tall, angular thinness is even more pronounced next to Amanda's petite curves. She has clear, dark skin and brown eyes, long black lashes and glossy, cherry-red lips. (We're allowed to wear makeup here, just not nail polish, which is irritating because my Essie collection took up so much space in my suitcase.) They're a very pretty pair, and they're standing so close together it makes it obvious they're tight.

"Yesterday," I say. I try to copy the stretch that Amanda's doing.

"Wow," Amanda says, letting out a low whistle, like there's something about my timing that spells trouble. "Your parents kicked you out right after the holidays. That's harsh."

Her words feel like knives. "They didn't kick me out," I say. I feel my lower lip tremble and try to make it stop. "They just, um, they wanted me to learn discipline."

"Ah, *discipline*," Ciara says. "That's what I promised my parents I'd learn here. It was the only way I got them to pay for it! It's super expensive to go here, in case you didn't know." I glance down at my hands. I feel like a spoiled brat for not thinking about that part of things. "And if you do well here you have a better shot at college," Ciara continues. "I have my sights set on Princeton." She gives me a smile that I'm pretty sure is genuine, and just like in the cafeteria last night, her glossy lipstick and perfectly styled hair make her look like a starlet at Sundance.

"So how do you know Joni and Jack?" Amanda asks. Her uniform hugs her figure a little more snugly than Ciara's and mine, showing off some pretty enviable curves.

"Joni's my roommate," I say. "And I met Jack yesterday."

Amanda's staring at me, and it gives me that funny feeling I get when someone's sizing me up. I'd really like her to stop. She and Ciara exchange a glance, and it makes me remember the way Amanda was secretly staring at Jack in the cafeteria.

61

I roll my ankle around. It feels a little funny, probably from balls-out sprinting over here. "Your shoes are so shiny," I say, pointing to the black shoes peeking out beneath Amanda's gray pants. Positive fashion commentary can be a lifesaver when you have nothing else to say.

Ciara starts stretching like Amanda, bending forward and shifting her weight into each leg, alternating like a metronome. "I'm on uniform duty right now," she says. "I've shined more TACs' shoes than you can imagine."

"Footwear and brass will be highly shined," I add, quoting what I read last night in the handbook Lt. Sturtevant gave me, along with something like: *Never mix articles of civilian clothes with your uniform. Your military uniform designates you as a special person: wear it with pride.*

Amanda and Ciara don't look very impressed that I read my handbook, so I change tactics. "Glossy, high-lacquered materials are emerging as one of the top trends to wear this fall," I say. "Boots, coats, etc. And they definitely photograph well."

Still nothing. Their faces are blank. I miss Andrea and Julia so much it's palpable.

A whistle blows and we all go silent and turn toward Sturtevant. "Sixteen laps equal one mile. Begin running now with your team." She blows her whistle again and Ciara and Amanda take off.

"We have to run *a mile* right now?" I say to their backsides, panicked as I try to catch up to them.

"Um, *yeah*," Amanda says when I'm in line with them,

trying to match my stride with theirs. She looks slightly regretful about having picked me as a teammate.

Shoes squeak over the gym floor as the cadets run. A *mile?*

Amanda, Ciara, and I run a lap in silence, and I'm already gasping for air when I ask, "So what's uniform duty?"

"You're gonna get assigned a chore," Ciara says, lengthening her stride. "Just try to make the best of it and pray you don't get bathrooms or the mess hall. Bathrooms are the most disgusting, and the mess hall is just publicly humiliating."

Amanda stops to tuck a wayward wisp of dirty-blonde hair into a see-through plastic clip, and I want to kiss her for the chance to catch my breath. I read the hair clip rule last night, too: *Females must pin hair above neck with clear plastic clips, or with any clip that matches hair color. Neatness is a priority, and essential to military appearance.* As different as my uniform is compared with what I usually wear, I have to say, there's something very regal about it. Each student looks like he or she has purpose, which is probably not something you can say when you walk into most high schools. I wonder if I look like that, too, even with my running shoes.

Amanda picks up our pace. I can tell by watching the two of them that Amanda's in charge. It's subtle, but the hierarchy is there, and it reminds me of how I feel when I watch Lia Powers rule her minions at school. I'm trying to keep up with them, but it's so hard—I'm panting rapidly to oxygenate my challenged cardiovascular system. Ciara helps by having me switch places so I can run on the inside and have less ground to cover.

While we're running, Ciara tells me about how she's from Brooklyn, and I tell her that my favorite clothing line, Vena Cava, was born in Brooklyn, and then Amanda says something I don't understand, and it must be an inside joke because they both start laughing.

I feel left out, which is probably dumb. But it's weird being so far from Andrea and Julia, and my sister, too. And, no matter how childish I feel for admitting it, it's not so great being this far from my parents.

"What's wrong?" Amanda asks.

The air in the gym feels too warm. I glance over at her, surprised at how quickly she picked up on my mood. She reminds me a little of Julia, at least in the perceptive way Julia can pick up on what someone else is feeling.

"I'm just homesick," I say, wheezing a little. I don't know how much longer I can run like this. "I'm really sorry, guys," I say. "I have to slow down."

Amanda rolls her eyes, and I'm so on the edge of what I can emotionally and physically handle that it almost makes me cry. By the seventh go around we're getting lapped by other students. I can see the backside of Jack as he passes, and it's like he's not even having to try hard to run that fast. His strides are long and relaxed, compared with his teammates, who look like they're sprinting. One girl tries to pass us and nearly knocks me over. She apologizes profusely and sprints away.

"I hear what you're saying about the homesickness," Ciara says, maybe trying to distract me from how badly this is going. "My girlfriend and I broke up before I came here. I miss everything about Brooklyn, especially her."

"That sucks," I say, which comes out like *su-uh-uhcks*, because I'm huffing and puffing. "But maybe you'll get back together this summer when you're home?" *Ho-oh-ome.* I sound like a deranged Santa Claus. And I'm probably in worse shape than him.

"The breakup needed to happen," Ciara says, her feet slapping the floor. "I just miss being friends."

Amanda has a funny look on her face. She doesn't say anything about being homesick, but I can see something painful behind her green-eyed stare. Maybe she hates her family or something; maybe she's glad she's here. Then she asks me, "Do you have a boyfriend?" And I say, "No," and she doesn't say anything else at all.

We run in silence the rest of the way. I'm downright dizzy by the time we get to lap thirteen. A few of the groups have already finished. We pass the fire alarm and I seriously consider pulling it. We run lap fourteen with only three other groups, and then the worst thing happens—I have to walk a lap. I'm honestly too close to death to not say anything, so we jog lap sixteen all by ourselves because every other group is done. My cheeks burn with shame, and I'm trying so hard not to collapse. And it appears nearly all two hundred cadets are giving me pitying looks! "This is going to tank our War Games ranking," Amanda says to Ciara.

"You're the one with plenty of wiggle room," Ciara says. "You're in the top twentieth percentile."

"I can't believe she made us walk a lap," Amanda says, like I'm not right there next to her! And like their precious War Games ranking is more important than my potential heart failure!

A whistle blares the second we finish. *"Attennnnnntion!"* Lt. Sturtevant yells, drawing the word out exactly like you always hear it in movies. Every student turns to face her, chins held high. I can't breathe. My legs are shaking and I have absolutely no idea what I'm doing. How high am I supposed to hold my chin? Are my feet supposed to be together or hip-width apart, like in yoga? I try to copy everyone else, but I'm so obviously an imposter, and Sturtevant so obviously notices.

"The fastest team mile was run in six minutes and thirty-nine seconds. Well done, cadets," she says, glancing over to Jack, Joni, and their teammate, a cute redheaded guy.

Of course.

Sturtevant has an iPad she must have procured while we were running/dying. She types something, and says, "That secures all three of your spots in the top ten percent of War Games selection."

I glance around and try to suss out how much everybody cares about this War Games situation, and it appears they really do. Nearly all the cadets are hanging on Sturtevant's words. I can see maybe two or three who look uninterested, but that's about it. Jack, Joni, and the redheaded guy

66

are smiling, and Sturtevant makes a face that looks like she's trying to smile, too. Then she strides over to me. "Brooks," she says. It's incredible how still and silent everyone has gone. Doesn't anyone have an itch or a cramp? "Stand like this," she says. My windpipe is still burning from exhaustion as Sturtevant places her hands on my shoulders, squaring them, and then positions my arms so there's a little space between my elbows and my body. She curls my fingers into a relaxed fist, placing them just behind my hip bones, not quite to my butt. Then she puts my feet together and turns them slightly outward. She's surprisingly gentle about the whole thing. When she's done, she checks me over and gives a curt nod. She leaves me standing there, and I have to say, it feels good to be in this position (and also not to be running). I'm almost feeling okay again, until Sturtevant announces, "This morning during combat training we will review the skills we learned last week. There will be a strong focus on combat training for War Games qualifiers."

My parents wouldn't even let Ella and me touch the vintage army figurine guys Grandpa Frank left us because they worried it would encourage violent play. Did they even *think* about this before they sent me here? I can barely throw a softball. How the freak am I going to defend myself in combat?!

I'm so sweaty I feel like I'm going to pass out as Sturtevant blabs on about how the War Games are a privilege, and something not every military academy offers. So many cadets are nodding—it's like they've all drunk the

War Games Kool-Aid, but I don't get it: What could ever be so great about extracurricular war activities that they'd all be so into this?!

"Washington, Moore, Brooks!" Sturtevant shouts.

Please don't be saying my name.

I turn, catching sight of Jack. He's watching me.

"Come to the front, cadets," Sturtevant orders.

Fear prickles my skin as I follow Ciara and Amanda toward Sturtevant. When I used to take chorus, we had this teacher who would make the worst singers stand up by themselves and sing first. It was so painful, and it's totally what's happening right now. My whole body is still shaking as we all stand there in front of Sturtevant, waiting.

"Self-defense is a necessary skill to master whether or not you are a military student," she says to me. She seems almost Zen, until she screams: "Boxing stance!" right in my face. She's so close I can smell her toothpaste. (Tom's of Maine Cinnamon Clove, the kind my mom buys for Ella and me even though we beg for Crest.) Ciara and Amanda jump into a wide stance and pop their hands up. I do the same, feeling ridiculous. I have no idea how to throw a punch, and I *really* don't want anyone to punch me.

"An effective boxing stance will allow you to move forward, backward, side to side, and in a circle," Sturtevant says. "Perhaps more importantly, it will signal to your opponent that you are trained and ready for a fight." A *fight.* Right. Sweat trickles down my back. *Please don't make me fight anyone, Sturtevant. You have to realize I don't know how!* "It will signal to your opponent that you're *not* about to be his next victim," she says.

Last year there were some muggings at the mall, and no one was physically hurt but we were all scared. Maybe I can learn to do this. Maybe I can protect myself.

"Bend more at the knee, Brooks," Sturtevant says. "Left foot forward! Right arm closer to your ribs!"

"Um, okay," I say, trying hard to do what she says.

"Don't speak to me unless I ask you a question, Brooks!"

That is so freaking rude.

"Right arm protects your ribs, right hand protects the right side of your chin, and left shoulder protects the left side of your face," Sturtevant instructs.

That's just a lot of instructions at once. I try my best to make my body look like Amanda's and Ciara's.

"Make a fist, for God's sakes, Brooks!" Sturtevant screams.

I do, and then she turns to the rest of the cadets. "This is your two-point cover, as everyone here besides Private Brooks is aware of," she says, and I can't figure out if she's being sarcastic or genuinely trying to give me a break. She pivots back to us. "Now get your left hands up at a forty-five-degree angle. Step forward and slide, cadets!"

What the flip? I don't know how to do any of this! I watch as Amanda and Ciara spring into action like trained Navy SEALs. They're way better than I would have imagined—especially Amanda.

I jump-slide forward with my fists cocked, trying to do

it like they did, but everything feels wrong.

Sturtevant grimaces like whatever I'm doing is physically traumatizing her. "I believe that's called a *sashay*, Brooks," she practically snorts, marching toward me. "Try again. Everything must be symmetrical. Slide forward ten inches, slide back ten inches."

I don't think that's the definition of symmetrical, but I don't say so.

"This time get your back heel off the floor and put a little more spring in your step."

I lunge forward and then back, trying to make my distance even.

Sturtevant shakes her head. Then she jumps in to demonstrate, lunging forward and backward. "Advance! Retreat!" she shouts. Her fists are up, and her body is coiled like a mousetrap ready to spring, and it dawns on me that she could probably end my life in less than five seconds.

She moves forward three lunges until she's a breath away from my face. It's actually really scary, and my chest is burning with how much I want to cry, how much I want to run back to Mount Pleasant and jump into my mother's arms. I fight back tears as Sturtevant shouts, basically in my face, "You are only as good as your weapons, cadets. How effective can you be?" She retreats three lunges back, and I stupidly think I'm in the clear until she practices her aforementioned "symmetry" and lunges three times toward me. "Strike!" she screams, and throws a punch directly at my face, missing me—on purpose, obviously—by the width of a hair.

I duck and scream. It's a pathetic scream, a whiny-baby scream, an *I don't want to be here can someone please call my parents* scream. It echoes off the wall and into the ears of two hundred cadets, reeking of defeat. Ciara freezes, and Amanda shrinks like she wants to be as far away from my misery as possible, but I can just see Joni in the front row of cadets; I can see her take a step toward me. Sturtevant pulls back, and there's a look on her face that might be regret, but I'm not sure because my eyes are welling up and my vision has gone blurry.

My cheeks burn with embarrassment and a single hot tear rolls over my cheek. What could possibly be the point of this stupid training when I'll never be as good as these other students?

I want to go home.

FIVE

I STOP SLEEPING THAT WEEK.

I get under my covers day after day with my strained muscles and my tired brain and I just lie there, replaying PT and all my academically exhausting classes, which are already way, *way* harder than at my old school (we've already had pop quizzes in trig and chemistry, and an oral presentation about our holiday break to deliver *in Spanish*, which, news flash: I don't speak).

We've literally run over ten miles since Tuesday, (I walked at least half of those miles while holding back tears), and I tried emailing someone in administration to see if I could get new shoes that fit right, but no one's emailed me back yet.

At midnight on Thursday I'm sweating/cold/having to pee/crying into my pillow/nervous/throw-up-y/staring at my phone and trying not to call my parents, who've spent their night texting me inane things like:

How did today go, sweetie? Was it better than yesterday? Did they let you sit out the obstacle course with your ankle still recovering?

I bet you did great!

Just say no to drugs!

The really weird thing about tonight is that Joni's not here. Her bed is neatly made, with the pillows standing at attention. She seems so rule-obsessed that I'm worried she's missing curfew because something's wrong, but I don't have a way of finding out without getting her in trouble.

This past week Joni's been really nice to me. She's not gregarious or anything like Andrea and me, or even quietly talkative like Julia, but I think she maybe likes that I'm her roommate. And her being quiet means I pay attention more when she does say something, and it's usually something helpful. Like yesterday, she told me to work on a breathing pattern to count my breaths when I run, and last night we worked on my two-point cover in our room.

Jack's been hanging around with us a lot, too, and he says most things here are mental, even if they feel physical. (And he's still so ridiculously hot that I practically need my new breathing pattern to calm down when I'm around him.) Sometimes I notice Joni looking at Jack carefully when he pays attention to me, like she's studying him. I don't think she likes him *like that*, but maybe she's a little possessive of him, and wary of me inserting myself into their friendship? Still, Jack and Joni seem like they're genuinely trying to help me, unlike Ciara and Amanda, who feel like they're more in it for themselves. I mean, they definitely haven't asked me to partner on anything again after I blew our run so badly. Ciara's nice enough, but Amanda seems to hate me more every day that I get closer to Jack and Joni. She either has a thing for him now, and Joni and I are just in the way, or she had a thing for him in the past, and now she hates Joni and me by association. It's not good.

I'm wrapped tight like a mummy in my covers as I text a little with Ella, who's awake, too, and telling me she's not speaking to our parents out of solidarity. When we say good-bye I start tightening and loosening my butt muscles (per a Dr. Oz relaxation technique), because I'm just so stressed out, but a moment later there's a knock on the door.

"Joni?" I whisper.

I prop myself up on my elbow and glance out the window to see dark sky spotted with stars. There's no sign of morning coming any time soon, only the outline of tree branches against the night sky. I reach for my phone for the flashlight but I can't find it in the tangle of covers. "Joni?" I call again, whipping off my sheets.

I shudder. Our room is freezing.

What am I supposed to do? I'm assuming I'm allowed to answer the door past curfew. Maybe Joni forgot her keys?

I tiptoe across the carpet. My fingers pause on the doorknob, and I've seen enough horror movies to know I shouldn't open the door, but I do anyway.

"Are you trying to get me caught, new girl?" a low voice asks.

My heart pumps faster as a large body pushes inside and shuts the door. I fumble for the switch. Light floods my room and illuminates an impish grin on Jack's handsome face. "Jack," I say. Relief fills me—*it's not a burglar; it's just Jack!*—followed by a slick rush of adrenaline—*holy crap, it's Jack!*

"What are you doing here?" I whisper.

He laughs again. "Looking for you," he says. And then adds, almost without missing a beat, "And Joni."

I live for the almost.

"She's out," I say.

"Is she?" Jack asks, but he says it like a throwaway, like he isn't actually surprised. He checks his watch. It's big and official looking like Joni's. I wonder if I was supposed to get one with my uniform. It's about as fashionable as overalls, which are only ever okay on reruns of *Friends*. "It's one a.m.," Jack says. He isn't wearing his uniform—just jeans and a jacket—and he looks way more devilish without it. "Officially the morning. You hungry for breakfast?"

I feel the grin spread across my face. This is why I've always gone to bed in a cute outfit: you never know when you could be called out of your home and into the public eye due to a natural disaster, an errant burglar alarm, or a hot guy wanting you to sneak out with him. "Hungry?" I say. "In the middle of the night?" I fake a yawn. "More like *tired*." But I'm smirking now, and when his eyes meet mine I know he knows I'm not tired at all.

"But breakfast is the most important meal of the day," he says, his deep voice confident.

"*True*," I say.

"And it's tradition," Jack says. "You have to break at least one rule during the first week of term."

"Well, in that case . . . ," I say, feeling like I could jump out of my skin at the prospect of breaking rules with him. Why is it so hard to be good?

"Exactly," he says, grinning. "Traditions are important. We should go." He grabs my coat and hat from the hook next to our door, then takes my hand and says, "*Shhhh.*" My fingers warm at his touch, and then so does the rest of me.

Nothing sounds better than escaping this week—leaving behind all the ways I've felt like a failure—but . . .

"What happens if we get caught?" I whisper.

"We'd get in trouble," he says as he opens the door. "So we better not get caught, Frankie." He squeezes my hand, and it sends something hot over my skin, and then he grins again, and it's all I need. I know this isn't a good idea: I know I don't know him well enough; I know I'm breaking the rules; and I know I've promised my parents I'll be better. But it's like this force that comes over me, like no matter how hard I try to be the person my parents want me to be, *I can't*. And since when is a little adventure a bad thing?

I step into the hallway and slip my feet into the snow boats I left outside my door. I laugh a little—a high-pitched giggle I barely recognize—as Jack leads me down the dim corridor toward a mirror at the end of the hall that reflects our glassy images. I feel like I'm watching someone else run toward the mirror, someone braver. *Someone foolish?* a small voice whispers, but I shush it down and keep moving.

Jack's hand is tight around mine and my breath comes faster as he pushes open the door to the stairwell. We race down the stairs, our footsteps nearly silent. Before I realize what he's doing, he grabs my shoulders and pushes me gently against the wall.

"Shhh," he says, a finger to my lips. I don't think I've ever been this close to a guy. Even when Josh kissed me, it wasn't like this. He didn't press his body against mine. This is something different. This is—

"Jack?" I whisper.

Is he going to kiss me? Do I want that? *No.* Well, *mostly no,* because I just met him and it might upset Joni, and plus I liked Josh five days ago, but God, Jack is *so hot,* so I kind of do want us to kiss right now, but—

Footsteps.

The soft padding of feet echoes from somewhere below us. "Stay here," Jack says. I feel cold the minute he pulls his body from mine. I really need to stop thinking people are about to kiss me.

Jack moves to the railing and looks down into the stairwell. We're on a landing just above the second floor; if this mystery person climbs toward us, we're trapped. Jack edges back to me. "It's probably a guard," Jack says. A *guard*? That can't be good! "If he gets off on the first floor, we stay put. If he starts toward us, we make a run for it." My heart is pounding so loudly in my ears I can hardly hear him. "Just follow me and do what I do," he says.

Nerves race through me. My eyes follow the cut of Jack's jaw, and I swear I can see the glint in his dark eyes even in the near pitch-blackness.

"*We can't keep hiding like this*," a girl's voice says from somewhere down the stairwell, and then another voice says something I can't quite make out—something whispered.

I'm not sure if it's the whispers and the darkness or the wonderful strangeness of being pressed against Jack, but suddenly time seems to slow. I feel like I'm suspended in this moment, like its unexpectedness has made it surreal. But then I look up to see Jack's dark brows stitched together. "*It's Joni*," he says into my ear, his voice urgent.

"Are you sure?" I ask.

Jack grabs my hand and pulls me toward the stairs. Considering I can count the number of guys who've taken my hand *on* one hand, it's not exactly easy to act normal about all of this. We start racing back up the stairs. "Why are we running?" I hiss as we near the door that leads to the third floor. "Is she going to tell on us?"

"She's not going to tell on us," Jack hisses back. Our footsteps are so loud they may as well be drumbeats.

"Hello?" Joni's voice whispers. I can hear how nervous she is—like she's trying to suss out if we're just other students breaking rules like she is, or if we're guards or TACs about to get her in trouble.

My hand sweats against Jack's no matter how much I will it to stop.

"Hello?" Joni calls out again, her voice hollow, and this time, it strikes me as sad. I'm about to call out that it's just me, so she won't be nervous, but then Jack tugs my hand and starts moving even faster up the stairs. He shoves open the door to the third floor and pulls me into the hallway. We zoom over the carpet, and I nearly crash into him as he stops short in front of my dorm room. "I don't want to get you and Joni off on the wrong foot," he says, not even out of breath from the sprinting.

I arch my eyebrows. What the heck is that supposed to mean?

"There's another stairway," he goes on, and I can feel the warmth of his hands through my cotton top. He nods over his shoulder toward the other end of the hall. "You can go back to your room, or you can come with me."

I lock on to his eyes, so dark and serious.

"*You*," I say. "I'll go. With you."

This time he doesn't take my hand. He sprints down the hall so fast I can hardly keep up. A door slams behind us: a few more feet and Joni will round the corner and see us. Jack shoves open the door to the stairwell.

"Why didn't we go this way the first time?" I ask as we slip inside, relief coursing through me. The hallway was still empty when we shut the door—Joni didn't see us, I'm sure of it.

"Because Lt. Sturtevant sleeps downstairs," Jack says. His voice is soft as we descend the steps. "Her room is right next to the stairwell, and I swear she has bionic hearing."

Freaking Sturtevant. That's all I need.

"Then you better shut *up*," I whisper playfully. "I already have one demerit!"

Jack laughs, and somehow not even the threat of Sturtevant can burst my bubble of giddiness now that I know we're safe from Joni seeing us, which obviously means my priorities are wildly out of balance. We go deadly quiet as we pass Sturtevant's floor, and then Jack inches an exit door open with a barely audible *click*.

"That was close," Jack says as we spill onto the quad, his words warm and heavy against my cheek. He opens my jacket for me to slip inside. He's so careful putting it on me.

"Too close," I say, but I can't stop smiling. I put a hand on my knee and try to catch my breath.

"We're not off campus yet, private," Jack says, reaching for my hand again. "No time for a breather." He guides me around a stone fountain. A sculpture of a woman in uniform rises from the center of a fountain, her carved medallions dangling from her granite chest. "This place is going to whip you into shape, Frankie Brooks," he says.

"Um, yeah, see, I'm actually very worried about that," I say as we make our way onto a sidewalk. "The PT is putting me over the edge. Literally every day I pull a muscle I didn't even know I had."

Jack laughs a little. Then he glances at me, and he must realize I'm not kidding because he says, "It'll get easier every day. It's hard for everyone when they start."

"I hope you're right," I say softly. "It's just nothing like my old school, and I *really* miss my family, and my friends, and my free time to blog and read magazines, and also the lattes my mom used to make my sister and me every morning before school. God, lattes! Have you ever had one made with camel's milk?"

"Um, no, I haven't," Jack says, but I can hear a smile in his voice. "But I was homesick when I started here, too."

Streetlamps illuminate our path. Jack has one hand holding mine and the other hand over his left eye. I'm about to ask him if he's all right, but then he takes a sharp right and we move off the sidewalk onto a grassy field. It gets darker and darker, but I can just make out a line of trees twenty-five yards away. I stumble over rocks and Jack catches me way too many times. My foot crashes into something that feels warm and I freeze, praying it isn't a dead animal. "Oh my God," I say, letting out a small scream I try to muffle that ends up sounding way too prissy.

Jack reaches into a deep pocket of his jacket. His handsome face is silhouetted against the dark sky. "Here," he says, passing something heavy into my hand that might be binoculars. "Night-vision goggles." I can feel the outline of them, and how solid they are, and then Jack takes them back and carefully places them over my head. I almost say I don't need them, but then he gets them on right and I see everything *in the dark.*

"Wow!" I say, like an idiot. But it's seriously so cool. There's a yellow/green tinge to the landscape but I can make out *everything*, including the grooves on the log I just tripped over, and two squirrels with glow-in-the-dark eyeballs staring at me a few feet away. It's so weird and cool and I'm so nervous that I burst out silent-laughing, and then Jack says, "Okay, Amateur Hour, let's keep moving."

"Don't you need these, too?" I ask when I finally get myself under control.

"I covered one eye back there so it's already adjusted to the dark. That's what you're supposed to do when you're about to be submerged in pitch-black terrain."

"Oh," I say, because it's a pretty good idea and obviously not something anyone ever taught me. I stare up at Jack, imagining what I look like with my night-vision goggles on. I've never accessorized quite like this.

"When I lost my hearing, my eyesight got crazy-good," he says. He smiles at me, and with the goggles I can make out each pearly white tooth in his crooked grin. "Even when I got my implants and I could hear again, I swear my eyesight stayed bionic."

"So you just carry these goggles around for us mere mortals?" I ask.

"Exactly," Jack says.

We push through taller grass, careful about our footing. "How old were you when you lost your hearing?" I ask.

"Six," he says.

I wait for him to elaborate, but he doesn't. What I want to say seems so personal I don't know if I should. I can't stop thinking about how scary that must have been, and finally, I just say, "You must have been scared when it happened."

"I do remember being scared," he says, "but what I remember most is my parents being *really* scared." He pauses. I feel him turn and take me in, and then he squeezes

82

my hand. "I don't remember it as well as I want to," he says. "What I remember is how it got harder and harder to hear things, like my mom's voice—that was the worst—and we didn't know what was wrong. Then *all* of my hearing went, and after like a million trips to the doctor I got these," he says, pointing to the implants.

We walk a bit longer. Why is it when someone shares something that makes him or her scared, you feel a real friendship start? Why do we all ever bother acting like we have everything under control? "Sometimes I don't know what to say when someone tells me something important," I tell him. "So I'm just going to shut up for a little bit so I don't say something stupid. And then I'll get back to you when I have something well thought out that conveys what I actually mean."

Jack lets out a laugh. "Okay. Cool. So I guess that means we have to hang out again?"

My insides flutter. "I guess so," I say. I'm so nervous it's hard to think straight. And it's taking so much concentration to escape from campus. My emotional and physical capabilities are already being way too challenged at this school. Why do I get the strange sense this is just the beginning?

The grass gets short again and Jack picks up our pace until I feel like we're flying across the field. It's so much easier with the goggles on. I feel awesome, like I'm on a secret mission or something.

"You doing okay?" he asks me.

"Just a little out of breath," I say. *And also my heart is racing,* which is both a result of being out of shape and also the fact that *we are sneaking out* and also *you are seriously so hot.*

"Are we almost there?" I ask, trying to breathe like I would into a paper bag.

"T minus two miles to go."

"What?!" I blurt. I haven't walked two miles except at the Westchester mall, which is different because I take lots of breaks to try on clothes and drink Frappuccinos.

"You're doing great," Jack says.

I am?

I concentrate on our feet passing over the uneven ground. Jack's Converse are getting soaked. Thank God I wore my boots. "So why aren't you wearing your uniform?" I ask him.

"I figured you'd be more likely to sneak out with me if I looked like the rest of the lame, nonmilitary guys you probably know back home," he says.

I stifle a laugh. "I guess your disguise worked," I say.

"I'll say," he says. He's being gentle and considerate about it, but he's basically dragging me. "Where are we *going?*" I ask as we bolt toward a fence.

"I promise it's not too much farther," he says. Then, maybe to distract me from the exertion, he says, "Joni told me you're a fashion blogger." I'm impressed that he got the term right and also that he's able to carry on a normal conversation as we basically sprint.

"Yes, I am," I huff, and he looks at me, but it isn't like the way Joni looked at me when I told her about my blog, and not only because I'm wearing the night-vision goggles and he's slightly neon-colored. It isn't confusion on his face; it's interest. The goggles make me sure of it. And maybe it's not romantic interest, but it's at least interest in what I'm saying. "So you think you can tell a lot by what someone wears?" he asks.

I can't tell if he's challenging me or not. Because obviously I agree with the whole *don't judge a book by its cover* mentality, but still . . .

"Don't you?" I ask. It seems so obvious to me I don't know how to answer the question any other way.

"Hmm. I never really thought about it," he says.

"You've never thought about *style*?" I ask, bewildered.

Jack laughs. "Maybe I have a little. And I can see what you're saying. My mom wears yoga pants and tunics, and she's pretty Zen. Or at least she used to be."

"Mine too!" I say, smiling.

"So what do our military uniforms say about us?" Jack asks. I follow his eyes to take in the gauzy clouds that lumber across the sky. They shroud the moon, and then clear to let light shine on our faces.

"That's the problem with uniforms," I say, trucking over the grassy field and breathing slowly. *In. Out.* "How are you supposed to express yourself when you're wearing the same thing as everyone else?"

"I guess you'll have to find a way to express yourself other than with clothing," Jack says. He seems to mean it lightheartedly, but I feel a little embarrassed. I know he's right: it's not like your clothes are who you are. But for me, it's always been the way I said hello to the world around me.

I'm quiet as we head toward what I can now see is a small break in the fence. "I guess to me style feels like a way to talk to other people without relying on words," I finally say.

He cocks a dark eyebrow, but nods like maybe he agrees.

We get to the fence. Jack bends and pushes aside a patch of tall grass growing wild even amid the snow. It makes me think of summer. No matter how much I love fall/winter fashion, my heart belongs to the warm weather. It's even worth surviving other teenagers—and worse, adult women—who wear short-shorts. (Why, God, why?)

Jack starts working at the fence. He's pulling it aside, gently but efficiently. He's noticeably big sitting there on the grass—he looks so much stronger than the guys back home. He yanks more fencing so the hole becomes almost wide enough that I could slip through. I glance around us to make sure no one's watching, but Jack doesn't seem nervous. He is totally and completely in charge, but not in a pushy way, just like that's who he is.

I take off the night-vision goggles and hold them in my lap. "I'm glad you came for me tonight," I say. Jack's dark eyes widen, but he doesn't say anything. He just stares at me. I made him nervous for the first time tonight—I feel it. My heart pounds against my chest like a trapped bird. His eyes are still locked on mine.

Kiss me.

The words come to me unbidden and I try to shake them off.

I just met him. Joni might not like the idea of us getting together because they're obviously best friends. I need to wait.

I inch away so nothing happens, no matter how much I want it to.

Jack doesn't say anything for a beat, and I can feel him trying to recover from whatever that was that almost just happened between us.

I run my fingers over a knotted tree root that snakes through the grass between us, and Jack helps me through the hole in the fence. He carefully protects my head so I don't hit the wire. *"Always take care of your fellow soldier,"* he says. "That's the Academy's motto."

I laugh a little, but what he said makes me think about tomorrow and how scared I am to do everything all over yet again, to be like a deer in headlights when Sturtevant springs something else on me. "Forget about what the Academy says," I say, feeling defiance surge through me like a shock.

Jack raises a dark eyebrow. "My kind of girl," he says, and my blood warms a degree. "Just for tonight, then," he says. "Tomorrow we go back to being rule-following cadets." He pulls back the fencing even more and follows me through. "You ready?"

We hold hands. I nod. I am.

SIX

THE TOMBS IS A RESTAURANT one mile south of campus. By the time Jack and I get there, I'm so cold I can barely feel my fingers, and tonight feels so strange I can hardly think straight. Not to mention my heartbeat hasn't normalized since we stepped off campus.

I let go of a breath as Jack leads me down the stone stairs toward a wooden door. I'm just going to take this one moment at a time. Nothing's happening with Jack and me, we're just hanging out. And I'm pretty sure that's not a betrayal of Joni—*yet.* The problem is I don't know because I've only had that one boyfriend, semi-terrible Carl Jensen, who had a pollen allergy and couldn't go outside for months at a time. (And I don't even want to think about what happened with Josh.) And even though I've read a lot of Ask E. Jean columns in *Elle*, and she gives great romantic advice, I can't recall anything relevant to my current situation.

The Tombs looks like it was built half underground, like some of the restaurants in downtown New York City that my parents have taken Ella and me to after seeing Broadway shows. There was this one time after *Cabaret* when Ella ordered coq au vin and convinced herself she felt drunk after realizing it was made with wine sauce. The head chef had to come to our table and assure her that the alcohol burned off during cooking, but that didn't stop her from needing to take slow, deep breaths while my mom patiently rubbed her back. The memory makes me ache with missing her. I wonder what she's doing right now. And if she's wondering the same thing about me, there's no way she'd ever guess I'd be doing this.

Light glows from the small, cloudy windows lining the side of the restaurant. Music pulses through the door, and when Jack swings it open, warm air rushes out to greet us. He unzips his jacket as soon as we're inside and I do the same. The night-vision goggles are tucked safely inside one of my jacket's pockets, and I feel weirdly reassured having them there. Maybe I should always carry night-vision goggles, even when I get back to Mount Pleasant. They're so much better than my phone's flashlight.

The restaurant has wooden beams on the ceiling and exposed brick on the walls. There are a dozen or so rectangular tables arranged in front of a stage. Framed photos of jazz musicians line the walls with signatures scrawled in black marker. There's a bar against the wall, too. Jack catches me looking at it and says, "They don't card here."

Yikes. Is this a bar or a restaurant? Are we allowed to be

in here? Military school is starting to make my rustic-chic mega party look tame. My parents would lose it if they knew I was in a bar.

I try to seem calm, casual. The smell of burgers and fries probably means this is mostly a restaurant. But what kind of restaurant is open at one in the morning?

"Should we sit?" I ask, my legs a little shaky.

Jack doesn't hear me over the music. He turns and calls out to a burly twentysomething guy. "Arturo!"

The guy—Arturo—lifts a meaty hand and breaks into a grin. He strides toward us and claps Jack's back. Jack's grinning when he introduces me as his new friend.

"Friend, eh?" Arturo says. The way he says it makes me wonder if he suspects we're more, and maybe that's because Jack always brings girls here. And not that there's anything wrong with that . . . I just mean I need to be careful, and not assume this is some real, actual *thing.* I don't need to embarrass myself like I did with Josh.

"Frankie Brooks," I say, extending my hand.

"Private Frankie Brooks," Jack says.

I kind of want him to shut up in case anyone else is here from the Academy. Should we really be so brazen?

We exchange *nice to meet yous,* and it's clear Arturo knows we're from the Academy and doesn't care, but I still keep my eyes out for people who could be military spies as Arturo leads us to a quiet table in the back. He sets down two menus. Jack pulls out my chair, which I don't think anyone has ever done for me besides my dad.

I don't bother opening my menu. "I didn't bring any

money," I say. Everything happened so fast at the dorm it wasn't like I had a chance to grab my wallet.

"No worries," Jack says, "my treat." He doesn't open his menu, either. "I'm still living large off my summer job shining rich guys' golf shoes."

I laugh.

"It sucked," he says, his eyes crinkling. At first he seems hurt that I laughed, but then he breaks into a grin. "Especially when the rich guys stepped in squirrel crap."

"Well, now I'm definitely ready to order some dinner," I say.

"I'm not that hungry," Jack says, so I say, "Me neither," because I'm worried he doesn't have enough money to pay for two dinners. One weird thing about Mount Pleasant is that most kids have enough money to do anything they want. One weirder thing is that some of them think that's the norm. "But I'm thirstier than I've ever been in my life because you made me take that ten-mile hike," I say, smiling as I sip the water Arturo sat in front of me.

We're quiet for a moment, listening to the music. When Arturo comes back, Jack orders us two sodas and French fries to share. I'm beyond relieved that he doesn't order alcohol, and maybe that means there's a speck left of the girl my parents would be proud to call their daughter.

Arturo heads to the bar and Jack moves his chair so that he's sitting right next to me. His nearness makes me so nervous I can hardly breathe. There's something between us that feels like a pull—I want to be even closer to him, but the thought of it has me so fluttery I can hardly take it.

I turn to him, gathering my courage. "So you and Joni . . . ," I say, leaving it hanging in the air like smoke. Because they're obviously extremely close, and I don't want to make any mistakes by hanging out with someone who someone else likes again.

"Me and Joni," Jack says, his words slow and careful. "What about us?"

"Friends?" I ask.

"Good friends," he says.

"Just friends?" I ask.

He meets my eyes. "Just friends."

I nod. "No history?" I ask, trying to keep my voice level. It wasn't easy to ask that.

Jack stares at me like he's trying to figure out what it means that I have these questions. "Lots of history," he says evenly, "but not the kind you mean." His gaze holds mine like he's challenging me, like he's trying to figure me out. Every second his eyes are on me feels like an eternity. I swear his cheeks flush a shade brighter, but then Arturo comes to set down our drinks and I have to pull myself from Jack's stare.

We say thanks for our drinks and Jack pushes the ice cubes down with his straw. "Our dads were in the military together," he says, watching the squares of ice bob back to the top of his soda. "Best friends since West Point." I recall the photo of Joni with the uniformed man on her desk—probably her dad. "We didn't always live close to Joni, except for a few stints in Florida, because our families both moved around a lot, typical military family stuff."

He shifts his weight. He must be a senior. His shoulders are so broad, and he doesn't have that same skin-and-bones look that most tall guys have when they're sophomores. "We saw Joni and her family at least three or four times every year," he says, "and you can get pretty close to someone that way. You basically see them grow up."

Right. And in Joni's case, he saw her go from the gangly girl in that photo on her desk to the very pretty fifteen-year-old she is now.

"Moving around so much was shitty because we never lived long enough anywhere to make close friends, which is probably why my friendship with Joni felt so important," Jack says, looking down at his hands, studying his short, bitten nails. "And, um, I guess sometimes I'm not good at making close friends because I just always think they'll be taken away from me, or me from them, like it was when I was younger."

I clear my throat. I want to say the right thing. "That makes sense," I say carefully.

Jack looks away like he's a little embarrassed. A breath later, when he turns to me again, his dark eyes are big and clear, but there's sadness there, too. It's like watching him remember something important.

"Joni's parents died two years ago in a car crash," he says.

My chest squeezes like a fist. "Oh no," I whisper.

"It was horrible," Jack says. "I was already in military school in Missouri, and my sister was at high school in our town, but my dad couldn't take knowing Joni would be here by herself at the Academy, mourning her parents alone, so he sent me here so we'd be together. Joni has an aunt she lives with now in the summers, but here at school, I'm kind of all she has."

"And your sister, too?"

Jack looks away, staring out a tiny window into the darkness, and then clears his throat. "Rachel was at the Academy last semester," he says. "She was kicked out."

"Kicked out?" I say. "Wait, *Rachel*? Was she Joni's . . ."

"Roommate," Jack says.

"Rachel is your sister," I say softly. Was it the academics that got her kicked out—not making the 3.5? Or the physical training, maybe? There are so many reasons I can imagine getting kicked out for here, so many things I could mess up.

"Joni told you about her?" Jack asks.

I shake my head. "I found a book in my room with her name in it," I say. I want to be nosy and ask exactly why Rachel got kicked out, but Jack changes the subject before I can.

"The Academy is one of the best military schools in the country," he says, and it makes me feel guilty; other kids would love to get into the Academy—but I'm here instead. Maybe I should try to be grateful no matter how scared I am. "But at my old school in Missouri I had this amazing English teacher who would go over my writing on the side," Jack says, "and he was teaching me so much stuff I couldn't get anywhere else. I tried to tell my parents I wanted to stay, but my dad gave me a long lecture about sacrifice: sacrifice for country; sacrifice for family; sacrifice for God. It's *in* him, I guess, because he's always been able to sacrifice; same with my mom. He'd leave us for months at a time when he was on tour, and we had to be okay with that. And I do want to sacrifice, too; I just didn't want to leave my friends and my TACs in Missouri to come watch over Joni."

Jack taps a finger absentmindedly along with the music. I want to say: *It's not fair that your parents sent you away to school to babysit Joni*, but I don't. It seems too harsh given what Joni has had to go through. So instead, I say, "I don't think it makes you selfish to want to stay somewhere that's good for you."

Jack smiles a little like he appreciates that. "I hope you're right," he says.

"I'm always right," I joke, and he laughs a little, but then his eyes go darker.

"Problem is, now I know how much Joni relies on me, so when I graduate in May that leaves her with no one, again."

He says it simply, and it makes sense. "I can help, too," I say. "I really like helping people, and Joni's my roommate, so that pretty much legally binds me and her as friends."

I try to smile. I feel dumb for saying that, like I was doing a commercial for myself. But I mean it—being kind is one of my good qualities, rather than all of the other things I've been doing lately that are not.

"Joni likes you, roommates or not," he says, and it makes me want to live up to what I promised.

We're quiet for a minute, and then I ask, "So you want to be in the military, too?"

"I do," Jack says. "But the rule right now is I can't serve with these," he says, gesturing toward his implants. "They might change the rule at some point. If they don't change it, though, I'm going to be a war journalist and write about what's really happening in the world."

I let this sink in—how driven he is to achieve what he wants. Obviously the fact is that for a lot of people, the military is their dream. I need to remember that. "You saying that makes me realize I need to appreciate being here more," I say. "It's been hard. I mean, I don't want to be here, if I'm being honest."

Jack's face dims, and suddenly I feel like a huge idiot for saying that. "I don't mean that as anything having to do with you!" I say quickly, suddenly really nervous. "I just mean I don't think I'm cut out for this, I mean, you know, fashion's my thing, not this."

"No, yeah, I get it," he says. He clears his throat, and it suddenly feels really awkward between us. "Anyway, at my old school," he says, a little distractedly, like he just wants the awkwardness to pass, "my writing teacher said to become a good journalist you need read thousands of newspaper and magazine articles. You work out your own style later—but first you need to get the rhythm of that kind of writing from reading other people's work."

"Is that what you're always carrying in that big folder? Newspaper articles?" I ask, and I can feel him looking at me as he nods, and then I realize I've let on that I've noticed him on the quad. "I saw you the first day my parents dropped me off," I say. "You were walking across the quad, reading."

He smiles, and then I ask the thing I'm trying to figure out about this place: "So are most kids at the Academy like you and Joni? They want to be military?"

Jack studies me. "Half and half," he says, running a hand through his spiky dark hair. "There are troublemakers and lifers. The troublemakers—like yourself, no offense—got sent here because their parents thought they needed military school. But you still have to be really smart to get in here. And it's not the kind of place that takes you if you did anything illegal, so even the troublemakers aren't *that* bad. The lifers plan to go into the military in some capacity. There are other kids here, too, like the ones who are trying to figure themselves out or escape stuff that happened at home. But those are in the minority."

I nod slowly. Serving in the military is Joni's dream, that's for sure, maybe passed down in her blood somehow from her dad. And it's Jack's dream, too, and he might not even get to do it!

I start thinking about all the things people want and don't get, and somehow that gets me worried again that there's maybe even a chance that Joni likes Jack, even if he says they don't have history like that. I liked Josh even though he had a girlfriend, and that felt so awful. The pain of what happened back home with Josh, and then with my family, swells like a knot in my chest, and I swear I'm going to break down and cry with homesickness any second, so I say, "We should go."

"Are you not having a good time?" Jack asks, his dark eyes heavy.

I get the sense that Jack's a good guy, but can I trust that feeling? I've been wrong so many times about guys, and stuff I think I understand until I realize I don't.

"It's not that—it's just . . ." *I'm really nervous being here at military school. I don't know what's going to happen to me. I miss my family. I'm worried I'm doing yet another bad thing right now. Also, I don't know what you and I are doing. I don't know if we're even doing anything. I don't know if you do stuff like this all the time because you're a senior. I don't know why you picked me to come with you tonight, and I don't know if it means anything at all.*

Jack long, dark eyelashes flutter as he takes me in. He looks unsure for the first time tonight, like he made a mistake.

"I'm sorry," he says.

I don't know what to tell him.

"I just need to get back," I say, my words so soft they're nearly swallowed by the music. I'm suddenly so sorry for all the terrible things I've done this year to my family—and to Lia, whom I passionately dislike but still regret hurting— and I feel like I can hardly breathe. I need to stop doing stuff like that. I need to leave this place right now and figure out exactly how I'm going to be good here.

Jack arches forward and takes my hand. I feel little sparks of electricity on my skin. "I get it," he says softly.

You don't—not at all. You don't know how bad I've been, you don't know hard it is for me to be better, and you definitely don't know how scared I am that maybe I can't change.

SEVEN

BY THE NEXT WEEK THEY'VE officially added me to War Games ranking, and *shocker*, I'm dead last. I can't stop sucking at every single physical thing Sturtevant makes me do. It's just so embarrassing. I'm not saying I want to be in War Games, but I also don't want to be literally *dead last* on a list of two hundred people. But any hope I had of moving a few spots up was dashed today in PT when we had to do monkey bars. Monkey bars! Like five-year-olds do at the playground! But you seriously can't believe how hard they are: I couldn't even get myself from one bar to the next. I ended up falling into a pit of wood chips, which gave me a huge splinter on my finger, which was bothering me so much I had to go to the infirmary so the nurse could tweeze it.

I glance down at my schedule to make sure I'm heading the right direction for Military Strategy. Most of my classes make me really nervous, but I actually really like Military Strategy, (and, of course, pottery, because I'd love to have my own line of handcrafted home goods one day, like when I'm seventy and retiring from the magazine world. I already made a mug last week that says FASHION SAVED MY LIFE!)

I fold up my schedule and keep walking. I can't find a bathroom, and I'm pretty sure I have mascara streaked all over my face from crying *again*, this time about the splinter. It was literally as sharp as a shard of glass!

Mess I went okay this morning. Ciara and Amanda insisted I sit with them, even though I wanted to find Jack and Joni. Jack's been so nice to me ever since we snuck out, even though he seemed a little embarrassed when he snuck me back into my room, like he'd messed something up.

And Joni's been so busy studying we barely have time to hang out, but today she came over to see if I was okay at breakfast after the wood chip incident. Of course Amanda gave us a death stare while Ciara picked at her omelet. I have no idea what happened between the two of them and Joni. I'm still sensing it's about Jack, but I don't even want to ask because I don't want to choose sides between them. I've never been someone to do that, really, because there's always more to the story.

Julia, Andrea, and I got along just fine at Mount Pleasant without being part of a certain group. Even though the three of us were best friends, we always had other friends in different social circles. So I'm not going to start allying myself with one group or another now. I know better.

Cadets brush past me, hurrying to their classes. My chest is so tight I can hardly take a breath. I need to find a bathroom but I don't think I can fix my makeup without being late to class, and you only get one warning for tardiness; the second time you're late to class you get a demerit. People must get kicked out of this place all the time! I pick up my pace, which makes me think about the sprints Sturtevant made us do this morning, which makes me want to cry again. I'm about to give in to the tears and make my mascara worse when I hear my mother's voice.

Just breathe.

It's what she used to say to Ella and me when we were little and devastated over something that felt so wildly important back then, like a broken toy or a lost doll, or a dance recital gone wrong.

Focus on your breathing, Frankie.

I hear her like she's right next to me, and instead of making me want to cry with how much I miss her, it steadies me a little. I watch my feet walk the hallway and I breathe.

In, out, in, out.

I smile a little. Maybe my mom's thinking of me right now, too.

I breathe deeply for another minute or two and I feel a little more okay. I feel *better*, at least, than before. And I'm starting to feel like if I suck so badly at physical stuff, then maybe I should focus on doing well academically at the Academy. I could get back the part of me I lost in high school, the part of me that liked to study and felt amazing when I got high grades.

Room 163.

Room 165.

A few more classrooms to go and I'm there, my arm muscles protesting as I push open the door.

MILITARY STRATEGY is written in blue chalk on the board like usual. Class size is smaller here for more "personalized attention." (#HowGreat.) There are three rows with six desks each. People are so prompt; there's still a minute to go until the bell rings, but I'm one of the last ones to show up. Again.

I spot Jack in the front row and a zing passes through me. The good thing about this school is that some of the military-specific subjects are offered to sophomores, juniors, and seniors, so we can actually be in the same class. I try to hide how nervous he makes me by walking right over to him like it's no big deal, acting like of course I'd go talk to him because we're friends. I try not to notice how many kids look at me funny. I try to tell myself it's because I'm new here, but I'm pretty sure it's because of all the embarrassing things that keep happening to me in PT.

"Want to sit together back there?" I ask, pointing to the back row, where there are two open spots.

"This classroom is too echoey," Jack says. "I gotta be in the front. Hang on," he says, and then he leans over to talk to the girl next to him. She looks up at me and smiles, and it's totally one of those smiles you give someone you feel super bad for, but I don't even care. She moves to the back row after low-fiving Jack like old pals. Everyone seems to like him here; I can tell by the way they cluster around him in PT and in the dining hall. He has a wide group of guy friends, but no one who seems to be his best friend or anything, and he doesn't pay particular attention to any girl except Joni. (And trust me, there are a lot of pretty girls who seem interested in him.) And he definitely avoids Amanda.

"Thanks!" I call to the girl, meekly.

"Sit down and take a load off, princess," Jack says. I can tell he's trying to make me feel a little better after this morning, but it's not working. All of my muscles are killing me as I lift my bag onto the empty desk. A few students turn to stare at us, but most glance back to their phones and books. "At my old public school the teachers wore FM systems," Jack says as I sit. "So they wore mics and their voices streamed directly to me, which was awesome. They don't have them here, which is BS, as far as I'm concerned," he says.

"Another reason you liked your old school," I say.

"Exactly," he says.

Two guys at the end of the row are laughing, and there's a girl near the window who reminds me a little of my sister. My heart does something funny as I watch her flip through her textbook. I imagine myself back home for just a second, working on my blog, going to school with Andrea and Julia like old times, spending time with Ella, sleeping in, eating non–dining hall food like Pinkberry frozen yogurt, and for God's sake—not working out.

Jack's dark eyes search my face. "You okay, Frankie?" he asks as I try to get comfortable in my chair. My thighs hurt so bad from the marching drills we had to do today. I don't think my legs were meant to stomp at right angles. God, what I wouldn't give for those relatively easy father-daughter Pilates classes back home!

"Just missing my family," I say.

Jack looks a little more empathetic than he did the night we were out together, but there's still the smallest flicker of doubt on his face, like he thinks I'm some faker who hates it here. And that's not entirely true; it's just that I'm so freaking homesick!

"Can we not talk about me falling into the wood chips?" I ask.

"Sure," he says, then, "It will get better, okay?"

I lower my voice so no one can hear us. "How can you know that?"

"Because being the new student sucks," he says. "You don't know what you're doing and you barely know anyone."

He smiles at me, not one of his wide, crooked grins, but a softer, careful smile. There's something so calming about his presence; maybe it's because he's strong enough to be my bodyguard. I don't even think Sturtevant could scare me with him around. "Maybe you'll even start to like it here eventually," he says. His voice is so hopeful.

"Is Joni starting to hate how I keep messing up?" I ask softly. "Am I embarrassing her?"

Am I embarrassing you?

I realize a beat later it's what I actually want to know. Because why is he so nice to me when I'm so bad at everything? He's one of the best students here—he's good at *everything*, and I'm just good at fashion blogging and cultivating a unique personal style.

Jack purses his perfectly bowed lips. I really hope he isn't hanging out with me because he feels sorry for me. The thought makes me feel awful.

He meets my eyes, and he looks like he wants to say something—I can see him thinking about it. But then he shakes his head like he's changed his mind. "Some of the kids here on are scholarship," he finally says, "and Joni's one of them. She has to do well here—and not get any demerits—so she can afford to be here. She's not going to endorse you, you know, answering your phone in front of the whole school and Sturtevant."

Heat rises to my cheeks. It's like Bad, Selfish Frankie all over again. Have I always been this way and just never noticed? My parents would be horrified at the way I acted the first morning in PT. (They would also probably be horrified at Sturtevant throwing a punch in my direction, but that's their own fault for sending me here.) "But it's not your fault you can't do all the PT stuff yet, and of course Joni's not mad at you," Jack says. "She likes you, actually. She thinks you have spunk."

"That's one way to put it," I say. I smile but Jack doesn't. He looks nervous.

"I think so, too," he says. He clears his throat. "You're so different, Frankie. It's kind of refreshing, actually."

My cheeks get so hot they must be streaked with pink, and Jack is probably noticing!

"And, um, the other night," Jack says. I can sense the girl on his right starting to listen, and I'm pretty sure Jack can, too, because he leans closer.

My pulse picks up speed trying to imagine what he's going to say. It's the first time we've been halfway alone since that night—we're constantly surrounded by other students in PT and in the dining hall.

"I just wanted to have fun with you," he says.

The bell rings, and I jump. I scan the classroom, but our teacher isn't here yet. "It *was* fun," I say, a little more defensively than I mean. The air smells like lemon detergent, and it's suddenly making me nauseous.

"I'm sorry if I did something I wasn't supposed to," Jack says. His words are slow and cautious, like he practiced them. It reminds me of Josh in my driveway, and I sit there, feeling my body go numb, not knowing how to respond. I'm not sure if he means sneaking out with me in general, or if he means how some parts of that night started feeling like a date, not like I'm the expert on dates or anything.

Jack's olive skin flushes while he waits for me to say something. When I don't, he says, "I just didn't mean for it to turn into something that made anything weird between us."

I sit still for a second, watching Jack's features soften. Maybe the words are similar to what Josh said after what went down between us, but the space between Jack's words is different. There's something *there*.

"I want to be . . . ," I start, but my voice trails off. I almost say: *friends*, but I stop myself. I'm not going to say I

107

just want to be friends because it's not the truth.

"Friends, right, I get you," Jack says, but he doesn't look like he gets me at all. He looks embarrassed, or confused maybe?

The classroom picks up with conversation and volume, like the rest of the kids are sensing our teacher's going to show any minute and make them shut up.

"Wait, Jack . . . ," I say, trying to find the right words. "Me wanting to leave had nothing to do with not wanting to be with you." I need him to understand. "It's not that at all. It's more that I'm starting to realize I need to try to be better here, and I guess, um, learn discipline and follow rules, and . . ." My voice trails off. "Because my parents want me to," I say.

I run my fingertips across my desk. Is that why? Or is it because a little part of me wants it, too?

"Oh, okay," Jack says, seeming surprised. "Then from now on we follow the rules. I'll help you."

I grin. "You will?" I ask. "I'd like that."

Jack nods. "Maybe we could even . . . ," he starts, but stops midsentence because our teacher has pushed open the door and is announcing his presence in a booming voice:

"Good morning, Albany Military Academy students! Forgive me for being late to enrich your minds today!"

Right; class. The whole point of Albany Military Academy: *disciplined education.*

Lt. Martin is full-blown brainiac material with his wire-rimmed glasses and tufts of graying hair above his ears, the kind of professor who makes you feel dumb just by looking at him.

"Intelligence analysis," he says, scrawling the words on the chalkboard right below *Military Strategy*, then turning back to us. "Why is it vital? What makes a mind—maybe one of yours—sharp enough to analyze the kind of intelligence that changes the outcome of an operation, or an entire war?"

In Military Strategy, I don't even bother jotting down fashion items to blog about like I do in Mount Pleasant in some of my classes, and not only because I'm trying to do better here academically but because this class is completely fascinating.

"The analyst must avoid projecting onto the intelligence what she *wants* her opponent to be thinking," Lt. Martin goes on. His eyes are like stones as he scans us, almost like he's searching out which one of us could be the next great US military intelligence weapon. "She must remove her personal biases to objectively consider and decode the material before her," he says. "So, how do we do that? We avoid, above all, mirror imaging. Do *not* assume that your opponent thinks like you; do *not* assume that she values what you value. Your opponent may consider great risk appropriate for what *you* consider small gain."

My mind wanders a *smidge*. Maybe because I can smell how good Jack smells. *Focus, Frankie, focus!* But seriously, what *is* that smell? It's like woodsy and boyish and maybe a little minty, too. And what was he going to say to me earlier? *Maybe we could even . . .* what?

Maybe I'll just write him a quick note—it's not like passing a note is *that* bad, nothing like answering my phone, which obviously was wrong. This is just a reminder that we have more to talk about after class.

Talk later? I scrawl on a piece of paper. I wait till I'm almost positive Lt. Martin isn't looking to pass it onto Jack's desk.

"Private Brooks!" Lt. Martin shouts.

Shoot! "Yes," I squeak.

"Class," he booms, "here I am blathering on about intelligence analysis, and I see Miss Brooks passing intelligence to Mr. Wattson!" Bile rises in my throat. I can't get in trouble again or I'll be at two demerits.

Lt. Martin laughs, but it sounds good-natured. He's still got a hand on his round stomach. "Oh, don't worry, Miss Brooks!" he says. "You won't get in trouble for passing notes here," he says, "but you should pay more attention, because your grade rests entirely on your test scores in my class: not on your effort; your listening skills; nor, in your case, on what I can sense is a winning personality."

At least someone gets me.

A few students chuckle, but I'm too wiped to care. I just need to survive this week. "I'm sorry, Lt. Martin," I say, and I find I actually am, because I like him, and I definitely love his class.

He nods. "Now, where was I? Ah, pitfalls to avoid in intelligence analysis." He turns and scrawls *rational-actor hypothesis* on the board, then points to it with his chalk.

110

"To fall into this trap is to assume that your enemy is acting rationally under the same standards of rationality you assume. This is war, people," he says.

Knock. Knock-knock-knock. KNOCK!

Raps that sound like a military code crack the door, and I turn to see a boy's face pressed against the glass. Lt. Martin strides across the room and opens the door. "Hello, Archie Hancock!" he says. "To what do we owe this pleasure?"

Archie's the guy who was on Jack and Joni's ridiculously fast-paced running team that first day.

"I'm here for Frances Brooks," Archie, says, looking down at the piece of paper in his hand.

"We were just talking about Miss Brooks," Lt. Martin says excitedly, like I've won a contest. The rest of the kids in my class look at me with renewed interest. The air is thick, like they're all anticipating something.

"Um, I'm right here?" I say, raising my hand halfway.

Archie breaks into goofy grin. "The new girl," he says in an amiable voice like we're already friends. It doesn't escape me that he could have called me something way worse—*the girl who answered her phone in PT, the girl who fell off the monkey bars, the girl who can't run or fight to save her life*—and that small kindness feels huge right now.

"That's me," I say, my cheeks warming. "Frankie."

Archie folds the piece of paper in his hands and turns to Lt. Martin. "Frances Brooks is being summoned to Lt. Sturtevant's office."

Oh God.

111

"By all means," Lt. Martin says. "*Take her.*"

The class is quiet while I gather my things. I try to breathe slowly, but I can't. Lt. Martin turns back to the chalkboard and Jack whispers, "Text if you need me." He scrawls his number onto a scrap of paper and our fingers touch as he passes it into my hand.

Archie closes the classroom door behind us and we start down a hallway with glass windows. Sunlight pours onto the floor.

"Thanks for being so nice back there," I say, wondering if he knows what I mean. Could he possibly understand how vulnerable I feel here?

"No problem," Archie says.

"Um, so do you know what this is about?" I ask as we walk over the sunlit tiles.

"I don't," Archie says. "And Frankie, I know we don't know each other, so I hope you don't mind me giving you advice. I just think maybe you should try to keep a lower profile here."

He glances over at me, and he must see the question on my face, because he says, "Maybe you could be a little more careful with who you fall in with at this school."

"Fall in with?" I repeat. Does he mean Amanda and Ciara? Or Jack and Joni? Those are the only people here I've spent a lot of time with.

We stop outside a door marked LIEUTENANT STURTEVANT. "You seem like a nice person," he starts, and I can't help but think he might not say that if he knew what I did back home. If he really knew me, he might think I deserved to be getting in trouble.

"Just be careful," Archie says, knocking on the door.

I don't have time to ask him what he means because the door swings open to Lt. Sturtevant dressed in full military regalia with a purple heart pinned to her chest. I don't think I've ever seen one up close like this, but I know my grandpa Frank was awarded the Purple Heart decades ago.

Archie straightens, so I do, too. Then Archie salutes, which I do not do. Lt. Sturtevant salutes back. I stand there, stupidly, and then I get that weird feeling I get in dreams when I walk into a room and everyone's talking about me.

Archie retreats into the hallway, and I follow Sturtevant to a mahogany desk in the middle of a green-carpeted room. Then she salutes again. I feel like I should do it because it's just the two of us, and not doing it feels wrong, so I fling my hand to my forehead and try to remember the way she adjusted my arm into place that first morning in PT. I'm almost sure I have it pretty close, so I hold it there for a few beats. Then I fall back on my memory of Tom Cruise's military salute in *A Few Good Men*, which we watched one random day in my old school when we had a sub in drama class. Tom really whips his hand quite aggressively back out of the salute, so I whip mine dramatically, too. It feels awesome, and it seems to have gone over well, because Sturtevant doesn't look mad or anything.

"Please sit, Brooks," she says, gesturing to a massive leather chair in front of her desk, which looks like something out of a movie set. There are stacked military manuals; a model airplane; a gold-dipped cannon figurine;

and, to top it all off, a tiny rifle inside a snow globe.

Here's the thing: I have to Instagram this. As nervous as I am about Sturtevant yelling at me, the images before me are too good not to capture them and show my readers. And it's not like we've started our meeting yet, so maybe she wouldn't even mind. "Just a quick photo opportunity?" I ask her carefully, slowly taking out my phone. "I have a pretty big online presence, so it would be great press for the Academy. If you could just hold still for a sec," I say, and then I angle the lens so that Sturtevant's visible behind her paraphernalia.

"*Private Brooks*," Sturtevant says.

Almost got it . . .

"Private Brooks!"

If I could just get the rifle snow globe in the bottom left corner.

"Put your phone away, private!" Sturtevant growls.

Snap.

I tuck the phone into my bag and give her a look that says *I'm so sorry* and also *I learned my lesson.*

"Private Brooks," Sturtevant says, definitely already forgetting how good my salute was. "This is exactly the sort of problem we're having with you here." A line marks the inch between her dark eyebrows, and a single drop of sweat beads on her reddish forehead.

"Do you mean me using my phone?" I ask. "I agree that it's been a distraction for me, and I'm definitely willing to work on it." I adjust my butt on the leather chair. I glance up to the bookshelves behind Sturtevant to see a slew of serious-looking hardcovers and a framed photo of her wearing army fatigues in front of a line of beige tents.

"The problem is not just your phone," she says.

"Well, what then?" I ask. Maybe my parents have de-enrolled me? Could that be?

"You," Sturtevant says. "*You* are the problem. Your attitude, your work ethic, and mostly just the day-to-day ways you manage to show me disrespect."

My mouth drops a little. The list sounds so long and foreboding when she says it like that, and I've only been here for two weeks! Sturtevant steeples her fingers, which I don't even think I've ever actually seen someone do. In Mount Pleasant, it's all about prayer hands and positions that express gratitude and openness. Sturtevant doesn't exude either. She procures a photo from her desk and passes it across the desk, and—oh, *no!* It's blurry, but it's obviously me sneaking past the guard that night I snuck out with Jack! My platinum-blonde hair is just so remarkable!

"You were seen last Thursday night off campus at oh two hundred hours with an unidentified male," Sturtevant says in the same tone the detectives use on *Law & Order*.

"I-I was, actually," I stammer. But I can't seem to finish my sentence. There's a photo, and I did exactly what she's saying I did—all of it—and what's the point of lying to her? "I'm sorry," I say, feeling my eyes well with tears. Is she going to call my parents? They'll be so upset with me. "I'm really, really sorry." I put my face in my hands. How could I have been so stupid to think someone wouldn't report Jack and me? Was it a townsperson? Or maybe an

115

undercover military employee of the academy? Or maybe Sturtevant herself woke up and saw Jack and me outside her room and followed us?

"Unfortunately, an apology won't cut it, no matter how sincere," Sturtevant says.

I look up from my hands to see that her expression has softened just a hair. I consider trying to cry harder, but I'm not that great of an actress.

"Who reported my misdoing?" I ask, thinking if I sound verbally adept she might lighten my punishment. What if it was a fellow student?

"We have reason to believe the person who came forward may want to protect the identity of your coconspirator," she says.

My *coconspirator*: Jack. And who would want to protect Jack?

Joni. Could it be? But why? She's been so nice to me!

"Really?" I ask.

I feel like I could help Sturtevant get to the bottom of this, which I soon deduce is not what she's after. She taps a thick finger against her desk. "The Academy does not tolerate illicit student activity," she says, "which is why the last student residing in your room was expelled."

Rachel.

Sturtevant pops her knuckles. It sounds like a warning. "This is the moment you tell me the name of the other student you were with that night," she says.

"Um," I stall. "I don't think I can—"

116

"*Now!*" Sturtevant yells, leaning forward and knocking her chair into her desk. The crash sends the flurries in her rifle snow globe fluttering.

"Anger has deleterious effects on your health," I say. "My mother says life is about forgiveness and an open heart."

"Your mother sounds lovely," Sturtevant says. "Name, please."

"Marie Brooks," I say.

Sturtevant clears her throat. "Not your mother's name."

I stare at her. She can't expect me to give up Jack. Who would do that?

"I'm sorry," I say. "I can't."

"Private Brooks," she says, "if you don't tell me who you violated code with, I'll award you with your second demerit. And since your chores haven't been assigned yet, I'll take special care to place you in the mess hall. Would scrubbing floors strike your fancy?"

I smile at her and watch as the corner of her lip twitches. I can totally handle scrubbing the dining room floors. Ella and I used to watch *Annie* all the time.

"Tempting, truly," I say. "But no."

Sturtevant's nostrils actually flare. She's so cinematic.

"Fine, Private Brooks," she says. "Have it your way. That'll be demerit number two, and you can report to the cafeteria on Sunday at 1800. One more demerit and you're out."

"What time is that?" I ask. "Like, in English?"

117

"Google it," Sturtevant snaps. She stands, which I take to mean I'm excused. She salutes, and this time I do it so dramatically that I almost knock myself out.

Note to self: tone down salute.

I'm walking toward the door when Sturtevant says, "Private Brooks?"

I turn to see her arched over her desk, ready to pounce.

"I hope you like hairnets," she growls.

EIGHT

I NEVER THOUGHT I'D ACCESSORIZE my look with weapons, but two days later I'm standing on a grassy field holding a bow and arrow, because *archery* is my newly assigned after-school sport.

Archery!

At least Lt. Sturtevant isn't teaching it. She's been riding me extra hard in PT, keeping her eye on me like she's just waiting for me to mess up or mouth off one more time. I keep wondering why it's so hard for me to be good, and if it's this hard for everyone. I think about Julia, and how she's always so respectful of authority. She would never Instagram her teacher.

(Though that photo *did* get over a thousand likes.)

To make up for my terribly disrespectful attitude problem, I've started studying way harder. Classes are ramping up in terms of intensity: I've managed to keep my GPA at

3.58, with trigonometry being the class that's by far the scariest. Tomorrow we have a quiz on sines and cosines, and I figured out I need to get at least a 3.25 to keep my average at a 3.5, which means tonight I'm probably not going to get to blog, *again*. Even Julia and Andrea have noticed, texting me things like: **you ok? Never seen you miss a post!**

But I can't get kicked out of here—I just can't. My stubborn streak is at a full flare-up: I miss my family so much, but even getting back to them wouldn't be worth the embarrassment of failing!

The TAC who teaches archery, Sergeant O'Neil, is male and wearing head-to-toe khaki, which normally I'd say was a huge fashion no-no, but I'm willing to look past it in the context of the United States military, because these are the folks who are protecting my rights to liberty and happiness and such. I wonder if there's a fashion designer who works on the uniforms the military wears? Probably yes, because there's a designer behind so many things you see, touch, sit on, walk on, kick, throw, or snuggle. It's mind-boggling.

Sgt. O'Neil paces down the line of cadets and hands out bows and arrows, and I can just catch Joni out of the corner of my eye, reaching out a slim hand to take her weapons. She hasn't returned to our room until past curfew for two nights in a row; I have no idea where she goes, but she must be pretty sneaky—she doesn't have a single demerit yet. It's interesting that she risks it considering what Jack told me about her scholarship, but I guess it must be something or someone really worth it.

When Joni sees me, her face lights up with a grin. Seeing her smiling at me like that, I just can't imagine she sent that photo to Sturtevant. I think, even by the time I left Sturtevant's office that day, I knew it wasn't Joni. She doesn't seem to have a mean bone in her entire body.

There are a dozen cadets standing in a straight line in front of six multicolored ringed targets placed forty feet away. I'm the only one who seems to be getting frostbite out here. Once we each have our weapons, Sgt. O'Neil blathers on about the parts of the bow and arrow—*sight window, arrow shelf, hunting stabilizer*—and gazes reverently at his own bow like it's a golden harp and not a killing machine.

"As you know," O'Neil says, "you will be selected for War Games based on your leadership qualities, strategic thinking, and, of course, your physical training. You will be scored individually during physical challenges and by TAC discretion. For those of you who are new here," O'Neil says, glaring at me like it's my fault, "that means you have much to prove." He looks a little smug, like he's enjoying lecturing me, *cadet #202 in last place!* "Remember that only the top fifty percent of cadets will qualify for War Games placement."

It still blows my mind that there's so much emphasis on being our best just so we can compete against other military schools, like a travel war team. "Thanks, but no thanks," I whisper to the girl next to me, who doesn't seem to agree with me at all.

"What was that, Private Brooks?" Sgt. O'Neil asks.

Shoot. "Um, nothing," I say. "I just had something in my throat."

Sgt. O'Neil straightens and looks annoyed. "As I was saying, the top fifty percent will have proven themselves true leaders," he finishes. I try to focus on what he's saying, but then he starts telling some story about how he placed top five in his very own War Games at the Academy back in 1999. I stifle a yawn. Do adults have any idea how inapplicable these stories are? Who gives a flip about 1999? I'm exhausted from waking up at five for weeks on end, and my arm already hurts from holding this stupid bow. I stare down the target, realizing there's no way I can hit it from all the way back here. I would literally take a pedicure-related fungal infection over this. Maybe even basketball.

"Today you'll be working in assigned pairs," O'Neil says, snapping me back to attention. "Personal scores will be recorded; this is not a group exercise. This is every man and woman for herself! You will be ranked solely by the number of bull's-eyes hit."

Maybe if I hit a bull's-eye I can finally get out of last place.

"Let the fun begin!" O'Neil shouts.

Fun? God, what I wouldn't give for my idea of fun: shopping with my mom; *Project Runway* binge-watching with Ella; and then all three of us heading to Relaxation Spa for aromatherapy and reflexology. I can't believe I never realized how easy my life used to be!

O'Neil glances down at his clipboard. "Randol and Jetson!" he shouts.

Someone's last name is Jetson? That's amazing.

"Levine and Davis!"

"Murphy and Brooks!"

Joni parades over to me, holding her bow and arrow with the confidence of a professional hunter. There's a shuffle across the grass as the rest of the cadets find their partners. O'Neil starts marking up his clipboard.

"Hey," Joni says.

I stare down at my bow. I need to tell Joni what happened with Sturtevant, and I'm really nervous.

"Frankie?"

I tilt my chin to look at her. I can feel my fingers getting sweaty on my bow even though it's freezing out.

"Are you all right?" she asks. Her strawberry-blonde eyebrows knit together.

"I snuck out with Jack after curfew the other night," I whisper. "And Sturtevant caught me. And now I got another demerit *and* I have to mop the dining hall!" My voice comes out in a hiss.

"You snuck out with *Jack*?" Joni asks. She checks over her shoulder to make sure O'Neil isn't anywhere near us. "Did Sturtevant find out about Jack, too?"

"No," I snap. "But can we please focus on me right now?"

"He could lose his scholarship to Cornell!" Joni says, all sniffly and defensive.

"Sneaking out was his idea!" I say. Then I click my

123

tongue. "Cornell?" I ask. Impressive. "Early decision?"

Joni nods.

O'Neil is talking privately with a cadet at the end of the line. I lean in close to Joni. "Do you have any idea who would have told on me?"

Joni's lips purse. She whispers, "Probably Amanda. I think she has it out for you, Frankie. She doesn't like Jack and me, and you've been hanging out with us so much . . ."

God, *Amanda*. What is her problem?!

"Attention!" shouts O'Neil, and now he's striding down the line toward us. I try to blend in and make my body look like the rest of the cadets', but I'm the only person wearing sneakers and also the only platinum blonde, and plus I don't know how to make my body that straight while holding my bow and arrow.

"Levine! Del Fico! Irwin! Randol! Brooks! Webb!" O'Neil shouts. "Step to the line."

I take a timid step toward a white line. "This is your chance to defeat your enemies with precision and skill! To make them suffer with *arrows of outrageous fortune!*"

"He was an English major," Joni whispers.

"Load!" screams O'Neil.

Load *what*? My arrow? How?

O'Neil turns to adjust a cadet. Joni's gloved hand is suddenly over mine, placing the notch in my arrow against the string of my bow. "Are you a righty?" she whispers.

I nod, afraid that if I look her in the eye she'll stop helping me.

"Then get your right foot back a bit to open up your

124

chest," she says. "Softer grip on the bow—open up your hand a little. *Good*. When O'Neil says *aim*, just bring your arrow back toward your face like Jennifer Lawrence does in *Hunger Games*, okay? Then look over the string so you can aim the arrow right at the bull's-eye."

"Aim!" calls O'Neil.

I yank my bow back like Joni said.

"Open up your chest more, Frankie!" Joni hisses. "Or you're gonna hit your—"

Too late.

"Fire!"

I let go of the bow and feel a split second of total *Hunger Games* awesomeness—I am J. Law! Hear me roar! But then I feel the opposite of awesome when the arrow slices like a deadly paper cut across my chest. "Ow!" I yell as my arrow flies through the air and sails five feet over the target. I'm in so much pain I barely even notice that I'm the only one who entirely missed the target. I double over, clutching my right boob. "Oh my God!" I say. "Am I bleeding?"

It hurts so bad I'm crying within three seconds, and then O'Neil is screaming, "Private Brooks!"

No, O'Neil. Please stay away.

Joni grabs my shoulders and tries to steady me.

"I said to open your chest!" she scolds.

I peek down to see if everything's still there, and there's totally a serious cut! (Okay, maybe more like a scratch, but still.) I'm so pissed that I pull at my bowstring, which is apparently a huge mistake, because O'Neil screams, "Don't dry-fire that bow, Brooks! You'll damage the equipment!"

Joni straightens. O'Neil is flying toward us. Joni backs up, but before she does, she gives my hand a squeeze.

"Get down on the mother-loving frost-covered winter grass and give me twenty, Brooks!" O'Neil shouts.

I turn to Joni as if somehow she can help me.

"Don't cry," she whispers. She narrows her light eyes on mine and gives me a small nod. "You've got this, Frankie."

Ugh! I get down on the grass and start doing my push-ups. Why is everything so freaking hard here?! *One, two, three, four, oh-my-God-five, are-you-kidding-me-six, seven-I-just-cannot, eight-nope, nine-I'm-done!*

I collapse onto the grass.

"Are you serious right now, Private Brooks?" O'Neil asks.

"I'm pretty serious!" I say, rolling over onto my back. Thank God my Academy parka is waterproof. "I can't do any more!"

"In five, four, three, two . . . ," O'Neil shouts, like I should be getting ready for a jazz solo. But the counting works, and suddenly I'm forcing myself to pop back up again. I do a set of four more push-ups, then I collapse again, and someone laughs.

"Private Davis?" O'Neil says. "Did you just laugh at a young woman who could one day be your fellow soldier? Get down on the ground and give me forty!"

Jennifer Davis—a girl I know from trig—stops laughing, and then joins me on the ground. I slowly finish my twenty (and by *slowly*, I mean slower than Jennifer does her forty), and when I get up, Sgt. O'Neil says. "I'd like you to try to hit that target again, Private Brooks."

"Oh, me too, thank you, sir, for the opportunity to try again," I say, and I smile sweetly so Sgt. O'Neil doesn't realize just how not thankful I am. Why is it so hard to cultivate gratitude when you're having such a terrible time?

Shopping, fashion blogging, aromatherapy with my mom and Ella . . .

If I could only click my heels three times and go home, even just for a little break!

I pick up my bow and arrow, because I'm not home, I'm *here*, and I'm going to make the best of it. I stare down the target.

Look out, Academy: you're about to see everything I've got!

Ready, aim . . .

Fire!

NINE

TWO HOURS AND ZERO ARCHERY targets hit later, Joni and I are sitting in a circle of desks in classroom 203 inside Flannery Hall. We're waiting for Lt. Sturtevant to lead our small-group leadership meeting, because, you know, the Academy is all about *leadership*. There are leadership seminars we have to attend twice a month, and then small-group meetings once a month with an advisor to develop a project we have to complete over the course of the semester. Of course everyone already knows what they're doing for their projects except me. Ciara is vice president of the LGBT club; Amanda organizes a group of ten students who go off campus and read to foster kids once a month (which surprises me, given she mostly seems pretty mean); Jack is the editor in chief of the school newspaper (and he writes nearly half of the stories, and they're *really* good), and Joni leads tours of the Academy for prospective incoming students. Joni told me Lt. Sturtevant pushed her to come up with an idea that would help her overcome her shyness, which I thought was cool. Not every teacher sees your weaknesses and tries to improve them.

I stare around the classroom. We must be in a social studies or geography classroom—there are maps and globes everywhere. It reminds me of my bedroom, where I have this funky light-up globe perched on my desk that Ella and I used to play with all the time. We'd close our eyes and spin it, and then point to a random spot and plan a trip. Ah, my bedroom. I miss my bedroom!

"How's your boob?" Joni asks me. "Did you slice it off with that arrow?"

I smile despite myself. "It's still hanging on, thank God. It's probably the only time having barely there boobs has worked in my favor."

Joni and I trade grins, and then she takes out a notebook and starts thumbing through it. I can see over her shoulder to all the detailed progress reports she's made for her leadership project.

I take out my notebook and stare down at a blank page. Normally, a blank page inspires me, but I just haven't had the time to give this much thought.

Windows look out onto the athletic field, and I can see two boys throwing a baseball back and forth. Leadership seminars meet during our personal time, which means I'm not going to be able to blog tonight, which is obviously not ideal. I just hope my readers bear with me through this challenging period in my life!

I turn back to the dozen or so kids in the circle. Jennifer Davis, the girl who laughed at me in archery, is here, too, avoiding my gaze. She's talking to another girl named Penelope who I know from Military Strategy.

Footsteps make me turn toward the door. "Good afternoon, cadets," Sturtevant says as she enters. She sits at a desk in our makeshift circle. "Welcome to your first small-group leadership seminar this semester."

"Good afternoon, Lt. Sturtevant," we say back. Sturtevant sits so erect it looks painful. We all sit up a little straighter, too.

"I'd like to dive right in and hear a pitch from you, Private Brooks," Sturtevant says, "on what you'd like your leadership project to be this year. Then we'll review the progress the rest of you are making."

"A pitch?" I repeat. I mean, obviously I haven't developed a pitch yet, because I've been so busy trying to learn hand-to-hand combat and not get demerits and keep my average about 3.5!

"Yes, that's what I said," Sturtevant says, opening her notebook like she's about to jot down all my brilliant ideas.

Joni's right next to me, and I can feel her stiffen. Sometimes it seems like she physically feels my pain. "Um, well," I say. Amanda's foster-kid leadership project floats through my head. I did tons of volunteering at home; that would be a pretty easy fit. "I'm heavily involved in community volunteering back home in Mount Pleasant," I say.

"That's nice," Sturtevant says. It doesn't even come out sarcastic; she sounds downright annoyed.

"I teach this very popular course at our local nursing home called It's Not 1952 Anymore," I say, "and I help old people, I mean, *the elderly*, navigate things like what to wear and how to text."

Sturtevant blows air between her lips. "Are you looking for some kind of award, Brooks?

"Um, no, of course not," I say. "I mean, unless you want to give me one."

Sturtevant gets a constipated look on her face. "I'm not sure how what you're telling me translates to your leadership project for the Academy," she says.

"Well, I could just bring my course back. I could go off campus"—*freedom!*—"and teach my course in Albany at a nursing home. The course was very popular. I always got rave reviews. So many elderly people want to dress fashionably, they just don't know how to make runway reality."

Sturtevant shakes her head. "I don't think so, Brooks," she says. "I'm pretty sure you can come up with something better than that."

Ugh! Why does she hate everything about me?! What could possibly be wrong with my idea?!

Jennifer Davis puts her fist to her mouth like she's trying not to laugh at me again. Joni shifts in the seat next to me. Sturtevant is writing in her notebook—God knows what—and Joni passes me a note that says, *Just tell her you'll go back to the drawing board. I'll help you!*

I clear my throat. "I'd like some extra time to go back to the drawing board," I say.

"That's fine," says Sturtevant with a disgusted wave of

her hand, like she doesn't even want to deal with me. "And when you come back to your classmates and me with an idea, let's keep in mind the standards of Albany Military Academy, and let's also keep in mind just how heavily this project determines whether you pass or fail your year here at the Academy."

TEN

FAILURE IS NOT AN OPTION, Private Brooks!

It's become my new battle cry, and I actually think it's working. I feel kind of psyched when I say it to myself.

On Sunday evening, Joni and I are sitting cross-legged on our floor, brainstorming ideas for my leadership project, and Joni is being super encouraging and saying things like: "Frankie, we can totally do this, we just have to come up with a single good idea!"

I have a notebook and a pen, and so far we've come up with two ideas:

1) Start a club for new students adjusting to life at the Academy, based on my experience. (Joni's idea.)

2) Start a Save the Rain Forest Campaign and make fashionable T-shirts to support the cause, based on the fact that everyone loves rain forests and fashionable T-shirts. (My idea.)

"The problem with the rain forest idea is that it has nothing to do with the military at all," Joni says. She puts down her pen and fishes through her handbag.

"Not everyone's does," I say as she yanks out a pack of gummy bears.

"Yeah, but Sturtevant is pushing you to come up with something really good," Joni says. She looks at me and pops a gummy bear in her mouth.

"Well," I say, "the problem with your idea is I don't think there are any new students except me."

Joni chews. She's so much more polite than me. She actually finishes her gummy bear before talking. "Then maybe you could write some kind of handbook that introduces any future incoming student to life at the Academy. You like to write."

"Not that kind of boring writing," I say, opening my hand for one of her gummies. She puts two orange ones in my palm and I stuff them in my mouth. "I just don't get why Sturtevant let Amanda do a volunteering thing for her leadership project and not me."

"Let's not focus on that, okay?" Joni says. "It's not productive."

"Fine," I say. I pull my hair into a ponytail. Most of it falls back out. "So, let's see, what if I did a bake sale? I'm actually terrific at making gluten-free muffins."

Joni pulls her knees to her chest. "Again, not military related," she says.

"I'll just write it down, as an option," I say. *Frankie's*

Glorious Gluten-Free Muffins!!! I write, because that's what my sister calls them.

"But how is that being a leader?" Joni asks carefully. "I think it's more like being a baker."

"Okay. I see your point," I say, and then I giggle, which starts Joni giggling, too. She's way more relaxed when it's just us hanging out in our room than she is at school.

"Jack said you're doing great in Military Strategy class," Joni says.

"He said that?"

Joni nods, and I feel myself blush. "Lt. Martin complimented me in front of the whole class and said I have some really out-of-the box thinking," I tell her. "It was amazing, basically the first thing I've done right since I got to the Academy!"

And it was especially satisfying because Lt. Martin and I got off to a rocky start after I passed that note to Jack, and then it got worse when he presented us with a battlefield type situation and asked us to write down what we would do in one hundred words or less, and my idea was only five words: *Lie down and play dead*, which Lt. Martin said was not in the tradition nor spirit of the US military. But then we got into these more complicated scenarios, more mental stuff, and he started getting really into my answers. My parents always say I'm good at knowing what will happen on TV dramas before they happen, so I just worked things out like that. Even Jack keeps whispering things like *good one, Brooks*, under his breath in Military Strategy.

"So what if you did something for your leadership project that had to do with military strategy?" Joni asks.

"Like what?"

"I don't know," Joni says, "you're apparently the military-strategy genius."

Maybe it's not true, but it still makes me smile.

"Listen, I gotta pick up a book before dinner," Joni says. "But I'll be home a lot this week and we can study together and think more about this, okay?"

"Thank you," I say, and I give her a hug before she leaves. How lucky am I that I got assigned to be Joni's roommate?

I make my way to my computer. It's Sunday, and I already finished all my homework due tomorrow, but for Wednesday, Lt. Martin assigned us fifteen hundred words to be written on any military strategy we deem fit to get our opponent to see things from our point of view.

#WhyDoYourHomeworkWhenYouCan . . . was once a scintillating trending topic started by moi on Twitter, but now I'm realizing if I don't go online until nighttime after my studying is done, the homework itself goes faster, and then I still have time left over to work on my blog. It's all about incentive, which, come to think of it, could be a good idea for my military strategy paper. I open up my laptop and write: *INCENTIVE IS WAY BETTER THAN COERCION: Give your enemy the right reason to tell you his secrets, and you'll feel so much better about yourself!*

I smile to myself. I think Lt. Martin would love that idea!

I close my Word doc and open up Safari. Tonight I have my first night on dining hall duty, which is obviously slightly terrifying, but since *I already finished my homework, thank you very much,* I search Instagram for hairstyles compatible with hairnets. Most of the photos I find show the hairnet starting farther back on the crown, which, unfortunately, I don't think is going to fly with the cafeteria people, since I'm pretty sure the whole point is to keep your hair out of the food. So instead I do some braids that circle the crown of my hair, which should still be visible through the netting. It's all very lunch lady meets *Game of Thrones.*

I have to wear my uniform even though it's Sunday, because that's the rule when you have mess hall duty. I check myself out in the mirror and it dawns on me that my black stiletto boots would look similar to my shiny shoes, and I could wear them tonight and give my blisters a few extra hours to heal from my still too-tight shiny shoes. I honestly don't think it would be a big deal, because it's not a weekday and we don't have any physical training, so what's the difference? I slip them on and check myself out. They're way less conspicuous than my running shoes, that's for sure. Plus I'm four inches taller and my pants look chicer and more streamlined—I'm like the Hollywood version of a butt-kicker.

Stiletto boots are a go!

It's 5:32—or 1732, according to the military—and I'm psyched because I have time to blog before reporting to mess hall duty.

My *Anna Karenina* paperback catches my eye from the corner of my desk. I still have another week to finish it, so there's probably no point in starting it now . . .

I tap my fingers on my desk. I have twenty minutes left before I have to get to the mess hall, so I guess I could split it evenly: ten minutes on my blog, ten minutes on reading for English.

I feel good about things as my fingers arch over the computer. I think my parents would be happy. I let go of a breath, and just like whenever I start to write about fashion, my stress disappears.

Très chic and utilitarian; the military has forever inspired fashion. Extra pockets, anyone? Aviator sunglasses? Who can resist a belt that cinches the waist?

I post a photo of Stella McCartney's Georgina Utility Tweed Jacket. It's mega expensive, so I also find a similar but cheap version from Forever 21 and link to that, too. Then I write a bit about why army-green joggers are the new leggings.

At 5:42, I start my reading, and it becomes clear that Anna Karenina understands exactly what it's like to be oppressed by social and moral laws even if she never went to military academy. I get caught up in the book and read a few minutes past the ten-minute mark, so then I have to run from my room and sprint across the quad to get to the mess hall on time, which is hard given that I'm wearing stilettos and my arm and leg muscles feel like jellyfish are attacking them from PT this week.

Inside the mess hall it smells like deli meat and starch.

The heat is cranking at least five degrees higher than any establishment should ever be. I knock at the door marked STAFF, and a fiftysomething woman opens it. "Frances Brooks?" she asks kindly. If she notices my stiletto boots, she doesn't say anything.

"Yes," I say. "Frankie."

"I'm Gloria," she says. "Come right this way." She smiles and I relax a little. She looks like a grandma who knits scarves and watches Lifetime movies.

I follow her into the middle of the cafeteria, past the salad bar and into the area where the hot food is served. She tells me to wait by the meat loaf, and then returns a minute later with a bucket of gray water and a mop. She's wearing a hairnet now, and passes me an identical one.

I try not to cringe as I put it on because I don't want to be disrespectful of her job, but I can't help it. I don't even know how to mop, and this bucket reeks of Clorox. At home we have a cleaning lady named Savannah who uses a homemade cleaning solution made of vinegar and essential oils like lavender. Why didn't my parents ever teach me how to clean?

"So, like, I'm supposed to mop in *here*?" I ask, gesturing to all the students grabbing trays and ordering food. I guess I thought I'd be in a more private place. I didn't realize I was going to be on display for the entire Academy to see me mop. Not like there's anything wrong with that. And I guess, well, maybe this is the kind of thing that will help me be *disciplined* and everything, it's just . . .

Gloria smiles. She's holding her mop like it's her

boyfriend, flush against her side and curled beneath her arm. "Yes, you're going to mop in *here*," she affirms. "The entire floor, which is fifteen thousand square feet. And also when one of your fellow students has a spill. Like right there," she says, pointing to a gross patch of tomato sauce.

She hands me the mop. "You have to use some elbow grease with this particular mop," she says way too loudly.

I'm already sweating bullets beneath my hairnet. "Um," I say, glancing between the tomato stain and Gloria. Is she going to help me?

She motions toward the stain.

"Right," I say. I think I'm on my own. I hold my mop with two hands and use my foot to nudge the bucket toward the stain. Water sloshes over the side of the bucket and onto my stiletto boot. Gross! I pick up the bucket and teeter over to the spot. This would be so much easier if I actually knew how to mop. I dunk the mop into the water, then pick it up and plop it onto the tomato sauce.

"No, no, no," Gloria says, striding over to me. "You need to drain the water first, like this."

The cafeteria has only gotten busier. Academy students are sidestepping Gloria and me to avoid the water I spilled. A beautiful girl with cornrows says "Poor thing" to her friend, who's chewing gum and staring at me. That redheaded boy Archie walks toward me, and he says, "Hey, Frankie," and I pause to say hello to him but then Gloria asks, "You see what I mean about elbow grease?" and there's an awkward moment when Archie looks like he can't decide if he should stop and talk to me or keep walking, and then he takes off. I can't blame him. Gloria is practically shouting her mopping tips as she slides the mop back and forth over the patch of tomato sauce. We both watch as the red stain disappears like magic.

"I get it," I say, nodding. "Lots of elbow grease."

She passes me back the mop. "See that juice?" she asks, pointing to a heart-shaped splatter of purple liquid near the pasta station.

Unfortunately, I do. I start to move my bucket toward the juice when I see Ciara and Amanda. They're standing in the lunch line behind Joni, whose face is flushed yet again. Amanda's closest to Joni, and she's saying something into her ear, and whatever it is makes Joni's eyes go bright with tears. Joni stumbles out of line, leaving her tray of hot pasta. Ciara stands there looking helpless, her eyes following Joni as she hurries through the cafeteria. I almost ask Gloria if I can go after Joni, but I stop myself. I can't mess this up.

Joni shoves through the side doors of the cafeteria and then she's gone. I take out my mop and start on the juice stain, trying to forget about Joni and whatever Amanda must have just said to make her so upset. I'll bring her some dinner back to our room when my shift is over so she isn't hungry.

Amanda and Ciara finish up at the pasta station and head toward Gloria and me. Ciara still looks a little thrown from the thing with Joni, and when she sees me she lets out a surprised laugh, then covers her mouth.

"Hi," I say, flustered.

Ciara says, "Hey," but Amanda stands there giving me the weirdest look, almost like she expected me to be here, mopping away in a hairnet. Maybe because she's the one who told on me.

I lift my hand into a wave. At least I don't have to wear sanitary gloves. We're all standing there and staring at one another when Gloria taps her foot.

"I should get back to work," I say, taking Gloria's hint.

Ciara starts to walk away, but Amanda doesn't move, so Ciara stops and just stands there waiting for Amanda, and the worst part is that I am, too. I can't explain it, but there's something about Amanda. It's like she stares at you for a beat too long, like she's trying to dominate you with eye contact. I want to come out and ask her if she told on me, but honestly, she makes me too nervous.

Students mill around us. A guy with a tattoo on his neck elbows another guy over the last lunch tray. We stand there, stone still, but then Amanda tips her glass to the side, just enough to spill a tiny drop of Coke on the floor that lands near Gloria and me.

"Whoops!" she says. She laughs, and I guess it's supposed to be a joke, but it definitely doesn't feel very funny.

"Amanda, seriously?" I say. I mean, come on.

"I should report you for misconduct," Gloria says, but she sounds unsure. I have a feeling Gloria has never reported anyone for anything.

"I was *kidding*!" Amanda says, her laugh slowing to a giggle. Her blonde hair is curled perfectly, making her look almost cherubic, which is false advertising.

I want to say it wasn't funny, or that it was immature, or something like that. But I feel about two feet tall standing there with my mop and my hairnet. For about the hundredth time since I got here, I just wish Andrea and Julia were here. Or my sister. I'd even take my parents right now! I just wish I could go home and have a night with my family snuggled on our big fluffy couch, watching a movie.

A heavy hand falls on my shoulder. I'm so revved up by the Amanda thing that I jump.

"Whoa, tiger," a familiar voice says. I turn to see Jack. He's wearing a hairnet and holding a scuffed red mop. The sight of him fills me right up—it's like his warmth conquers the frigid chill Amanda unleashed.

"Why are you wearing that?" I ask, smiling even wider as he gives me his crooked grin.

"This thing?" he says, touching his hairnet. "Because it looks so good on me."

Amanda's staring from Jack to me. She's frowning, and I think back to how Archie warned me about falling in with the wrong people.

"Come on," I say, giggling a little. "Why are you wearing a *hairnet*?"

"My Missouri hat didn't go with this shirt?" Jack tries again. He's smirking this time.

"Jack," Gloria says warmly.

Jack sings "Gloria" the way it gets sung in Catholic mass, with two dozen syllables stuffed into one *Gloria*: "Glo-o-o-o-o-o-o-o-o-o-o-oria!" and Gloria beams like it's the funniest thing she's ever heard. And maybe it's not, but

143

there's something about Jack that's contagious. I can feel myself beaming, too.

Amanda rolls her eyes. "Let's go," she says to Ciara, and they take off. In the absence of Amanda's cold front, I can feel the cafeteria's buzzy feeling again. Laughter and conversations twine together around us as silverware clinks.

"The thing is," Jack says to me, "I have to get in trouble every so often so I can come see Gloria."

"And if this floor don't shine like the top of the Chrysler Building," Gloria says.

"Annie," I say, smiling at Gloria's quote. "I was just thinking about how my sister and I used to watch it," I tell her, and she winks. I like her. Maybe this won't be so bad.

"Can't say I've seen it," Jack says.

Gloria and I exchange a look like *what a travesty.*

"You've never seen *Annie?*" I ask.

"Maybe I saw it a while ago," Jack says, grinning.

"Maybe it's your favorite movie and you're embarrassed to tell us," I say.

"Maybe," Jack says. Then, to Gloria, he says, "I'll take it from here. I can help her."

"I see you've already helped yourself to my favorite mop," Gloria says.

"Old Faithful," Jack says, running his hand lovingly over the thing. He dips it down and kisses it mock-passionately.

"Oh, for heaven's sake," Gloria says, and then, to me, "I'll be in my office if you need me." She glances at her watch. "You've got one hour to cover the whole floor, so

144

work quickly enough that you can grab some grub before the dining hall closes."

I start to thank her, but she's already retreating to her office.

"So," Jack says.

"So," I say.

"Want help?"

I chew my bottom lip. I should just be polite and accept his help, but before I know it I'm saying things I probably shouldn't. "Why are you always being so nice to me?" I ask, my words soft.

Jack's long fingers curl around the mop. "I'm a sucker for lost causes," he says. "And you've gotten in trouble like three times since you got here. And two of those times were my fault."

"I've actually only gotten in trouble twice," I say.

"Are we not counting the note you passed me in class?"

"We're not," I say.

"Okay, then," Jack says, rubbing his jaw like he's considering this. "PT and sneaking out with me."

The way he says it . . . *sneaking out with me* . . . gives me shivers. I've never snuck out with anyone before. And I know I'm supposed to be good here, but all I want is for Jack to come to my room tonight so we can sneak out again. How am I supposed to stop wanting to do these things?

Jack isn't smiling anymore. He's looking at me like we're alone together, and like he knows how much I want to be alone with him. I try not to look away like how I always used to do when Josh looked at me at school; I want to be braver. So I hold his eyes with mine, and then he's the one blushing and looking away. He runs his mop over a clean patch of floor like he's just looking for something to do. "I told Sturtevant it was me you were with," he says.

"You did *what*?" I ask. "You shouldn't have done that!"

Jack shrugs his big shoulders. "It seemed unfair that you got stuck mopping and I didn't. I don't have any demerits this year, and my college only finds out if I get kicked out. One little demerit was worth it." He smiles. "And the idea of hanging out with you wasn't all that bad, either," he says.

He's making me really, really nervous.

"Now get to work, Annie," he says, nudging his mop into mine. "It's a hard knock life or whatever."

"This from the guy who never saw *Annie*," I say, surprised that I can even attempt a joke with how jittery I suddenly am. Jack smiles again. I take out my mop and plop it onto a patch of floor.

Mostly we mop together in silence. It's kind of Zen watching all the grime disappear, and my mind drifts off, and somehow I find myself thinking about sines and cosines and all the other things I studied this week. I'm working so much harder here—it's like the part of my brain that only had room for fashion is slowly letting a few other things in. I got an A- on my trig quiz—enough to keep my overall average above the 3.5 mark. Now I just need to figure out the right leadership project. But how am I supposed to be a leader here when everyone knows I'm the worst at everything?

I glance up at all the kids passing us to get their dinner. I expected that other students might make fun of us, but no one does. I'm not sure if that's because I'm with Jack, who stands protectively near me the whole time we mop, or because they've all had mopping duty, too, and know it sucks, or because most of them are just genuinely kind. I think it's a combination of all three.

Right before seven, when my left elbow is killing me from the weird position that mopping requires, Jack asks, "Want to get sandwiches and eat outside?"

"*Outside?*" I ask. "Like in the winter?"

"It's fifty degrees out," he says, smiling as he takes off his hairnet and sends his near-black hair standing on edge.

"You're insane," I say, "but I'll do it."

We carry our buckets to the side of the cafeteria and tuck them behind one of the food stations. I'm wishing for him to put his arm around me or make any kind of contact as we maneuver through the students, but he doesn't. He pushes the exit door, and the blast of fresh air that greets us feels like relief.

"Warm," Jack says. "For January."

The stream of students leaving the dining hall has petered out to a trickle, but Jack still keeps his voice quiet. "I need to talk to you about something, because I'm worried it's gonna mess things up for you here."

My heart beats faster. I hold my turkey sandwich in the air, waiting.

"When I first got here last year, Amanda and I hooked up," he says, and my eyes widen at how plainly he says it. "It was a mistake. I didn't know her well enough to know it wasn't a good idea, and I shouldn't have done it. After we got together she hooked up with someone else the same night, and Joni and my sister, Rachel, walked in on them, and they told me what they saw. Amanda thinks that's the whole reason she and I never turned into something. She was probably just embarrassed, and she blamed Joni and Rachel no matter how much I tried to tell her it wasn't that." His dark eyebrows knit together. "I'm almost positive she's the one who got Rachel kicked out by sending a picture of her out after curfew, and now I'm worried she's after you."

"It's what Joni thinks, too," I say. "I asked her who she thought ever would have told on me, and Amanda was her first and only guess."

A pit forms in my stomach. Jack's hands go into his lap like he's unsure of what to do with them. "I'm sorry I've made things harder for you here," he says softly, his eyes darkening.

I want to reassure him that it's not his fault, but that's not entirely true.

"It's not all you," I say. "It's just being new, and trying to figure things out, and my body is literally killing from PT and my brain is hurting from the classes. This place is really different than my high school or anything else I've ever done." I gesture to my uniform. "Even the uniform thing." I take a breath. "It's just so hard not to want to go home, at times."

Jack inches closer to me. Being alone with him like this is all I've been able to think about, and now it's happening. I panic a little. I pick up a twig and start drawing in the dirt by our feet so Jack can't see my face.

"I can see Amanda doing it," I finally say. No matter how sorry I am for whatever makes her this way, I *can* see Amanda orchestrating something cruel.

"She's had a shitty go of it," Jack says. "Her parents took off when she was eight and left her with an aunt, and when she stopped being easy to take care of, her aunt shipped her here."

I bite my bottom lip. That's awful. "So what do we do?" I ask.

I expect Jack to shrug, or look hopeless, but he doesn't. He runs a hand through his hair and looks at me with an intensity I haven't seen before. "We protect you and Joni from Amanda."

The winter sky is nearly black. Streetlights cast a golden glow on the sidewalks that run along the perimeter of the quad. I want to ask the obvious question: Are you protecting me because you like me and you're worried it will upset Amanda?

Or am I reading everything wrong just like I did with Josh?

Still. Joni. She's starting to become my real friend—it's something I can feel deep in my bones. "I just, I want to be sure about Joni," I say. "Do you think there's any chance she likes you a little?"

"Not even a little," Jack says. "You're gonna need to trust me on this." My breathing quickens as he leans closer.

"Frances Abernathy Brooks."

My name sounds totally different than I've ever heard it. I whirl around to see Lt. Sturtevant. Jack and I scramble to our feet and salute.

"Should I report you for your footwear?" Sturtevant asks me, gesturing to my stiletto boots.

I glance down at them. They couldn't possibly look more amazing peeking out from my pants.

"Another demerit?" Sturtevant asks.

"No, please," I blurt. I can feel Jack straightening next to me. "My shoes are too tight, and I emailed someone in administration weeks ago and they said I'd get a new pair ASAP, but they haven't arrived yet, and my feet are bleeding with blisters and I'm out of Band-Aids and I'm really sorry. I'll wear the right shoes tomorrow for PT even if they're too small. Please don't report me." I'm blabbering, and I'd probably start crying if my eyeballs weren't too tired to make tears again today.

Sturtevant stares at me, and I know it's not just my footwear she's reacting to: it's me. It's like I'm always trying to get my way, and I'm not disciplined the way these other kids are; I bet most of all of them would have just sucked it up and worn their shiny shoes.

Sturtevant looks at her watch. "Both of you need to get back for recall to barracks. Private Wattson, go ahead. I'd like to speak with Private Brooks."

Jack leaves for his dorm, glancing over his shoulder to lock eyes with me. I quickly look away, feeling my cheeks heat. I try to meet Sturtevant's gaze, but I'm just so nervous.

Her voice is a notch softer than usual when she says, "Private Brooks, I'm increasingly concerned you don't understand what's happening here." She lets out a breath. "You're ranked two hundred and two out of two hundred and two cadets. With the exception of one of your teachers, the TACs here have no problem keeping you there until you show us something—*anything*—and the part I worry you're not understanding is that an expulsion from the Academy doesn't just mean you get sent home; it means there's a permanent expulsion on your high school transcript. Your high school in Mount Pleasant won't allow you to transfer back in regular time unless you've successfully matriculated here."

Oh my God. "You mean I'd have to repeat a grade?"

"That's exactly what I mean."

My heart pounds so hard and fast I feel like it's crawling up my throat. Another year home in Mount Pleasant? Another year I'd have to wait for fashion school, for my real life in New York City to start? My friends moving on without me?

"But I'm doing so well in Military Strategy!" I blurt. But even as I say it, it dawns on me that it's the only thing class I'm really excelling in. In my other classes I'm just barely keeping the 3.5. And of course I suck at all the physical training!

Sturtevant's watching me almost like she almost feels sorry for me. "And that's a good thing," she says, "but we need to see more, Private Brooks. You don't need to excel at the physical training in order to stay at the Academy," she says, "only to qualify for War Games, which at this point looks highly unlikely for you. However, to stay here, you must complete physical training to the best of your ability, and that means you have to try your hardest and show us *improvement*. And you absolutely must stop disrespecting me, my colleagues, and the United States military, which is exactly what you're doing when you photograph me in my office or wear high heels with your military uniform."

Guilt pounds me. I need to fix this—I need to fix *me*.

"You're excused, Private Brooks," Sturtevant says. "Please think about what I've said."

I head across the quad on shaking legs, unsure of how in the world I'm ever going to be able to do what I know I need to. What if the only way to learn discipline is to truly follow the rules for the first time in my entire life?

ELEVEN

I FLING OPEN THE DOOR to my dorm room, praying Joni's there so I can tell her what Sturtevant just told me, but she's not!

I plunk down on my bed and text **SOS** to Julia and Andrea, and a second later they FaceTime me from Andrea's bedroom. When they pop onto my screen, the sight of them floods me with relief.

"You look awful," Julia says.

Andrea elbows her. "You have no filter. Right, Frankie? She needs a filter."

"I miss you guys," I say, feeling so scattered I hardly know where to start. "And even supermodels look worse on FaceTime. It's been proven."

"We miss *you*," Andrea says.

"I had to mop the mess hall tonight," I say, already feeling a lump in my throat. "Because I got in trouble with my

TAC, and then she talked to me tonight about how I have to be better here and stop getting into trouble or I could get expelled, and . . ."

"Who's Zack?" Andrea asks.

"Not Zack. *TAC*. Tactical officer."

"Expelled?" Julia repeats. "What did you get in trouble for?"

"Um, well, a few things," I say, making myself tell them no matter how embarrassed I am. "I answered my phone in PT that morning, and then I snuck out with that cute guy Jack I told you about, and I got caught. Someone—I think this girl Amanda—sent a picture of me out at night to Lt. Sturtevant, who's like this scary headmaster lady in charge of me." I picture Jack giving me his number that day in Military Strategy, and the way his dark eyes crinkled at the corners, and how concerned he looked when I had to leave class for the lieutenant's office. "Today I wore stiletto boots instead of my uniform shoes, and . . ."

"Wait, you snuck out with a *guy*?" Andrea asks

"Well, not just any guy: Jack."

She still looks shocked, and I get it, because I've never done anything like that before, unless you count my kiss with Josh, which she doesn't even know about. And it's not like I was trying to keep what happened with Jack from them, and I'm sure I would have already told them if I were still there, but Facetime is different, because what if Andrea's parents (or, worse, her witch-tastic older sister) are right outside the room and can hear our conversation?

Julia doesn't seem that surprised. This year she told me:

Adolescence is a time of vital brain development, Frankie. We have to lay down the proper neural pathway for our future. I wasn't concerned about my neural development, but now I'm second-guessing myself.

Jesus. And now I'm crying.

"Don't cry," Andrea says, sniffling. She always gets weepy when someone else cries. It's her only soft spot, really. Last year one of her competitors got wind of it and used it against her during a tennis match by pretending to sob while playing.

"I can't seem to stop doing stuff I'm not supposed to," I say. *I also kissed Josh. I also cheated on a test.* "My parents would freak out if they knew. And if I get expelled, that means I'd have to repeat sophomore year in Mount Pleasant! You guys would be juniors, and I'd still be a sophomore!"

Andrea gasps, and I cry harder. Julia says, "Frankie, *listen*," and I do, because Julia always knows. "You just need to figure out how to be yourself there *and* follow all the rules."

"Get serious," Andrea says to Julia.

"But what if *myself* is bad?" I ask Julia.

"You're not *bad*," she says. She taps a finger against her computer screen like she's trying to touch me. Technology is so weird. "You're *you*, Frankie. A total original. So don't worry about how you snuck out, just don't do it again."

It's the simple-but-good kind of advice you read in *Seventeen* magazine, the kind of advice that sounds like a no-brainer but actually works if you follow it. And maybe I can follow other kinds of rules, the ones set in place by the

Academy to make me stronger and more respectful. Maybe if I tried to follow the rules a little bit closer and attempted to learn *discipline*, I'd do better. Even if it was more boring.

"Now, how can you get back on this lieutenant's good side?"

I sniff. "I have this leadership project I'm supposed to pitch to her at our next meeting," I say. "We have to develop some big idea we work on to demonstrate what great *leaders* we are. I just have zero good ideas right now."

Andrea wipes her tears. Julia says, "Make it something only you could do," and then there's a knock at the door.

"Hang on," I say to Julia and Andrea. I move across my room and open the door to see Archie.

"Frankie, hi," he says. He's holding a shoe box. "For you," he says, passing me the box.

"Where did you get these?" I ask. I've been waiting for these shoes for weeks!

"Sturtevant," he says plainly. "I'm on errand duty."

Lt. Sturtevant must have figured out a way to get me these after our conversation. . . .

"Who's that?!" Andrea yells from inside my room. "What a hottie!"

Archie glances to the screen and looks mortified when he realizes we're on FaceTime. "Sorry," I say to Archie. "She has no filter." I'm about to say something else, but then Archie politely excuses himself like some kind of concierge.

"Thanks!" I call down the hall after him.

I shut the door and bring my new shoes in a size seven

over to my desk. "You're ridiculous," I say to Andrea, who's laughing. I lift my shoes out of the box for my friends to see. I'm embarrassed, not by the uniform shoes, but by the fact that I got myself sent here in the first place.

"We're gonna need those J. Crew rhinestone shoe clips you wore last summer," Andrea says.

I try to smile, but Julia doesn't. Instead, she moves a little closer to the screen, and says, "You can do this, Frankie, I know you can."

TWELVE

IT'S WEEK FOUR AT THE Academy, and I start trying my best—my real, actual, true best. I flat-out confess to Joni that I need her to help me be disciplined and study, and just like she promised, she starts staying in our room instead of going to the library or wherever she usually goes to study. Every night she sits right across from me at her desk, and every time she senses me getting fidgety, she says, "Ten more minutes and then we take a quick yoga break."

The sixty-second yoga-pose breaks actually work so much better than running to the basement vending machine for snacks, which is what I did the first few weeks I was here. It also feels good to have Joni physically next to me, even if she's just quietly studying. I got an A on that Military Strategy paper about incentive, and another A- on a trig quiz! Spanish is still proving especially hard.

There's, like, twenty pages of reading assigned per class, and the words on the pages are written *in Spanish*. And in chemistry, I'm trying so hard to keep up after what I did in chemistry back home. I'm never going to even be tempted to cheat again, because this time I'll be ready for every test. Plus, working more efficiently means I'm able to allot twenty minutes to blogging each night, so I've been more consistent about getting my posts back up and running.

There are so many miserable days of physical training (and I still haven't done better at any of the drills!) that I can barely walk by the time I show up at the gymnasium on Friday. I scan for Jack and Joni. I pass two boys doing burpees by choice, an exercise Sturtevant makes us do that not only sounds disgusting but also burns the living crap out of your leg muscles. I swerve through a group of girls talking about War Games, and then arch onto my tiptoes to look over their heads for Jack. He's usually easy to find because he towers over almost everyone.

Watching Jack every day in PT makes me like him more than ever. He's the fastest, strongest, most agile, *and* the most determined, but it's even more than that. His face gets this look when it's time to do a drill, like every moment is wildly important, like he's imagining being in combat. It's like he has to be the best, but not for something small like bragging rights. You can tell by watching him that he's in this for things much bigger than him.

It's 0529 and I'm pretty sure Sturtevant's gonna blow her ear-blasting whistle any second. I finally spot Jack and Joni standing together in the far corner of the gym. Joni's stretching her quad with her leg kicked back and listening carefully to something Jack's saying. Jack sees me and waves. I walk toward him, trying to clear my head, but it's not easy. I want to be alone with him more than ever. I can't stop thinking about what it felt like to have his fingers laced through mine the night we snuck out, and how I want that again and again. And it's like that night happened, but then we pulled everything back when I told Jack I needed to be better. Now he's trying so hard to help me be better—giving me tips in PT, taking me to a study group for Military Strategy, and basically just not sneaking out with me, and I don't know how to tell him how much I like him, or how even if I don't want to sneak out again, I *do* want to see him again alone like that night weeks ago.

I make my way toward Jack and Joni, ducking as I pass Sgt. O'Neil and two more TACs I don't recognize with matching clipboards and grim expressions. This week O'Neil assigned us a paper to write for archery about the staging of Shakespearean battles. As if I don't have enough work to do in all of my academic classes! Though I do think I can turn that project into a blog post if I incorporate Shakespearean costumes. . . .

I get to Jack and Joni, and Jack holds up his hand to high-five me. I reach up, and he raises his hand just enough that it's out of my reach. "Hey," I say, simultaneously thinking how lame it is that this is the quintessential joke guys have invented since the beginning of time, and also that I'm so glad he's doing it because it means I have to step closer to him to try to reach his hand. "Are you rubbing in my shortness?" I ask as I jump up to slap his palm with mine.

"Hardly," he says. "I'm congratulating you on getting out of last place for War Games."

"What?! Are you serious?" I ask him. Can that be?!

"I checked it this morning," Jack says.

"You're cadet one ninety-one," Joni says.

"Oh my gosh!" I say, and then Joni puts her arms around me in a big hug. Jack and I exchange a nervous glance over her shoulder—for a second he looks like he's going to hug me, too, but then he just stands there fidgeting. "Listen, you obviously got out of last place because of your mad strategic-thinking skills," he says, "but there's a chance you can do something physical today to impress Sturtevant and move up even higher."

"Are we hula-hooping?" I ask. "Because that's a physical thing I'm surprisingly good at."

"Um, no," Jack says. "Rumor has it we're doing the high ropes course."

"Oh," I say, my War Games buzz crashing a little. "High ropes?"

I try to act natural; I'm trying to get better at taking things as they come. But I was just getting used to regular PT. I'm not ready for anything *high* or having to do with *ropes*.

I exhale. I don't have a choice. It's another thing the Academy has made loud and clear for me: I'm not in charge. At home, my school taught so many touchy-feely concepts reinforced by the parents in our community, mostly focused on us teenagers being in charge of our own experience. My mother has actually said things to me like: *If you don't want to do your homework, perhaps you could talk with your teacher about an alternate project tailored more to your interests.* That would never happen here. And surprisingly, it's almost more reassuring to know my place rather than having to constantly try to figure out where I stand.

"The high ropes course is *fun*, Frankie," Joni says. "I promise. Hard but fun."

Jack clears his throat. "There are some kids who are gonna freak out up there and fall, and no offense to them, but maybe this could be a chance to move up even a few more spots in the War Games rankings. It just takes balance and confidence."

Balance and *confidence*. Can I do that?

Sturtevant blows her whistle and we all straighten. "You'll follow Sgt. O'Neil and me through the back door, and we'll train outside this morning," she says. She looks a little tired today. She doesn't say anything more—she just swings open an exit door and cold air rushes in. We exit through the back of the gym, and I realize I've never seen this part of campus. The sun is just up. Light pours through the trees' bare branches in pure, white rays. O'Neil says something about how *the gloomiest night will wear on to a morning*. The temperature is somewhere in the forties, so being outside is like trying to exist in a refrigerator, which I find uncomfortable. Why are these people all so outdoorsy? And where are the ropes?

To our right along the outside of the building are boxes filled with helmets in varying sizes. I'm relieved that they have ones marked EXTRA-LARGE. "Select your helmets in an orderly fashion," Sturtevant says. It can't be a good sign that we need helmets, but at least I find one that fits. I strap it on as Jack talks to Joni and me about a reporter from the *Wall Street Journal* who's teaching an online journalism course he wants to take, and it makes me smile because he so obviously loves what he loves, and of course I can relate to that.

I spot Archie. "It must be so nice to have such a modestly sized head," I say to him as he selects a helmet from the box marked MEDIUM. Sturtevant's whistle blows again, and she and O'Neil lead us around the side of the building. That's when I see them:

The ropes.

I tip my helmet head way up and take in a rope course that looks both like a twelve-year-old boy's dream and also my own personal nightmare. Two wooden poles the width of telephone poles (but taller) shoot up into the sky. Terrifying makeshift ladders constructed by brick-sized slabs of wood are nailed into each pole. At the top of each pole is a landing spot—almost like a platform, the kind of thing trapeze people wait on before flying through the sky with their death wishes. The two poles are about a basketball court apart from each other, and they're connected by trails of rope like some kind of makeshift bridge only an insane person would want to cross. My head is still at an awkward angle as I try to take it in, and then just like that—as fast as a sneeze comes on—I start hyperventilating. I've never hyperventilated before, but I know that's what's happening as soon as it hits me. It's like I can't get a breath in, so then my body starts trying to get one thousand breaths in all at the same time. I open my mouth to call to Jack and Joni—they're right in front of me facing Sturtevant—but they don't see me or hear me because I'm basically a silent movie. I'm trying to move my mouth around words but sound won't come out. I can't stop breathing so fast.

My legs wobble. I lean a little to the side and then a hand grabs my elbow. "Frankie?" Ciara says. She whirls me around. "Uh-oh. Okay. Get down." She shoves me to the ground and for a second I think she's attacking me, which seems unfair because obviously I'm hyperventilating and can't fight back. We're in the back row of cadets and I'm pretty sure no one else has noticed Ciara engaging me in combat, but also I don't even care too much about that because I feel like I'm dying anyway, which I've felt at least six times since arriving at the Academy.

Ciara curls my spine and pushes my neck forward and my head down. "I used to get panic attacks," she says, shoving my face toward the dirt. "I know what to do. Put your head between your knees and breathe." That's when I realize this is her version of helping. And she might have dislocated my shoulders, but the position of having my head way down low to almost the dirt automatically slows my breathing. *In. Out. In. Out.*

"Brooks!" Sturtevant screams. My helmet rests against tiny pebbles—I didn't realize I was so flexible.

I lift my head a little and see Joni staring down at me. Jack's there, too, now, bending to help me, but Sturtevant's already moving through the cadets, shouting, "Clear out!"

Sturtevant squats. I can see her shoes—they're *so* shiny. I would normally be scared, but I'm having that post-near-death-experience feeling where something just happened but you're still alive and therefore flushed with euphoria. "Hi, Lt. Sturtevant," I say to her feet. "Your shiny shoes look so nice."

I lift my eyes to see her lips purse. I can see up close they're quite chapped.

"Brooks, are you going to be able to participate today with the rest of us, or do I need to send you to the nurse's office?"

If she had offered a spa appointment, I might have taken it, but I don't really like the nurse here. It felt like she was purposely trying to hurt me with the tweezers when she was removing my splinters a few weeks ago.

"I don't need to go to the nurse," I say, finally catching my breath. "I'll be fine."

"Good," Sturtevant says. "You'll also be going first. Stand up."

What?! "Oh," I say, "I've actually never done something like this, so maybe—"

"Do you know why you moved up a few places in your War Games ranking?" Sturtevant asks. She doesn't wait for me to answer before yelling, "It's certainly not because of anything physical you've done here at the Academy! It's because your Military Strategy teacher seems to think you have some aptitude for the subject. So why don't you get off your butt, stand up, and actually try to do something

165

that requires physical strength as well as mental clarity."

"Um, okay," I say, shaky as I push to my feet. Sturtevant is holding a red harness—like the kind of thing you would maybe put a horse's head in, but bigger. Faster than I can say *this sucks!* she's looping it beneath my crotch, and then around my hips, securing it so tight I'm not sure if I'm going to be able to breathe ever again. No one could hyperventilate in this thing, at least.

"You will use these carabiners to secure yourself to the safety cables," she says, loud enough for everyone, not just me. She's holding up ropes that are attached to my harness. On the ropes are heavy-duty silver clips. "Being attached to the safety cables is your lifeline," Sturtevant says. "This is not a team exercise. You—and only you—are responsible for making sure you are attached and therefore not at risk of falling." She turns to me. "Climb, Brooks!"

"Right now?" I ask. "The pole?"

I can see the muscles in Sturtevant's neck pulsing. "*The pole*," she says.

Oh my God. I turn to see Jack and Joni. Joni gives me a thumbs-up, and Jack gives me an even bigger and more crooked smile than usual, and I know it's meant to be their votes of confidence, but I just don't know how this is going to be possible.

"What if I fall off the ladder?!" I ask Sturtevant, my voice way more panicky than I want it to be. And obviously I want to do the thing she said—*have physical strength*—but seriously, it's not like I'm going to be attached as I'm climbing. And the pole is really high!

"Are you serious, Brooks? Can you not climb a ladder?"

"I don't know!" I say. "I've never climbed one! In my town we have workers who do things like painting and other ladder-type jobs." I know I sound like a princess, but at this point, I just want to stay alive. What if I panic and jump off the ladder?

"I'll spot her," O'Neil says.

"Thank God," I say.

Sturtevant puts her hand to her temples. "I'm getting a headache from the sound of your voice, Brooks," she says. "The rest of your activity will be completed in silence, or you will earn a demerit."

A demerit for talking?! I walk on trembling legs toward the pole and O'Neil follows. Adrenaline is pulsing through me, but O'Neil looks pretty calm standing there in his parka, and then he says, "Up you go," and I start climbing because I don't know what else to do.

The wood-slab ladder isn't as rickety as it looked from afar, I'm happy to report—the rectangles of wood feel sturdy beneath my feet. I climb, trying really hard to not look down because I know I'll freeze if I do. *Just try your best, Frankie*, I tell myself. And I try to remember what Jack said: *balance and confidence.* If I just make it even a little way across the rope, I could maybe get myself a few spots ahead in War Games. I could even get into the eightieth-some-thing percentile! That would be such an improvement.

"Climb through the square!" O'Neil shouts from below, which is the most obvious statement anyone has ever made, but I don't say so because it would be rude and also I'm not

167

allowed to talk. I climb higher and higher until I'm almost there. I can see a square of blue sky, and then I'm climbing right through it. I scramble onto the wooden ledge. I expect to feel relieved—I made it to the platform!—but suddenly I'm more terrified than ever. I'm on all fours on the platform, staring out at the ropes. There's one thick rope that I'm obviously meant to walk on, and then two thinner ropes that are positioned to be "railings," except I'm pretty sure railings aren't supposed to swing in the breeze. Is everyone freaking serious with this?! A quick moment passes in which I consider the possibility that this is all a joke—some kind of initiation prank that everyone else is in on. But Sturtevant doesn't exactly seem like the kind of person to mess around, and hazing is forbidden at the Academy.

I can't seem to get out of my crouched position. I know it's the next step, but I can't seem to bring myself to stand up.

"Stand up, Brooks!" Sturtevant shouts from below. Her voice sounds wobblier carried on the wind.

It's weird. Now that I'm not allowed to say anything, it's hard to stall. Maybe that's why Sturtevant made me shut my mouth. I'm just awkwardly hunched over on all fours like a drooling baby.

"Make your body erect like a glistening skyscraper!" O'Neil shouts from the grass, and I make the mistake of looking directly down at him through the hole in the platform. Ah! He's so tiny! I am seriously so high up! What if I fall off the platform?!

I'm frozen in the cat/cow yoga position Joni makes me do in our room —it's like I absolutely can't move.

"Brooks, you need to stand up and clip your carabiners!" Sturtevant yells.

I can't! What if the wind blows and pushes me right off the platform? It's way windier up here than it was down on the ground. But I can't tell anyone that because I'm not allowed to talk!

Sweat beads on my neck. Oh my God! I just have to do this. I have to stand up. This is too mortifying to be on all fours. A squat—I'll do that next and then push up to a stand. *One, two, three . . .*

I'm squatting!

Standing is next. I know how to stand: I do it every day. It's just that I'm so high up. I'm so incredibly high up. I'm . . .

I'm standing! Like an erect skyscraper!

"Clip your carabiners, Frankie!" Sturtevant shouts.

It's the first time she's ever called me Frankie, and she's reminding me to clip myself so I don't fall. Maybe she secretly cares about me? Or maybe she's just worried about bad press for the Academy if I drop to my death.

I look down at her because I have to make sure I'm clipping these things to the right places. About three feet above the rope railings there are two cords secured from the telephone poles. I'm pretty sure that's what she wants me to clip them to. I stare down and try to do charades to show that I want confirmation that I'm clipping my *lifelines* to the right place so I don't perish. I catch the eyes of two hundred cadets staring up at me. They're so clearly enthralled; they look like they're watching a reality TV show and I'm the train-wreck star.

A few cadets even hang their mouths in O shapes. I see Jack and realize it's the first time I've ever seen him look scared. Which reminds me that I need to get my carabiners on right because then I'll actually be safe if I panic and fall off the platform. I wave around my carabiners, and then clip the metal to the cords, waiting for Sturtevant to scream any corrections. Finally she says, "Good, Brooks! You're secured! Now walk!"

Right: the tightrope part. There are the two rope railings for me to hold on to, and then the tightrope for me to walk across. If I just hold these railings—I reach out, and suddenly my hands are around them, but I'm still on the platform. I'll lean a smidge forward. Oh God.

The rope railings are bristly beneath my palms. They're pretty thick, and if I could just use them to balance myself it might be possible to walk the tightrope. All I need to do is put one foot on the tightrope. First just the front half of my foot . . . I take one small step and there we go . . . oh my God! My hair is soaked with sweat beneath my helmet, and every inch of my exposed skin is sweating, too, so that when the cold breeze hits me I feel ill.

You have to do this, Frankie. Worst thing that happens is you fall, but the harness will catch you. Okay. Right. I count to three in my head, and step off the platform.

I'm on the rope! I'm like that famous 1970s tightrope

walker who walked on a rope between the World Trade Towers!

Just one foot in front of the other. I take another step—now I'm walking—really, truly walking, like a person with a destination in mind. Someone whistles from below—I think it's a cheering kind of whistle meant to encourage me—but I don't dare look down. I just keep going. It's exhilarating! I'm way up here! In the sky! Walking!

"Good work, Brooks!" Sturtevant shouts. "Keep going!"

I don't say *thanks*, but I think it. I just keep trucking on: right foot, left foot, right foot, left foot. I'm gripping on to the railings like my life depends on it, because it kind of does. Whoa! Another breeze hits—why does the wind feel so strong? Is there a storm coming or something?

Oh no. I'm wobbling—I'm definitely wobbling. I know I'm about to fall. Yep. Definitely about to fall . . . maybe falling . . . I'm totally falling!

No!

I kick one foot off the rope like I'm a gymnast trying to balance myself. I don't even know where the instinct comes from: I hate gymnastics! It's a breeding ground for eating disorders. But here I am, balancing myself in some kind of gymnast balance-beam pose that defies the laws of my athletic ability and gravity.

A collective *ooooh!* comes from at least a hundred cadets below. Others shout, "No!" and "Hold on!"

Why are they allowed to talk and I'm not?!

I'm still in the gymnast position. My right thigh muscle

is burning from trying to balance all my weight on that leg. I just need to lower my left leg back down toward the rope. Slowly. Down . . . down . . . down . . .

Score! Both feet are back on the rope. I want to clap for myself but that would mean letting go of the rope railings.

I have to focus; I have to keep going. Right? Isn't that what I'm learning here? That no matter what crazy situation you're put into—no matter how foreign it is, and how challenging—you just put one foot in front of the other and keep going?

The wind picks up even more, but I'm okay. I'm almost there—I think I'm going to make it to the other end! I pick up my pace—*right, left, right, left, right, left*—faster and faster—I've got this!

Until I don't.

Suddenly the rope starts sloping up to meet the second platform, and it becomes tauter like a straight, hard line on an incline instead of a softer, pliable thing. Another gust of wind hits and just like that I'm *off*. There's no balancing; there's no saving myself. I'm off the rope just inches before I would have made the platform. I can see it as I fall.

No no no!

My large head starts falling fastest. I'm pointing down toward the ground and convinced I'm about to hit the dirt when my carabiners snap me upright and stop me in mid-air, and then I'm dangling with my arms splayed like a paper doll.

I feel tears start as I swing back and forth, but I swallow them back with everything I have. I'm not going to cry.

Not today—no way. Not when I did way better than I ever thought I could.

Sturtevant helps lower me down. "Well done, Brooks," she says. At first I think she's joking, but then I look up into her face and see how serious she is. She's proud of me for making it as far as I did.

"It was a good walk," she says.

I stay still as Sturtevant unclasps my carabiners. I look out at all the cadets, and I can't stop grinning when they start clapping.

THIRTEEN

THE NEXT DAY I'M PACING one of the Academy's outdoor training fields when I see it: my War Games ranking!

I've been pressing refresh on my phone all day. Sturtevant must have just changed it, and my name is right there, glorious as ever: Frances Brooks, Cadet #172. That's the eighty-sixth percentile! How awesome is that?! The thrill is so great I can barely even feel the pain from where the harness rope-burned me while saving my life.

Last night on my blog I posted about the ropes course, linking to all kinds of live-action ropes course shots I found online. (I wish Sturtevant let me take pictures of myself during PT, but obviously that's a big no-no.) Anyway, it's getting me thinking . . .

What if I can figure out a way to involve fashion and blogging in my leadership project for the Academy? I keep thinking of Julia's words: *Make it something only you can do.*

I don't quite know how I'll do it . . . but I just feel like there has to be some way to make it work, because here's the thing: my military-style posts are getting more comments than any other posts I've written this year. My readers all agree that army-green joggers, aviator sunglasses, and military-style jackets really set a woman apart and communicate strength. Maybe if I want to make my mark at the Academy, I have to do as I'm told without losing my joie de vivre and passion for fashion; and maybe I need to revolutionize the way military style is seen by my fashion community!

Enter: my first military-style photo shoot for *FreshFrankie*.

I came up with the idea late last night and asked Jack and Joni to be my models. First they got all shy and said no, but when I explained I was trying really hard to cook up a good idea for my leadership project, they caved!

It's just a kernel of an idea . . . but what if I could figure out how to showcase military fashion? Would Sturtevant ever go for that? I'm not sure how it would work . . . some kind of slide-show presentation online? But I'd have to make it way different than my blog . . .

I obviously need to think about it some more.

Now I'm waiting for Jack and Joni. I've been here on the athletic field for nearly an hour, scouting out my location and coming up with some ideas for shots. The photographer (me, in this case) should always be early to a shoot. I've learned just how much the photographer runs the show from watching behind-the-scenes footage on *W* and *Vogue*'s websites.

The art director is important, too, which I gathered from the time my dad got me an informational interview with the accessories director at *Self* magazine, which was amazing. The whole way down to New York City my dad lectured me on how the vast majority of the world is without money or connections, and how I had to figure out a way to give back to the world even if I decided to work in fashion. Here's the thing: I *do* know how fortunate I am, and of course I plan to give back. Duh!

It's Saturday, which means I'm not wearing my uniform, but I *am* wearing an amazingly chic military-inspired outfit, if I do say so myself, which includes light green utility jeggings, a hip-length cinched jacket with extra pockets, and a structured messenger bag to hold the semiprofessional Olympus camera my parents got me for Christmas last year. I'm also wearing riding boots and my new fashion staple: aviator sunglasses. I don't know how I've lived this long without realizing they're by far the most stylish kind of eyewear. And you can get them at the drugstore for like nine bucks!

I check my watch. I still kind of can't believe I convinced Jack and Joni to do this, and I'm praying they won't bail. Wind whips the platinum pieces of hair across my face. I swipe them out of my eyes, scanning the field for my friends.

"Frankie!"

I turn to see Jack and Joni walking beneath the goalposts. Jack stands taller when he's wearing his uniform, and he doesn't stuff his hands into his pockets like he does in street clothes. Joni's dressed in uniform, too. As much as I love the capriciousness of fashion and the changing moods and seasons, Jack and Joni's military uniforms look totally and completely right on them no matter where they are. I'll have to remember to work the timelessness of military fashion into my post. I really think *military chic* is going to be a new movement for my readers. How totally inspiring!

I wave as Jack and Joni come closer. Jack grins, his dark eyes crinkling. "Do I look fashionable enough?" he asks me.

"Yes, you do," I say, trying to sound professional. I want to add: *You look fantastic*, but that might be overkill, even if it's the truth. "Should we get to work?" I ask, my voice fluttery. I gesture toward the obstacle course set up on the PT field. There's a rock wall, a balance beam, a tire footwork course, a two-handed vault, and a whole bunch of other things that look ridiculously hard to do, but maybe if I keep building strength, eventually I'll be able to conquer them.

We walk silently toward the obstacle course and I see a lone medicine ball left behind. I try to tuck my hair behind my ears, but it's no use. The wind is picking up, sending Joni's strawberry-blonde hair flying, too. Jack glances at me again, and I look away, hot with nerves, trying to concentrate on the winter grass beneath my feet.

We stop in front of the wooden rock wall. It's about eight feet tall, spotted with little plastic imitation rocks you could grip to climb up and over. We stand there considering each other, and then Joni looks at me pointedly and says, "We should get started, Frankie. I have to study for a French quiz."

"Oh, okay," I say quickly, feeling a little weird. It's strange—sometimes things are okay when we're all together, but sometimes it feels like three's a crowd. "So how about we do some poses here," I say, pointing to the rock wall, "and I'll photograph you guys."

"Poses?" Jack repeats.

"Just natural stuff," I say as we stare at the thing. I have a little bit of a sick feeling when I think about Sturtevant making me climb it on some future morning. I take out my phone to get some music going to relax Jack and Joni so they're game for the shoot. They burst out laughing when a Rihanna song plays. "Rachel," they say at the same time.

Joni tells me, "Rachel had this crazy way of moving her legs like Rihanna does in the video." Then Joni tries to do the crazy movement with *her* legs, and it just looks so ridiculous that we burst out laughing.

We joke around a little more, and when I get the sense they're relaxed enough, I say, "Jack, how about you start to climb, and Joni, maybe you look up at Jack like you want his help, and Jack, you reach down and grab Joni's hand."

"Frankie, this isn't 1950," Joni says.

"No, of course not, I didn't mean it like that," I say, embarrassed.

"How about Joni and I race to the top," Jack says.

"Yes!" Joni says, grinning.

I don't even need to say *Go!* before they're latching on to rocks and clambering up the wall. I fumble in my bag

178

for my camera, barely able to snap a few shots before Jack and Joni reach the top, high-fiving each other and arguing over who won. They're laughing as I snap a few more pictures.

"My fingers touched the top first and you know it," Jack says.

"It's not my fault your wingspan is seven feet," Joni says.

I check over my shots. Some of the shots are blurry with motion, but there are a few that are perfect. The best one shows Joni at the top laughing with her head tilted back while Jack grins up at her. I thought I was going to want to show something that felt like the military to me—something tough and sweat-inducing. But this moment, with them having achieved something separately and yet still somehow as a team, feels even more like what the Academy is trying to teach us.

I'm quiet while they catch their breath. I think about how the military is so much more than these kind of drills—so much more than training and teamwork and everything they're teaching us here. It's certainly more than goofing around and talking about military fashion—even I know that.

"Why?" I ask as they shimmy down the rocks. For a moment I don't even think they've heard me. "Why do you guys want to be in the military?" I ask nervously. "I want to understand, and I don't think I do."

Joni and Jack push off the wall and land in a muddy patch of dirt. They're standing together, united by their feat, and they're watching me, waiting.

Jack looks at Joni. "You first?" he asks, and it seems more out of politeness than wanting to avoid the question.

"You," Joni says softly.

Jack kicks at the ground, his shiny black boot leaving an imprint in the grass. "It's always felt to me like something inevitable, a feeling I knew I'd never be able to shake. *This*," he says, gesturing around himself like he means not only the three of us, but something way bigger: the school; the state; the country, "is worth protecting, and I guess I grew up wanting to protect it." Jack's blushing a little. It makes me wonder if he's ever said this out loud. "If that's through being in the military, or being a war reporter and showing the world what the military is really like . . . I want to do that."

"And there are other people and their families far away, too, who deserve protecting," Joni says. "It's not just our country."

"Right," Jack says, "I didn't mean it like that."

"I know you didn't," Joni says kindly.

"It's not going to be an easy life, of course," Jack says. "But it's the only life that's ever made any sense to me. I'm gonna be one of the people who tell the truth about what's happening. I'm going to be a part of it no matter what."

The air between us is cold and still. There's no bugle call, no one shouting instructions, no one threatening demerits. There's just the three of us. The obstacle course suddenly looks kind of beautiful in the fading winter light.

"We have so much here," Joni says softly. "We're so lucky. And I guess, just like how some kids are pulled toward being artists or doctors, being in the service is what pulls me."

The wind works through my hair and my fingertips prickle with cold. "Thank you for helping me get it," I say. I have a lot more to learn, but it won't just be about discipline; it'll be about a way of life that millions of our countrymen and countrywomen undertake, which I know maybe sounds dramatic (who uses the word *countrymen?*), but it's true. How can I not think more about the men and women who leave their families to keep me safe?

Joni leans back and gazes into the sky. Jack seems lost in thought, too, toying with a tiny crease on the sleeve of his uniform. I watch his hands smooth the fabric, and think about how Albany Military Academy is full of more surprises than I could have imagined. Maybe this won't be the life I choose, but if I hadn't come here, all of this would have remained a mystery.

We're all quiet for a while. And then Jack's face goes darker, and I get nervous that something else is coming. "The other thing about being here is it strengthens you for real life stuff, which for me, lately, is the problems my family is having."

I stare at him, waiting for him to explain.

He lifts his eyes to meet mine. "I've been wanting to tell you something, Frankie," he says, clearing his throat. "A couple months ago my parents decided to separate."

I put down my camera, letting his words sink in. "That's awful, Jack, I . . . ." I try to form a sentence in my head that will make him feel better, but nothing comes.

"It sucks," he says. "And right now it's even worse for Rachel because she has to deal with their fighting all the time because my dad can't afford to move out yet. My mom and dad and Rachel keep calling me so upset over all different stuff, and I feel, like, a million miles away and I can't do anything. Everything about it kills me," he says.

Before I can think about what I'm doing, I reach out and squeeze Jack's hand. My skin feels like it's on fire. I quickly let go, and Jack turns to me, his eyes searching my face. The silence between all three of us suddenly feels awkward.

"You guys are gonna be okay," Joni finally says. I can tell by the way she says it that she already knew about Jack's parents. "No matter what happens, your mom and Rachel are strong. So is your dad. So are you."

"Rachel's also a raging pain in the ass," Jack says, smirking just a little, enough to shift the mood.

"Crazy how you can love your family so much and they still drive you nuts," I say. I look over and see Joni flinch, and my heart stops when I think about Joni's parents being dead. "I'm sorry," I say, "I shouldn't have said that."

Joni shakes her head. She doesn't seem upset. Instead she says, "There was this one time when we were white-water river rafting in Montana, and my mom fell overboard, then a second later my dad lost his balance and fell overboard, too. But my dad always swore that he had jumped overboard into the rapids to save her. My mom and I laughed so hard every time we heard him try to tell people that story, because we knew he'd just been clumsy and fell into

182

the water. But he was so stubborn. His inner Navy SEAL wouldn't admit he'd lost his balance like any other dad could have," she says, letting out a soft laugh. "It's hard when you lose what you thought you would have for so many more years. Family is everything." She glances up from her hands and looks at both of us. "But so are friends," she says.

I smile at them. My friends, my *true* friends—who else would stay behind in our room to help me study, or confess to sneaking out to help me mop, or go out of their comfort zones to model military uniforms for me?

I think about what today could mean. I could show all my readers what happens at military school—the friendships, the hardships, and the lessons we're learning. I could show what it looks like to be here, why we wear what we wear, how it helps us perform and work together to be in uniform.

And I could go so much further with it as my leadership project, because what if changing wartime fashions reflect more than just practicality and style frivolity, but an entire country's mood and outlook?

Can I make this work? Could I do something so big and awesome that it saves me from getting expelled, *and* happens to be something I truly believe in?

FOURTEEN

I FEEL A LITTLE BRAVER after my talk with Jack and Joni and this week of PT. (I bounced up to the seventy-ninth percentile after my Military Strategy teacher made a surprise appearance in PT, and I was one of only thirteen cadets who solved the puzzle he gave us! Even Jack and Joni didn't get it, and they were so impressed with me!) I feel brave enough that I decide to finally tell Andrea and Julia the truth about everything that happened before I got here, and when their sweet faces pop up on FaceTime, I just blurt it right out. "Guys, I have to tell you something. Josh Archester kissed me on New Year's," I say. "And I kissed him back."

Andrea almost chokes on her Luna Bar, but Julia barely looks surprised.

"I always told you I thought he liked you!" she says.

I try to smile. Six weeks ago that would have made my

year. But too much has happened here. I feel out of sorts being away from my friends and my family, but I also feel like something new is starting here, even if the road has been bumpy. And Josh feels far away from this place. And also from our last conversation, he might have been a jerk, and I guess so was I for kissing him.

"It was a mistake," I say. "And it's not the only one I made." I lower my voice. "I also cheated on my chem test."

Julia makes a face like *are you freaking kidding me that's terrible!* But now it's Andrea's turn not to look surprised. "I did that once, too," she says.

Julia whips her head around to stare at Andrea. "You guys!" she says.

"I'm not going to do it again, ever," I say.

"Me neither," Andrea says.

"Okay, good," Julia says. "Frankie, about Josh. I mean, none of us even knew him that well . . . including *you*. Maybe you should take it slow with this new guy at school. *Jack*," she says, dramatically saying his name like soap opera actress.

I nod. I know she's right. There were so many things I made up in my head about Josh, and then it crushed me when he wasn't who I thought he was.

When Andrea, Julia, and I finally get off FaceTime, I whip out my phone. **Want to meet up?** I text Jack. **Coffee? Dinner at mess hall?**

What I'm really thinking is: *Want to get to know each other and keep being friends first?*

But of course I don't text that.

I'm nervous waiting for his reply, so I busy myself arranging a few pictures on my desk—the one of Ella picking out watermelons at a farmers' market; my parents and me at a music festival in Rhinebeck; and then the one of Julia, Andrea, and me getting ready for homecoming. It's my favorite picture of us; we didn't realize that Ella was taking pictures, and we were all just sitting around in our pajamas eating pizza. Our fancy dresses were hung behind us on my closet doors. Julia had just made a joke about this guy she liked who used to have lice in kindergarten, and how she couldn't get that out of her head every time they kissed, and Andrea and I were laughing while Julia looked at us with this hopeless expression on her face. I think about my sister taking that picture, how she always wanted to be a part of our friend group, and how lucky I was that Andrea and Julia always treated her like gold.

Today when my sister and I talked, it was the first time one of us didn't cry saying how much we missed each other. I can't believe this is how it's going to be when I go to college. It's hard to live with someone your whole life and then just stop.

My phone buzzes. **Come on a run with me around the lakes.**

Oh my God. Is he serious?

Are you trying to kill me? I write back.

You need to start training outside of just PT.

"Just" PT? I write. **PT freaking kills me!**

Just come, he writes. **I'll go easy on you. No more than one mile. Promise?**

Deal. I'll pick you up outside your dorm in ten.

I grab my Academy parka from my bed. I kind of can't believe I'm agreeing to this. I look in the mirror and frown when I see my hair: my normally sleek lob is spiking everywhere from the forty-mile-an-hour winds in archery today. What is it about the Academy—it's always so freaking windy here! Though the gusts today totally worked in my favor: I hit the bull's-eye for the first time—twice! (I also almost hit Sgt. O'Neil . . . but still!) Joni says there's a good chance the bull's-eyes will up my War Games ranking, which is a serious miracle. Or maybe it's actually from hard work?

I dig through my purse for my keys and decide to forget about my hair, because my goal is to transcend any sort of teenage obsession with beauty and focus on exuding inner beauty, which everyone knows is the ultimate fashion statement.

#Duh.

My stomach is burning as I lock my door, which is either because I'm nervous about meeting Jack or because Sturtevant made us do eight hundred crunches in PT. Sometimes I think she's purposely trying to injure us, and the early morning wakeup calls are already nearly the death of me. The physical rigors of this place are *so* much worse than I imagined, which is saying a lot given how dramatic my imagination is. Even the mopping I've had to keep doing each night on dining hall duty seems to be toning up my triceps.

While I'm waiting for the elevator I call my parents

back—my mom has called twice today. My dad picks up on the first ring. "Hi, sweetheart," he says. "How's it going there?" I can hear the concern in his voice. I called home crying so many times the first few weeks that I think he just expects it now. But come to think of it: I haven't cried in several days!

"It's good, actually," I say. "I think I might be starting to like it." I think back to that afternoon with Jack and Joni on the obstacle course, and our talk about their plans to be in the military, and how I still can't imagine what it would be like. "Grandpa Frank," I blurt.

"What about him?" my dad asks.

"He was in a *war*," I say.

"Yes, he was," my dad says, like he's not sure what I'm getting at.

"What did he say about it?" I ask.

"He . . . ," my dad starts. "He didn't like to talk about it, Frankie."

He sounds uncomfortable, but I can't help but push.

"And you didn't ask him about that entire part of his life?" I ask.

There's silence on the other end. And then my dad says, "I didn't," and somehow it doesn't surprise me. He wasn't close with his dad. Sometimes I think it's one of the reason he smothers Ella and me.

"Dad, I think you should have asked," I say softly.

My dad's quiet, and I feel guilty for calling him out about something so sensitive, so I switch gears to how my GPA is hovering just above 3.5. My dad tells me he's so proud, and then he says how my grandfather would have been so proud to see me doing well at his school. It fills me right up.

My mom gets on the phone next, and says, "Sweetie, I was just going through my sweaters, and there's a few I'd like you to have for this winter, so Dad and I were thinking we could come pick you up this weekend and bring you home, and—"

Bring me home to get sweaters? Now she's really reaching.

"Mom, no. I'm sorry," I say. "I need to study all weekend and put together a presentation for my leadership project, and—"

"Study? A leadership project? That sounds wonderful!" my mom says, sounding nearly as excited as she was when I went vegan for a few months in eighth grade. But what's she going to say if Sturtevant doesn't approve my project and I get expelled?

Shudder.

I check my watch. Jack's meeting me downstairs in a minute. I take the stairs so I won't lose service, and my mom and I talk about my dad's new SoulCycle class, and how Ella has taken something of mine to school every day in case she misses me, and how my mom had to tell her she couldn't bring one of my sports bras because that was inappropriate, which makes me laugh.

Then my mom asks me about my blog, which she doesn't usually do. I tell her it's going okay, and that I have an idea for a new post about fashion trends to try based on your astrological sign, and she says she'll be sure to look for it, and then I say, "I wish you would always read my blog."

My mom's quiet on her end of the line. "I do always read your blog, Frankie," she says. "Every entry; so does Dad. We have since you started it."

"You have?" I ask, my voice echoey in the stairwell. They never talk to me about it, so I always assumed they didn't read it.

"I just, I don't know much about that stuff," she says. She laughs, almost nervously. "I live in my yoga pants, and I was a hippie before that. Fashion isn't exactly something I know."

"I don't need you to be an expert in it," I say, sitting down on a step.

My mom's quiet for a beat. Then she says, "I can tell what a good writer you are when I read your blog posts."

My chest squeezes. We talk a little more, and when I say "I love you," she says it right back. I can hear how choked up she is when we say good-bye.

I descend the rest of the stairwell and work my way through the lobby, past the poster advertising the senior class dance. Jack hasn't said anything about it. I'm going to need to act cool if he tells me he's taking someone else.

Outside, crisp evening air fills my lungs. I sit down on the grass and wait for Jack. I pick up a stick, and then I do the thing Ella and I always used to do when we were little: I trace little rivers across the dirt, curving them together in figure-eight patterns, the muscle memory from my child-hood so strong it feels like I've always done this. It's funny how you slip so quickly from playing in dirt to avoiding it. When does that happen? Can we ever go back?

My chest feels tight when I think about Ella and all those years of playing together. I worry about her, about her nervousness, and how sensitive she is. Is she really going to be okay this entire semester without me? Did my parents even think about her when they did this?

Did I think about her when I threw that party, when I did all that stuff that got me here?

"Frankie."

I look up to see Jack. His broad shoulders are hunched and he looks sheepish. "Are you okay?" he asks.

"Yeah," I say carefully. I'm wary to tell him about how homesick I suddenly am. "I'm just thinking about my little sister," I say. "I miss her."

"Do you still want to go back home?" he asks, his voice careful.

I let go of a breath. "Sometimes," I say, because it's still the truth, no matter how much better it's been going here.

Jack nods. "I understand," he says, but face goes cloudy, and I have the feeling he doesn't. Or at least, he can't help but take it personally.

"Let's run," I say, words I never thought I'd utter.

Jack takes off and I laugh as I try to catch him. Maybe I'm imagining it, but the running feels a lot easier than it did that first day at PT so many weeks ago.

Dusk falls around us, the sky slowly and surely melting into a lavender blanket. We take a path that brings us to two ponds, maybe about a half a mile all the way around each one. We're so incredibly quiet——there's only our breath and our footfalls. I don't think I've ever been alone with a guy and not tried to fill the silence with nervous chatter. We go all the way around one of the ponds before I interrupt the quiet.

"Break?" I say, pointing to a fallen log near the edge of the pond. "I'm sorry. I'll keep working on it; I just need a quick breather."

We sit. "Does that mean you'll keep running nights with me?" Jack asks. "And then after our run we can grab sandwiches? It's my routine," he says quickly, before I can answer. "I want you to do it with me."

"Okay," I say, breathless. "I'd like that."

His face breaks into a grin. "We'll add a mile each week until we get up to five. We'll stay at five for a solid three weeks and then jump to seven."

"Are you going to make a runner out of me?" I ask, trying to make my inhales slow and even, doing the breathing pattern Joni taught me.

"I think I am," he says, and we grin at each other.

The sky darkens until we can see stars and a crescent moon.

"Gorgeous night," Jack says.

I love how he talks like a writer. Most guys don't use the word *gorgeous*. My heart picks up as I take him in: the way his olive cheekbones go a little pink when he's cold, his deep dark eyes that look like they hold secrets and other important things. Every time I hang out with him I feel more drawn to him—and not just to some idea of him—the real him.

I remember so clearly the first night we snuck out together, when Jack lent me his night-vision goggles and told me about his bionic eyesight. I look up at him, wanting to know so much more about him, and then about what I need him to know about me.

"I'm trying to be more honest," I start, "and I want to tell you something."

Jack's quiet, waiting for me to go on, and I can feel all the things I want to get off my chest, but it makes me nervous, too.

I almost just want to jump up and start running so I don't have to say anything, but instead I stay still and go for it. It's what being brave means, at least to me in this moment. "You know the other day you said you made some mistakes with what happened with Amanda?" I ask. "I just want you to know that I made a lot of mistakes at my old school, too." I swallow and brush blades of dead grass off my coat. "I kissed this guy who had a girlfriend." I meet Jack's eyes. "And I applied to this school called American Fashion Academy, secretly, and all I wanted was to go there. But my parents found out about a party I threw, and about a few other things, and I ended up here."

"You didn't want to come here at all, did you?" Jack asks. He's staring at me like he's trying to figure everything out. But there are so many mixed feelings I have about the Academy, and just because I put up a screaming fight not to come here doesn't mean I don't recognize that parts of being here that feel right.

I shake my head. "No. I didn't want to come here."

"Are you glad you're here now?" Jack asks.

I swallow. The answer is *yes*, but it surprises me so much I have a hard time saying it.

Jack eyes darken and a look passes over his face I can't read.

"I have a lot of issues with trust," Jack says, and I can't figure out if he's just changing the topic, or if he means he can't trust me now that I've said what I have. "We moved around so much when I was younger I never found a group of people I could rely on, and now, with my parents separating . . . I just have a hard time having something and believing it's not going to be taken away."

It's comes out so plain and true that even though I didn't have to go through what he did, I understand exactly what he means.

"I guess, with you," he says, "I haven't been able to figure out if you care about this place or if you're just suffering through it until you can get out of here."

"Care about this place?" I ask. "Or care about you?"

Jack blushes. "Both, I guess," he says.

"Well, *both*," I say. "I care about the Academy, and I definitely care about you."

There's a long beat between us, and my heart starts going so fast I can feel it in my ears. I try to breathe, and then I say it: "And I cheated on a test!"

Jack's dark eyebrows shoot up.

"I cheated," I say again. "I'm a cheater." It feels so good to say the words out loud, to get them off my chest. "Or, I *was* a cheater. And that's why I'm here."

Jack nods. He doesn't look too horrified or embarrassed for me. But I wonder if everything I'm saying is making him doubt me.

"You're not a *cheater*," he says. "You just cheated once. If you put your mind to it, you won't do it again. My old writing teacher used to say that your gut knows everything, and if you check in with it you'll know right away if something is a bad idea or a good idea."

But then, what about . . .

"What about that night we snuck out?" I ask. "That was wrong, wasn't it?"

Jack's cheeks go even brighter. "It didn't feel wrong to me," he says softly.

"Me neither," I say. Maybe it was against the rules, and I'm not saying I'm going to do it again, because I'm not. But it didn't feel *wrong*.

Sparrows chirp from the branches above us, and I suddenly feel like maybe everything is going to be okay. I need to talk to Joni—it feels only fair to tell her first how much I like Jack, to make sure she knows I'm not going to get in the way of their friendship.

Jack comes closer until we're inches apart. I want so badly to sink into his arms. His lips are right there—if I just leaned forward a breath I could kiss them.

"Jack," I whisper.

He doesn't say anything. He just holds my eyes with his.

195

"I have to talk to Joni," I say, and I have this wild feeling that he knows exactly what I mean even before I say, "I just want to know that this is okay with her." He doesn't move. He's still looking at me like he wants something from me, and I'm terrified and excited because I'm pretty sure I know what he wants. But if does like me, if this is real, I can't do anything until I'm positive Joni's okay with us being more than friends, and that she knows I'm not going to take her best friend away from her. I promised I would put her first, even if that means not getting exactly what I want, and the only way for me to do that is to do the right thing and ask her myself—*tonight*.

I stand with shaking legs. "Can we keep running?" I ask, trying to keep my voice steady, suddenly needing to run so I can burn off this nervous energy.

"We can," Jack says, straightening to his towering full height. "And Frankie?" he says, his dark eyes bright. "The next move is yours."

FIFTEEN

HEY, JONI, I TEXT THAT evening during our study
period once I've finished my homework. **Are you still out
studying? Can we talk?**

I glance around our empty room, already missing her
after only an hour apart. It's our first night studying apart
in a long time, but Joni had to meet her lab partner earlier
in the evening. And she warned me I needed to practice
being disciplined by myself, so that I didn't always rely on
her as a study partner.

Studying solo actually went pretty well. I finished
a take-home trig test faster than I thought, leaving me
enough time to write a blog post about these insanely
amazing scarves by Turkish designer Asli Filinta. And I
worked more on the actual writing of the post, making
sure it was strong editorially, rather than flipping around

197

and clinking on a million fashion links and reading other people's articles.

I almost feel like I'm in late elementary school again, before I got sucked into the internet. Joni makes me put my phone away with hers under her bed, and we don't check them until we've finished our homework each night, and it feels so good not to have to be connected to everyone and everything every five seconds. And my grades are *so* much better: I'm up to a 3.67!

Sure, Joni texts back. **In library in the Flag Room. Meet me here? Table in the back.**

See you in five minutes, I write.

I hurry through the cold and get to the library, a brown-brick building with mosaic windows that reminds me of a church. Maybe it once was one. I push through the doors, showing my student ID card to a librarian at the front desk wearing a feather headpiece.

"Nice headpiece," I say. You don't often see fashion-y headpieces in suburbia, and she's really rocking it.

"One more hour till recall to barracks," the librarian reminds me, smiling as she gingerly touches the feathers.

I head past rows of books toward the Flag Room, a white-walled room decorated with various American flags and framed photos of generals and other honored military personnel. I push through the doors and spot Joni at a far table, eating Pirate's Booty and staring at her computer. The screen casts a glow onto her features, making her look even paler than usual. There are four girls sitting a few tables away, and another group of guys—one with a

198

split lip and a black eye—sitting near a window. The Flag Room isn't one of the study rooms designated as a silent room, so it should be okay for Joni and me to talk, but I'd rather these kids not hear what we're saying.

"Hey," Joni whispers when she sees me.

I sit. All the tables are white, too, with sculpted silver chairs that look futuristic compared with most everything else at the Academy.

Joni studies my face. "You okay?" she asks. Her lips are glossy with a fresh coat of the cherry Chap Stick she likes.

"Um, I am," I say, trying to adjust my butt on the seat to get comfortable. I want to leave my coat on because I'm still shivering, but I also don't want to give Joni the impression that I'm ready to bolt at any second, so I take it off and drape it on the back of my chair. "So," I start, leaning closer, nervous. Please let this conversation go well! "I wanted to talk to you about something, about your, um, feelings, and my romantic feelings, and um . . ." My voice is rising and comes out strangely defensive, like I'm accusing her of something.

"My romantic feelings?" Joni hisses.

"No," I say. "Well, mine, and your feelings about . . ."

"Frankie, please, keep your voice down."

I turn to look around me. A girl sitting at a table near the door has turned her head to stare at us. I make my voice way quieter, and say, "I just need the air to be clear between us, so I wanted to ask you if—"

"Are you seriously doing this here?" Joni growls.

"I-I," I stammer. "I just, I need to know how you would

feel if I—" I try, but Joni interrupts me.

"I don't know what you're trying to say, but I don't appreciate you questioning me here like some *interrogation*."

"Interrogation?" I say. "I'm not—"

"You're putting me on the spot," Joni says. She swipes away a strawberry-blonde wisp of hair that caught on her eyelashes. "I *really* don't want to have this conversation right now."

"I'm sorry," I say. "I was just . . ."

I don't even know what to say to her. This wasn't how I thought this was going to go. "Look, Joni," I start, but it's no use; I don't even think she can hear me anymore over the clatter of books and pens she's shoving into her bag. "I just think we need to be honest with each other," I press on, determined to do this.

Joni slams her laptop into her bag.

"Not here, not now, Frankie!" she says, sounding almost desperate.

"But I—"

"I mean it, Frankie, *shut up*."

My jaw actually drops. I can't even remember the last time someone seriously told me to shut up. "Joni, what's going on?" I ask, but she's already slinging her bag over her shoulder, heading to the door without a glance back.

I lean against my chair, stunned. Tears prick my eyes. I get up to chase after her, but she's so much faster than me. Everyone here is! We maneuver through stacks of books and past a librarian wheeling a cart and calling out, "Girls, slow down!"

"Joni!" I yell.

"Be quiet!" hisses a student with a shaved head studying at a cubicle.

Joni pushes through the front doors and I'm hot on her heels until we hit the open quad and she starts literally *sprinting*. I have zero chance of catching her. I run as fast as I can, and then double over and try to catch my breath. I lose sight of Joni, of course, and when I finally get my cardio-vascular system under control I hobble across the rest of the quad until I get to Lyons Dormitory. Is she even going to be in our room? I show my ID card to the security guard, who still pretends not to know me, and I take the elevator to our floor. I don't have to bother with my key in the lock because I can hear Joni sobbing inside our room.

A pang slices my chest as I push open the door. Joni's slumped on her bed with her face buried in her pillow.

"Joni," I say, my voice raspy. "I'm so sorry, so so sorry." I go to her bed and sit on the edge. I rub her back gently until she finally catches her breath. "I just really like Jack, and I want to make sure it's okay with you if we start being more than friends, not like I even know if he even definitely likes me, but I think he might? I don't know! I have this terrible problem of not getting when a guy likes me or not, so I . . ."

Joni's head snaps up. "Wait, that's what this is about? It's not about me?"

"Well, it's about you and me, because Jack's your best friend, so I wanted to know how you would feel . . ."

Joni swipes a hand over her eyes. "I already know you

like Jack," she says. Then she adds, "Um, it's kind of obvious." Her cheeks are flushed from crying. She lets out a big breath, and her skinny, freckled fingers toy with the hem of her uniform. "I would never stop you guys from being together, because I know it would make you both happy. Of course, I worry I would lose you guys a little bit; I mean, you're my best friends here." Color rises to her cheeks, like she's said too much.

But I can't stop smiling. "You're my best friend here, too," I say.

Joni clears her throat. "I need to tell you something," she says. "I guess, in the library, it's what I thought you were asking me about. Um. My romantic feelings." She takes a huge breath. "I'm a lesbian, Frankie," she says.

I sit up taller. "You are? That's awesome! I'm so glad you told me!"

Joni looks at me and lets out a little laugh, but then she's suddenly sad again. She exhales. "It's complicated," she says. "I'm not ready to come out yet."

"Well, you just did a great job telling me," I say. "That has to be a good start."

"Because I trust you," she says, and it fills me right up. "Jack knows, too, of course," she says, shaking her head slowly. "He's like my brother. And he's my only real friend here, before you came, I mean." She clears her throat. "I'm just not ready to tell the whole world, and it's really complicating things, because . . ." Her voice trails off, and I get the sense she's not ready to tell me more. She switches topics, and says, "I could tell you and Jack had chemistry that first night," she says. "I know him *really* well, and I know when he's interested in someone."

My heart hammers at her words. She knows him better than anyone here, and she thinks he likes me. I try to stay calm, try to focus on what she's saying and not make this moment about me, because it's clearly not.

"I hope I didn't act too weird about it," she says. "At first I worried if you guys started spending every minute together that I'd be without my best friend."

I squeeze her hand. "I'm not going to take him away from you. No way."

"You should go for him," she says, squeezing my hand back. "He's awesome."

We smile at each other and my pulse goes even faster. Joni thinks Jack likes me, and she's okay with us getting together, which means there's nothing in the way of Jack and me now, and something about that, no matter how much I want it, scares me more than anything.

"So what are you going to do?" I ask Joni. "Maybe there's someone here you could talk to, to get advice about how to come out, I mean, when you're ready."

Joni lets go of a big breath. "I don't know what to do. When my parents were alive, everything was so much easier. Sometimes I'm so exhausted from missing my parents that I feel like I don't even have the energy to do anything outside of what this school demands, like make new friends and come out and be the real me. And I never got to tell them," she says. "My parents. I never got to tell them I'm gay. And I don't even know how they would have taken it, but I still wish I could have that moment, even if it wasn't perfect."

We're both crying when we wrap our arms around each other. When I imagine what it's like for her without her family, it makes me want to never let her down. "I promise you I'll keep your secret for however long it's a secret, and that I'll be there for you whenever you decide it's not," I say into her embrace, holding her even tighter. "And I promise no matter what happens, you won't ever lose me."

SIXTEEN

A FEW NIGHTS LATER I'M blogging about how Coco
Chanel's rise to fame began during WWI, and how that's
likely because her no-frills approached to fashion coin-
cided with the severity and practicality of the time. My
blog comment section has been livelier than ever, and
this post might be another hit! I keep trying to brainstorm
exactly how to turn my love of fashion into my leadership project, and I have a few ideas, but I keep coming up
against one huge problem: Sturtevant wouldn't even let
me teach my fashion course at a nursing home, and I have
a sinking feeling that's because she thinks fashion is point-
less and superficial. So how is she ever going to approve a
fashion/military leadership project? I don't want to sell out
and do the kind of leadership projects everyone else is. But
how am I going to convince Sturtevant?

Right before lights-out, I shut down my computer.

I don't try to write just five minutes past the mark like maybe I would have weeks ago. Figuring out how to be creative within the confines of the Academy feels like it's finally getting a little easier—I'm not perfect, but I'm getting there. (And I'm also in the seventieth percentile for War Games—seventy-second, to be exact—because of my accidental windstorm bull's-eyes!)

I pull the covers all the way to my neck and think about Jack. The weather plummeted to single digits this week, so we haven't run since my talk with Joni, which means we've had zero alone time. I just don't know what he's thinking after our conversation at the lake. Does he trust that I like him, and that I'm not some flight risk? We're so different—he's so disciplined and sure of himself. I've been trying hard lately to balance studying with blogging, so maybe I'm actually getting more disciplined, too . . . but still, do opposites really attract? Or is that just stuff people like to sing about in pop songs?

I check my phone. There's only another minute to go before lights-out and Joni still isn't here. I want to ask her where she goes when she breaks curfew, but even though we've gotten so much closer, she's still way more private than me. I don't want to push.

Right before lights-out, Joni bursts in our room and says, "Hey!" Then she gets her hair shiny and perfect with a few rapid-fire brush strokes. She's like a race car driver changing into her pajamas at top speed, and then flipping off the light, shrouding us in darkness. There's only the glow of her phone.

"Is that a new perfume?" I ask. She smells like lemon.

"Um, I don't think so," she says quickly. "And do you know you're cadet 136? That's the sixty-eighth percentile!"

"I am?!" I blurt. Sturtevant must have just adjusted it! We did this sidestep drill in PT where you have to shuffle sideways over ropes like I've seen NFL players do on TV, and apparently I'm weirdly adept at moving laterally, which was a surprise to everyone, especially me. Sturtevant said I should take up tennis, but I told her I'm conflicted about that sport because I hate those all-white outfits.

"I think it's because you made it over the climbing wall for the first time," Joni says. "It's so much harder to do without the fake rocks. I can't believe they took those off. Maybe you're at an advantage since your tiny feet can fit through the cracks?"

I totally almost forgot how I got over the climbing wall for the first time!

I can feel myself flush with pride, even though sixty-eighth is still far from fiftieth percentile, and the final War Games rankings are going to be posted next week.

"Hang on," Joni says, "lemme turn off my phone, and then we need to debrief about the archery drills O'Neil's adding tomorrow, because it's like this army crawl drill and I have some tips for you that could bump you up even more, and . . . oh God."

"What?" I ask from my bed.

Joni's staring hard at her phone. "Okay, it's not a big deal . . . it's just, it looks like someone posted a photo of you when you fell off the monkey bars . . ."

"What?!" I shove off my covers—I need to see the picture. I stumble over the carpet to my desk and open my laptop. The screen glows like a light bulb.

"What are you doing, Frankie? You're gonna get us in trouble!"

"It's only a minute past curfew," I say. I click and find the photo. "Ugh!" I yell. It's a picture (posted anonymously!) of me lying facedown in the wood chips beneath the monkey bars! And the three other students in the photo are all adeptly swinging from bar to bar! And then beneath the photo is a caption that reads: *Which one of these is not like the other?*

"It's not that big of a deal," Joni says. "I mean, everyone already saw this happen, and this is just silly that someone would post it."

I stare down at the image of me lying in defeat—it's *everything* I've been trying to work so hard not to be anymore! "It's like proof I don't belong!" I say, feeling my cheeks get hot. I don't want to cry about something so stupid as this picture, but it's embarrassing.

"How can you say that?" Joni asks. "You *do* belong, Frankie, you're doing awesome here!"

I turn to Joni. Tears fill my eyes. "Do you really think that?"

"I *know* that," Joni says.

The sound of a key grinding into our door's lock makes us both turn. The door swings open, and Sturtevant's unmistakable frame is silhouetted in our doorway.

Oh my God.

Sturtevant flips on the light. Her makeup-free face is scowling with lines that frame her chapped lips like parentheses. She's wearing her starched uniform and staring at me like we're on the battlefield and I'm her sworn enemy.

"And this demerit," she says, "would be your third and final."

The way she says it strikes me as sort of overdramatic, and frankly, I'm really only comfortable with my own overdramaticness. A part of me wants to be mouthy, because that's my defense mechanism when I'm embarrassed, but there's another part of me that doesn't, the part of me who admittedly wants to make War Games, the part that wants to stay here, to keep trying. And that part of me is probably why I start crying.

"Wait," Joni says, but Sturtevant shakes her head like I'm some pathetic stray poodle mix drooling on her floor. I have to stop crying all the time!

"Give me one reason I shouldn't have you expelled," Sturtevant says.

Because I don't want to have to repeat a grade! Because I don't want to have to wait an extra year to get to New York City and start my fashionista life! Because I don't want my friends to move on without me!

I could say those things, because they're true, but instead I say something else that's also true. "Because I want to be here," I say, my voice quavering.

"But that's not enough," Sturtevant says, and I know she's right.

Joni's quiet. The air goes still. What I want feels like it's floating between all three of us like butterflies. But I have to say it. "I have no excuse for what I was doing and I'm sorry," I say, "but please, let me stay." I meet Sturtevant's eyes. "Let me prove to you I belong here."

Sturtevant stares back at me, and this time I don't break her glance like I did that first day I met her. She gives me a curt nod.

"One more chance, Brooks, and that's it," she says. "Here's what you're going to do to prove to me that you belong here. By Sunday you'll arrive at five p.m. at my office with a clear plan of your leadership project for my approval. If I don't approve your leadership project on Sunday, you will be expelled effective immediately. You will pack your bags Sunday night, and you will be sent back to Mount Pleasant, where you will repeat your sophomore year of high school."

I shudder.

Before I can say anything, Sturtevant whips her hand into a salute. Joni and I jump from our beds and salute back.

My hands are shaking, but I still reach for the brand-new pot of La Crème lip balm on the post of my bed. "Here, take this," I say, carefully holding the balm out for Sturtevant. "It works wonders on dry lips."

"Frankie has a lifestyle blog so sometimes she gets beauty samples," Joni says both nervously and proudly. "*FreshFrankie* dot com."

Sturtevant looks down at the chic pot of lip balm nestled in my clammy palm. She looks kind of offended that I called out her chapped lips, but she takes the lip balm.

"Good night, cadets," she says, flipping off the light and closing the door behind her, leaving us standing there in the darkness.

I turn to Joni. I can just make out her form in the darkness. She lets out a big breath of air and then opens her arms. I'm hopeful and giddy as I fold into her embrace.

Lt. Sturtevant's keeping me here even though I made a mistake, at least for a little longer. She's asking me to prove myself, and she's maybe even hoping I do.

SEVENTEEN

THE NEXT MORNING THERE ARE a dozen naked plastic bodies lining the perimeter of the Academy's swimming pool. The air is hazy with the thick stench of chlorine particular to the grossness of indoor pools—it might even smell worse than the gym—and my bathing suit is gaping in all the wrong places because I had to borrow one from school, which is obviously disgusting and potentially unsanitary, even if Sturtevant assured me it had just been laundered.

Blue kickboards are stacked in piles at the edge of the pool, and two diving boards jut over the water. There's a record board with swim times, and then the standard felt signs that advertise things like: *Albany Military Academy: Section Title Champions, 1987, 1991, 1997, 2004, 2010.* (People get so excited about athletic achievements, and I just want to go on record saying that maybe we should value other things in relation to how they'll be valued later in life, like creativity and/or communication skills.) I'm standing next to Joni, who looks amazing in her perfectly fitting bathing suit. We're both gazing at the plastic dummies, and I'm wondering what god-awful thing O'Neil and Sturtevant have planned. Now that I've just made it into the sixtieth percentile, I don't want to mess it up by being a terrible swimmer, which by the way obviously I am.

"CPR training?" I guess beneath my breath. Why is PT always so unpredictable?

"Way worse," Joni says cryptically. "We're going to need to save those dummies."

Red, white, and blue lane lines dissect the pool into eight lanes. Sturtevant and O'Neil are pouring water samples into little test tubes like scientists. I secretly scan for Jack. I barely slept last night after Sturtevant busted into our room. Every time I tried to fall asleep my thoughts alternated between ideas for my leadership project and thoughts of how close I came to getting into trouble and then, of course, thoughts of Jack.

The tile is cold beneath our feet, and something about standing around barefoot at the pool reminds me of being a little kid with my mom and Ella at the YMCA, and how Ella and I would freak out laughing at how the old ladies paraded around the dressing room with their droopy boobs on display, which made my mom roll her eyes with exhaustion and lecture us on *respecting and accepting the female form*.

I scan the pool, trying not to be nervous. Sturtevant and O'Neil are still arguing over the test tubes—I can hear Sturtevant say the pH is too high. I spot Ciara and Amanda across the pool, deep in conversation. I'm assuming Amanda's the one who posted the picture of me in the woodpile, because as far as I can tell, I haven't made any other enemies here. So should I be afraid of her? Or should I just try to have empathy with whatever is going on with her? I'm still upset about the picture, but Jack texted me late last night saying, **I know you've probably seen that photo, but don't waste your time worrying about it, bc we have more important things to think about, like getting you into WAR GAMES!**

It made me feel a lot better. Friends are the key to life, I think.

"You ready to save lives?"

I turn to see Jack. He isn't wearing a shirt and I might pass out at the sight of him. His shoulders are broad and smooth and his stomach has all these muscles that I've only seen on Olympic athletes and Abercrombie & Fitch models. His skin is so olive and gorgeous even though it's winter, and I'm suddenly really embarrassed, like he caught me peeing in the pool or something. I try to straighten so I won't look so shrimpy in my gaping bathing suit.

I watch his long lashes blinking at me and try to pull myself together. He looks even hotter than how I imagined him last night as I was falling asleep.

"So that's what we're doing today?" I ask. "Saving lives?"

"Oh, definitely," he says. He high-fives Joni, then returns his gaze to me. "See those naked bodies?" he asks me, his voice low. Hearing those words out of his mouth makes me blush. "Sturtevant's about five minutes away from throwing them in the pool and making us jump in after them."

"Are you freaking serious?" I say. I try to take a breath, but the hot, chlorinated air sticks to the inside of my lungs.

"So serious," he says, and I can tell he's trying to hold back a laugh.

"You enjoy watching me suffer," I say, kicking at his bare ankle.

"Maybe a little," he says.

Lt. O'Neil shouts out something about how all of us better stretch to keep our muscles warm because we are *T minus three minutes from getting in this mother-loving water and learning how to save a life, and that life might be our best friend's life in a cold-blooded war and dammit if we don't take that more seriously by stretching instead of standing around like useless pelicans.*

Jack reaches his arms behind his back to stretch his shoulders and Joni and I do the same. I want to just stand there and stare at his stomach muscles, but I don't, obviously, because I'm civilized. Mostly.

O'Neil tosses two plastic bodies into the water. Then he leaps into the water like it's no big thing, somehow managing to keep his head afloat while simultaneously grabbing the bodies and swimming them toward the opposite end of the pool.

"Um, guys, I'm getting really nervous," I say. "I'm not exactly a great swimmer. I'm more into reading magazines in the shade than going in the pool."

Jack scans to make sure Sturtevant's still busy testing the chlorine and pH levels and O'Neil's still busy saving fake lives. He turns back to me. "You just go like this," he says. He demonstrates how to jump and do a partial scissors kick to keep your head afloat. "It's called a lifesaving jump," he says. The muscles in his legs ripple so beautifully that of course I have to ask him to demonstrate it again just to be sure I've got it. "And then you scoop your hand under the dummy's arms and over their chest like this," he says, and before I realize what's happening he's got his arm over my body—his strong grip holding me tight against him. I seriously might die. I can hardly breathe it feels so good to be in his arms. "Oh my God," I say, because I actually can't help the words from escaping my mouth.

"You guys, seriously?" Joni says.

Jack lets me go and I try to breathe. I contemplate getting in the water and pretending to need his assistance so he has to do that move again. Jack's smiling at me—he wanted a reaction and he got one. *The next move is yours.*

"I've got it," I say. "The lifesaving jump, I mean."

Joni rolls her eyes and it makes me think back to our photo shoot when I started worrying three was a crowd. My head spins with the memory of that day, and it's like the extra adrenaline I have in my body from Jack touching me makes me connect that image to something else—an idea. I've been spending all of this time researching war-time fashion and changing moods and trying to figure out how to combine that into a leadership project. What if the answer is to showcase all that research in a military-inspired fashion show? Forget just making something online! I could have Academy students live-model the looks just like Jack and Joni did at our military-inspired photo shoot! What if that's how I proved myself a leader to Sturtevant?

"I might have an idea for my leadership project," I say slowly.

"T minus one minute!" O'Neil shouts from the pool, where he's now doing some weird pull-up exercise against the steely metal edge. "Stretch your shoulders specifically. Mentally prepare yourself to thrive with less oxygen."

"Less oxygen?" I squeak, but Jack and Joni don't say anything. They sling their arms behind them in what I guess is a shoulder stretch. Do these types of exercises just come naturally to them?

They both look at me expectantly. "You were saying, about your leadership project . . . ," Jack says.

"Well, it would be like a fashion show that raised money for charity!" I say. Oh my God—this might be it! "See, it's like a military-style fashion show," I say, my thoughts racing. My parents donate to, like, a million charities, and one of them is a nonprofit that provides recordable books for military parents to make for their kids so they could hear their voices each night reading a story while they're deployed overseas. What if my fashion show raised money for it? "And the tickets I sell for the fashion show could raise money in a highly creative way to support the troops!"

"That would be awesome!" Joni says.

"But do you think Sturtevant would agree?" I ask, my

voice getting fast. "Because if she doesn't approve this on Sunday, I'm expelled. You heard her, Joni."

Joni's face gets serious. "I mean, I'm pretty sure she'll like it," she says.

"She'll definitely like that you're raising money for something positive for soldiers," Jack says.

"And if you bring a lot of military history into the show . . . ," Joni says.

"I will," I say, "and you'll help me, right, like you said last night?"

I try to mimic Jack and Joni's swim stretches, which basically entail clasping my hands behind my back and bending forward.

"Of course," Joni says.

"You'll model one of the looks for the runway?" I ask. We're both hanging our heads way down as we stretch, and I stare at her upside-down face and try to read it. Would she do it for me?

Joni goes bright red either from her head being flipped over or from my question. She drops her arms back to her sides. "Why can't I say no to you?" she says, and I grin.

"You've always wanted to be a supermodel," Jack teases her.

"You're not off the hook," I say. "I'm going to need a hot guy like you to contribute his body for styling."

Joni stares at me, looking stunned that I said that. *I'm* sort of stunned that I said that. Did I just call him hot?

Jack crosses his long, muscled arm over his chest and

starts up a new stretch. "Frankie, be serious," he says, like he thinks I was kidding about him being hot and/or modeling for my show.

"I *am* being serious," I say. "As you may or may not know, I plan to become a huge fashion editor before age thirty or die trying."

Jack laughs and I get that warm feeling again. I try to ignore what it feels like to have his eyes on my bare collarbone, my shoulders.

"You know, Ciara has a great voice," Joni says tentatively. "Maybe she could open up the show with a rendition of 'Let It Go.'"

We glance across the pool to see Ciara and Amanda still deep in conversation as they stretch. I'm relieved they're not looking at us, because I'm sure they'd be suspicious if they caught us staring at them.

"'Let It Go'?" Jack repeats.

"The song's a little childish," Joni says, "but you should hear her sing it."

"Childish?" I say. "Have you listened to the lyrics? Have you internalized them? Could there be a more vital message for our generation? That would be perfect!"

I crane my neck to make sure Sturtevant and O'Neil are still occupied. O'Neil is dripping wet and conferring with Sturtevant over the pH levels. I try to ignore the fact that I'm going to have to get in the water, wrap my arms around one of those stupid dummies, and try to save its life.

I glance back to Jack. "I need you," I say.

He blushes a little. "Tell you what, Frankie," he says slowly, a grin breaking out on his face. "I'll do your fashion show."

I let out a little squeal, and I swear Joni tears up, but maybe it's just the chlorine.

"On one condition," Jack says.

"Anything," I say.

"You accompany me this weekend to the Marine Corps Snowball," he says.

My heart stops. "The dance?"

"The dance," Jack says, and his voice is so intense it makes me feel like I can't breathe, like this moment is happening and I just need to get inside of it, to live it right now and then again and again, whenever I need to remember the magical things that happen every day when you're not even ready for them.

"Are you *asking her out*?" Joni asks, smiling.

"More like I'm his charity case," I say, trying to sound light. "First it was the mopping, then private running training, now a dance?"

Jack laughs. "If you'd rather mop or go for a run this weekend, we could do that instead of the dance," he says.

"I thought you weren't going to the dance," Joni says, her voice teasing. "You're asking her so last minute, Jack." A smile plays on her lips. She's enjoying watching us squirm.

Jack clears his throat. "Sorry about the last minute-ness," he says to me, sort of seriously. "Dances aren't usually my thing. But I thought with you, it would actually be fun."

I bite my lip and look at Joni. She gives me a small nod,

and I say, "I'll do it on one condition," my heart feeling like it's about to beat out of my chest.

"Now *you* have a condition?" Jack asks, laughing.

"You have to promise to get a bunch of guys to do my fashion show," I say. I stick out my hand. "Deal?"

"Deal," Jack says, grasping it. His touch sends little pricks of something hot over my skin.

A whistle blows. "Attention, cadets!" O'Neil shouts. Maybe the chlorine is too high? Is he canceling today? "You will be paired in groups of two," he says. "Seven dummies will be scattered in the pool per round. Each dummy weighs one hundred and thirty-five pounds. You will dive to the bottom of the pool and drag your dummy to the side of the pool, where your teammate will help pull him to safety and administer CPR. And then you'll switch."

What?! Is he freaking kidding?! I glance at Jack and Joni, but they don't seem scared. I took a babysitting class when I was twelve and learned CPR, and I'm pretty sure I can remember the moves, but how in the world am I going to rescue a one-hundred-thirty-five-pound dummy from the water?!

Lt. Sturtevant shouts out names and pairs us up. I'm with one of Jack's senior friends named Jeff who has said hi to me a few times in PT and seems pretty nice.

We line up behind the starting blocks at the end of the pool, and Amanda's name gets called right after mine. She and her partner are directly behind Jeff and me. I turn to watch her try to dodge a cold puddle of water, and she stares back at me, practically glaring. Sturtevant is shouting out names, and I feel like I can barely breathe from the combination of Jack asking me to his dance plus the chlorine plus the lifesaving task ahead of us, but I still gather up every ounce of courage I have left, because with everything that's happened with Amanda, I don't really know what's going on with her, but I know she shouldn't be treating me like this. I didn't do anything to her. And I'm sick of being scared of her, and worried about what she's gonna do next. "I know you took that photo of me sneaking out," I say to her. "I know you sent it to Lt. Sturtevant. And I'm pretty sure you posted that other embarrassing photo of me in the wood chips."

Her expression stays way too neutral. "So what if I did?" she asks, her words flat.

My partner gives us the courtesy of pretending not to hear what we're saying. He absorbs himself in adjusting the tie of his bathing suit.

I stare back at Amanda. I cull from everything I've learned since I've gotten here about not backing down from intimidation, and I don't say anything: I let my inner strength and my (slowly) improving outer strength convey what needs to be said. At first I almost think Amanda's about to laugh in my face, but then she breaks eye contact with me. The skin around her hairline flushes and she looks down at her feet.

"Leave me alone, Amanda," I say, my voice steady. "I'm not here to hurt you."

Amanda doesn't say anything. And then whistles start

blowing and everyone goes quiet again. The divers start rescuing the dummies; the land rescuers perform first aid. I try to study how Jack and his partner do it, then Joni, and then I try to visualize how I'll do it. It's like a steady rhythm of work for the next hour, until it's my partner and me standing at the edge, our turn to learn how to save lives. I stare down the pool, breathing deeply to quiet my thoughts and steady myself. When the whistle blows, I take a leap into the unfamiliar water.

EIGHTEEN

"CRANK IT UP!" CIARA SHOUTS over the sound of Joni's hair dryer.

I turn up the George Ezra song and Ciara does a dance move straight out of the 70s. Joni bops her head along to the lyrics:

Give me one good reason why I should never make a change . . .

"I love this song," Joni shouts as she smooths her hair with a bristle brush.

It's Saturday night and the three of us are in Ciara's room getting ready for the Marine corps dance. I really needed tonight after the previous week at school. I nearly drowned in the pool the day we did lifesaving, and it also dropped me back into the seventieth percentile for War Games ranking. Ugh!

I holed up and whined about it for a few days, but then Joni reminded me I didn't have time to whine if I was going to make my presentation to Sturtevant on Sunday (tomorrow!) for my leadership project.

She's right, obviously, and I've been working on it like crazy! Joni also said sometimes if you hold a goal right in the front of your mind, it makes the work so much easier. I keep visualizing myself tomorrow, standing in Sturtevant's office, doing my presentation for my (potential!) fashion show, doing my absolute best job of convincing her why I deserve to stay. I feel like I've come so far here, and now it's not just about surviving, it's about proving to Sturtevant and everyone else that I'm good enough to have a place here.

"A room of my own," Ciara says to me while Joni blows her hair dry. She gestures around the tiny room like it's a palace. Apparently she got a single because her roommate complained to Lt. Sturtevant she was morally opposed to Ciara being gay. Ciara told me it was the only time bigotry had ever worked in her favor.

Ciara's walls are decked with tear-outs from fashion magazines along with photos of Celine, her French Bulldog, and one of her and Amanda in uniform at what she tells me was Academy's freshman orientation. (By the way: this week Amanda mostly avoided me, but then two days ago in PT, she shared her water with me because I forgot mine. Even if we don't become great friends, I want us to be civil, so that's progress, at least!)

Above Ciara's desk is taped a picture of a boy with golden-brown skin in his twenties wearing an army uniform in the desert. He's got the bottom of his boots lifted, and across both rubber soles scrawled in marker are the words: *I will miss you every step of the way.* My heart catches when I see it. Ciara says to me, "That's my cousin Bobby. He emailed that picture to his mom when he got overseas." Ciara and I trade a glance, and she says, "I look at that picture when I'm having a hard day."

I swallow down a lump in my throat. Joni turns off her blow dryer, oblivious to our conversation. "You know how my date asked me to the dance?" she says. "He was like, 'Will you go to my dance, and also is your friend okay—the one who couldn't save the dummy?'"

I scowl at her. "My CPR was perfect," I say proudly. "And I wasn't the only one who couldn't save the dummies."

"But you were the only one who almost had to go to the infirmary for water inhalation," Joni says, barely able to stifle her laugh.

Ciara snorts. "The look on Sturtevant's face when she realized she had to jump in after you was priceless. Like she was annoyed enough at you that you couldn't save the dummy, and then she had to get her uniform wet so you wouldn't drown."

Joni's laughing so hard she smacks a hand on her leg. "I think she actually has a soft spot for you, Frankie, that's the best part."

"Well, you guys better hope she likes my proposal for my leadership project tomorrow," I say. "Or she's gonna kick me out whether she likes me or not."

"She's gonna like it, Frankie," Joni says, and we smile at each other.

Joni seems okay that we're hanging out with Ciara; she was a little nervous Amanda would show up, but I reminded her we'd be together, and that I also kind of sense things with Amanda are going to be easier from here on out. I think she respected it when I stood up to her at the pool. Why else would she share her water? And I noticed she didn't turn away when I waved to her and Ciara at lunch yesterday.

Joni's going tonight with a senior guy from her leadership group. She says she's made it very clear to him they're just friends. It makes me happy to think she's making another friend besides Jack and me.

Ciara moves to the mirror and examines her reflection. She opens a tiny velvet pouch, retrieving gold pyramid stud earrings. Behind her, Joni slips into a simple black shift dress. When Ciara turns and sees Joni, she says, "Wow! You look gorgeous."

Joni goes bright red. "Oh, um, thanks," she says. Then she turns and busies herself buckling her patent-leather heels.

My phone chimes and I see a string of texts from Jack:

I'm thinking you're a hydrangeas lover because I saw them once in my mom's Elle Decor

Not like I read Elle Decor

Wait no flowers bc Joni's allergic . . . so . . . Candy? Or no bc you're sweet enough already? Whoa. Lame. I'm gonna delete this.

No! I accidentally pushed SEND!

I laugh, wanting to tell Jack that he's making my day

with all of the thought he's putting into this, but I don't know how to write that without sounding cheesy. So instead, I write: **J you don't need to get me anything. I'm psyched just to hang out with you.**

A dance; slow music; me in a dress: I shudder when I imagine everything that could happen between us tonight.

"This looks like a torture device," Joni says, holding up my eyelash curler.

"It makes your eyes pop," I say, and then I get an idea. "Let me do your makeup! Please?"

"Um, no," Joni says.

"Come on, it'll be fun. And I'll post before and afters on my blog, and if you hate it, I'll interview you and you can talk about the evils and artifice of makeup. It's always good for me to have another opinion on *FreshFrankie*."

Joni agrees, and then Ciara says, "Do mine, too," and I hear my sister's voice warning me about eyelash germs. Ciara's smiling as she edges closer to Joni. I like Ciara a whole lot more when she isn't around Amanda. She's so much more relaxed, so game for anything.

A Prince song comes on, and I start curling Ciara's lashes and do a teeny tiny smudge of eyeliner. "It'll be sexy and subtle," I say. Ciara's perfume—something lemony and grassy—fills the air between us. I finish her makeup and start on Joni, carefully slipping the curler over her lashes and pressing down as she prattles on with the reasons she doesn't think her date is hot—too short; already potentially balding. I go along with it because obviously she hasn't told Ciara yet that she's gay. Seems to me like Ciara would be a pretty great person to tell, but maybe Joni's worried about exposing herself to Amanda's closest friend.

"So, who *do* you like?" Ciara asks, her voice even. She's staring at Joni like it's just the two of them. I start doing makeup on Joni's right eye, smudging a little liner beneath her lower lid, then the top, and that's when I notice sweat beading her hairline.

"Are you okay, Joni?" I ask. I put a hand on hers. She's clammy.

"I'm fine," Joni says quickly, snatching back her hand. "I just need some air. Meet you guys downstairs?"

"But I only did one eye," I say, the liner poised in mid-air.

"I'll think I'll survive," Joni says, and then shoots us a smile that she obviously has to force. She grabs her purse and scrams.

The door shuts behind Joni. I glance at Ciara.

"That was weird," I say.

Ciara considers me. "Yeah," she says, glancing at her phone. "We should probably go down to the lobby and check on her. Our dates are going to be here any second."

I take a quick breath. I can't wait to see Jack. I hope he likes my dress, but I have to keep in mind that my dress is a) amazing, but b) a fashionable girl dresses for herself, not guys or society (reference *FreshFrankie* post #457: "Will Wearing a Jumpsuit Leave You Dateless? Who Cares? They're Worth It!"), which is why I chose an Alexander Wang black minidress with a neon yellow cutout just above my right hip.

And #sidenote, I'd like to add that my bare arms look amazing from the eight-thousand push-ups I've done since my arrival at the Academy. And I feel *strong*, which isn't a word I would have ever used to describe anything other than my fashion sense before Sturtevant repeatedly kicked my butt during PT.

Ciara and I zip our phones and keys into our purses. In the hallway, we pass a poster that says DON'T JUST READ TWITTER. Jack's name is listed along with two others I don't recognize. "What's this?" I ask, stopping to check out the poster.

Ciara squints. "Jack did that last year, too," she says. "He and some other guys and this girl named Priya give a talk about news outlets and international relations type reporting they think Academy kids need to know about. Jack makes it so funny. He's a great public speaker."

I swell with pride. Ciara must see it on my face, because she says, "Easy, fangirl."

"I'm not a fangirl," I say. "I'm just very supportive of people I care about doing creative work."

Ciara keeps giggling and I give up trying to play it cool. "Whatever," I say. "I may also have a minor crush on him."

"Minor?" Ciara repeats.

I jab the elevator button a few times, not meeting her glance. "Okay, fine. *Major crush*," I admit.

"He likes you, too, you know," she says, and I try not to let on how unbearably fluttery that makes me. What if Jack tries to kiss me tonight? What if I try to kiss *him*?

The next move is yours.

I'm buzzing with nerves as Ciara checks a text from her date, Dhruv. "Always freaking late," she grumbles.

I've never met him, but Ciara told me that Dhruv Gupta is a senior who's been one of her best friends since the two of them took over the treasurer and vice president roles in the LGBT club, which Ciara refers to as the table tennis club because apparently they play Ping-Pong at their meetings before discussing any pressing issues, which sounds like how my mom's book club is really a wine club. Dhruv is openly gay like Ciara, and Ciara told me them going together is a way to make a statement on heteronormative pairings.

We wait for the elevator in comfortable silence, and I almost want to tell Ciara how easy it is to hang out with her without Amanda around, making things tense. But then I consider Amanda's situation at home, and I say something different. "It's good that Amanda has you," I say. "It seems like you're a loyal friend to her."

"Yeah. Well, our friendship makes my life complicated," Ciara says. "But I don't have a perfect family life back home, either, and you can only understand that when you've lived it, like Amanda has. She's been there for me, and so I want to be there for her, too."

The elevator doors open and we get inside. I don't want to pry further and I don't want to pretend to give advice on something I don't completely understand. I shouldn't have been so quick to pass judgment on their friendship in the first place; my mom always says you never know what makes friendships, relationships, and families tick. So I just say, "That makes sense," and Ciara smiles at me like she's grateful that I understand.

When the doors open on the ground floor, Jack's standing there in uniform like something out of a movie. He looks gorgeous in his crisp dress blues, the uniform cadets wear for special occasions. Gold buttons parade down the front of his dark jacket and a white belt with a gold buckle cinches his waist. Pins decorate the lapel. He's so gorgeously tall, and he's holding a copy of March *Vogue*. "Better than flowers?" he asks, passing it into my arms.

"Six hundred pages of spring fashion?" I say, pressing the magazine to my chest, and then kissing it to make him laugh. "Um, yeah."

"Get a room," Ciara says to my magazine and me, and then excuses herself to call Dhruv.

"You could be on the cover of *GQ*," I say appreciatively, taking in Jack's six-foot-four frame in his uniform.

"No way," he says. "I only model for your blog."

"The comments are still flowing in on that post," I say. "It was shared two hundred times."

Jack smiles. And then he says, "You're the one who looks like a girl in a magazine."

"You like this dress?" I ask, surprised.

"Well, not really, but I like you," he says. I burst out laughing, and then he does, too. "No, seriously, you look amazing in it," he says. "Even if there's a big hole in the side."

"It's a cutout!" I say.

232

"It's a hole," he says. "But at least your hip won't overheat at the dance."

I laugh again, and then I try to be polite and thank him for taking me to his dance, but he waves me off. "You might want to wait and see my dance moves before you thank me," he says.

Ciara peeks her head back inside the lobby. "Guys!" she calls. "Dhruv's going to meet us at the gym. And I can't find Joni."

"Lemme call her," I say.

"That's a purse?" Jack asks as I rummage through my clutch for my phone. "It looks like an envelope."

"It's a miniclutch," I say, "just enough room for a phone and credit card. I had to take my key off my key chain."

"All in the name of fashion," Jack says.

"Always," I say.

The phone only rings once before Joni picks up. "Frankie!" she says, sounding out of breath. "My date got here early, so we just decided to head over."

"Oh, okay," I say weakly. Why didn't they just wait for us, like we planned? "I guess we'll just meet you there."

"Great!" Joni says, way too enthusiastically. "Bye!"

"Is she okay?" Jack asks.

"I think so," I say, and we stash my magazine in Ciara's mailbox. Jack helps me slide into my coat, which is wildly unnecessary, but also really cute.

We walk across the quad, and Jack asks Ciara, "You ever play Ping-Pong with Dhruv?"

I squeeze his arm. He's making an effort with her, no matter what he thinks of her friendship with Amanda.

"All the time at LGBT meetings," Ciara says. "You have, too?"

"There's a table in our dorm's basement," Jack says, "and Dhruv's Ping-Pong skills are legendary. It's a transcendent experience watching him play."

I laugh. He has a weird sense of humor. I like it.

"And you, Frankie?" he asks as we traipse through the cold. It's dark, and the ground is soggy with the memory of snow. "Ping-Pong? Horseshoes? Any random athletic skill you'd like to share with us?"

"You may have noticed I suck at everything sports-related, even games," I say, dodging clumps of mud. I'm trying to keep my vintage Ferragamo heels from getting ruined.

"I don't think you suck at anything," Jack says.

Ciara glances at me. I can feel myself blushing.

"Your bionic vision must not be working in PT," I say, elbowing him and trying to laugh it off. "I also suck at French. I picked French at school so I could go live abroad in Paris for a few years and work at a fashion company like Dior. But it turns out *mon français est épouvantable.*"

"But that sounded pretty good," Jack says.

"It's the only thing I know how to say, really."

"It could get you pretty far, though," Jack says. "If you just warn the French how terrible your French is, and say it with that charming smile of yours . . ."

"You speak French?" I ask him.

Jack nods. "We lived in France for five years while my dad was stationed there."

"That's my dream," I say.

"Really? To be a military brat?" Jack asks.

I start at the dark note in his voice. "No," I say quickly. "To have parents who raised me in France for a few years, just so I could learn the language and adopt the effortless cool of the French."

I'm trying to be funny, but I can sense Jack's mood has shifted. "It wasn't all that great," he says.

"Leaving your friends and living somewhere you didn't even understand the language had to be hard," Ciara says, and I wish I had thought to say that, instead of the stupid thing I actually said.

"Yeah," I agree, dumbly. *Say something else, Frankie.* "Parents don't always think about their kids, I guess."

Jack glances at me. "It's not like that," he says. "It's not like your parents, where they always have a choice in where they'll work and live. My dad had orders."

This is getting worse by the second. Every time I think I sort of understand military life, I so clearly don't. "I'm sorry," I blurt. "I didn't mean to sound naive."

Jack lets go of a breath. "I don't expect you to know, I just want you to understand."

I can hear in his words how much he wants me to get him. I imagine Jack and Rachel's life now, and how after all that they sacrificed they still have to deal with their parents splitting up. We step onto a sidewalk, our path illuminated by antique-looking streetlamps. My arm is still linked through Jack's when Joni rounds the corner of the PT building and spots us.

"There you are," she says, glancing at Ciara, then at Jack and me. Her right eye looks bigger than her left because I only did the mascara and liner on that side. She introduces me to her date, and then we all head toward the PT building, which is decked with multicolored streamers. There's a huge sign hung above the entrance with spray-painted letters that read:

ALBANY MILITARY ACADEMY MARINE CORPS SNOWBALL DANCE THE NIGHT AWAY!

The brick wall of the PT building looks black and shiny in the darkness, and I can't explain it, but the night feels magical, like we're about to go have an adventure in the place that pushes me to my limits every day at the crack of dawn.

Jack must see it on my face. "You look happy," he says.

"I am," I say. "No one's going to make me do push-ups tonight."

"We'll see about that," he says, and I laugh, giddy as we walk through the entrance. It's already so different from any dance at my old school. Officers mill about wearing their fancy dress-blue uniforms, the American flag stands proudly on a gold-painted pole, and a boy in uniform plays "Taps" on his bugle. My chest swells at the sound. These are the things that feel special to me here, the constant reminder that we're all a part of something so much bigger than we are, that our country is something we all share, something we can all be proud of and feel love for.

Jack squeezes my hand and leads me toward a long folding table with a few seniors I recognize from PT sitting on metal chairs and holding clipboards. A red, white, and blue banner hangs above their heads. One of the girls grins when she sees Jack, then jumps up to hug him, and the second girl crosses us off her list. She looks at me sweetly and says, "Have fun, Frankie." Then she leans closer. "You answering your cell in PT this semester was truly hilarious."

Hilarious? Or just plain rude and disrespectful? I try to smile, but I'm still nervous when I remember it. It's not who I want to be anymore.

We head into the gym, and standing at the entrance are Lt. Sturtevant and Sgt. O'Neil. They're both decked out in their fancy uniforms—they look pretty awesome—and the craziest thing happens: I salute. It happens, just like that. It feels like the right thing to do.

Sturtevant and O'Neil salute back, and then, even crazier: Sturtevant smiles at me.

One more day until I present my leadership project to you, I think as I return her smile. By this time tomorrow, I'll know my fate, and the thought makes me go warm all over as we head into the gym. I try to put it out of my mind, but it's hard!

In the gym, I'm surprised at how many Academy kids are out on the floor dancing. Everyone looks so formal and distinguished. Some are wearing suits and dresses because

237

we're allowed to wear street clothes, but most of the guys are in their dress blue uniforms, and a lot of the girls are, too. The mix is nice, actually.

Tonight there's going to be a presentation of service awards for the seniors who've made the biggest contributions to the community, and all the plaques are lined up on a square table beneath the basketball hoop. Streamers and posters hang on the walls, and bowls of punch, Doritos, and pretzels are on two large tables tucked into a corner. A sequined disco ball hangs from the ceiling, and it's spinning slowly, casting speckled light over the walls, bleachers, and dancers.

"Dance?" Jack asks me.

Katy Perry comes on over the speakers, and Jack says, jokingly, "OMG! It's my favorite song!" I'm about to laugh, but then he pulls me toward the center of the gym, grabs my hips, and starts dancing.

"Whoa," I yell over the music. "Seriously?"

"What?" he says, smirking.

"You said you were a bad dancer!"

"No, I didn't," he says, his grin widening. "I said you had to see my dance moves before you thanked me." He steps away from me and starts dancing crazily—it's like his feet are doing one thing and his arms are doing another, but the whole thing together goes completely with the music. It's all I can do to keep dancing. I want to video this for my blog, but then I hear my mother's voice: *Don't let technology take you out of the moment, Frankie!* So I just watch, and everyone else does, too. The crowd pulls back to surround

Jack in an amoebalike circle that sways and clumps as more people join.

Everyone's shouting and cheering and Jack's soaking it up, but instead of seeming like a show-off, he just looks like a guy who's having a great time. He throws his head back, grinning up at the disco ball as his arms whirl and his legs move faster than I realized was humanly possible. Everyone's laughing and clapping, and it's like his energy is contagious, and I don't want to be apart from him for another second, so I jump right into the middle of the circle and start dancing. Everyone cheers, and the few people who know my name shout it out. I'm laughing as I twirl around the circle, right up until Jack pulls me to him and sways my hips in time with his. The rest of the kids start to move toward us, closing the circle until everyone's dancing in a mash again. I'm exhausted by the time a slow song comes on. I rest my head against Jack's chest, and he kisses the top of my head. His dark eyes are bright even in the darkness. He leans close and whispers into my ear. "Wanna get some air?"

I nod, breathless. I do.

Jack grabs my hand and guides me through the crowd. I love how his big, warm hand feels holding mine, and I love what it feels like to be the girl he wants close to him. I know I haven't known him for that long, but everything I know about him, I really like. Isn't that the way it's supposed to be?

Jack leads us into the lobby, not bothering to wave to the girls collecting tickets. He's looking down at our hands intertwined, and there's an expression on his face that I can't read.

"This way," Jack says, pushing through the glass doors. He leads me down the steps and around the side of the building.

"Where are we going?" I ask. "It's freezing!"

"You'll see," he says.

I follow him carefully across a stone path, careful not to trip in my heels. "Slow down!" I say.

"Sorry," Jack says. "I forgot about your five-inch heels."

"I didn't want to dance with your belly button all night, Freakishly Tall Guy."

"Fair," he says. But instead of slowing down, he scoops me into his arms.

"Hey!" I say. I'd tell him to put me down, except I really don't want him to. The night is darkening around us as we move between two brick buildings. The moon is gone, leaving us in pitch-darkness.

"A little longer, princess," Jack says, winding along the stone path.

I try to laugh but my head is swirling.

"This is sort of like a scary movie," I whisper.

"Has anyone ever told you that you're overdramatic?" Jack asks. The lack of moonlight between the buildings makes it hard to see his face.

"My mother," I say. "All the time."

The buildings open up to a square courtyard. A stone patio surrounds a willow tree lit up with Christmas lights. Jack's still holding me, and I can feel him watching my reaction. I turn to him. "It's beautiful," I say, my voice soft.

His face breaks into a wider grin than I've ever seen on him. "You like it?" he says.

"I love it," I say. "Wait, did you . . . did you put these lights up?" I ask, so nervous that I'll be wrong and embarrass myself for asking.

"I did," he says, blushing.

I can't bring myself to speak. It's by far the most romantic thing anyone has ever done for me. (It's maybe also the only romantic thing anyone has ever done for me, but that's another story.) Jack's eyes travel over me and I can barely stand still beneath his gaze. Finally he clears his throat and looks away.

"Willa," he says, nodding at the tree. "That's what I call her. You should see her in the spring, when she's all flowery and stuff."

"Flowery and stuff?" I repeat, laughing.

"I don't want to seem too romantic," he says, and my heart beats faster and faster.

"Too late," I whisper as he lowers me gently to my feet. I want him to kiss me so bad I can hardly bear it.

Buzz! Ding!

My phone buzzes and chimes inside my clutch, and the sound feels so discordant with how quiet the night is that I unzip the thing to turn it off.

"Are you going to answer your phone?" Jack asks, and there's a nervousness in his voice that makes him sound unfamiliar.

"What? No," I say. "I'm turning it off, so it doesn't . . ."

I want to say, *so it doesn't ruin this moment,* but I know it already has. God! I fumble inside my clutch, my fingers shaking. I pull my phone out to switch it off. There's a missed call from my parents, and a text that says **call home**.

"Frankie?" Jack says, his eyes on the screen.

"Um, I should call my parents," I say, "in case something's wrong. It's really unlike them to text me that."

"Of course," Jack says carefully. "I'll just give you some privacy."

I nod. I'm halfway between wanting to kill my parents for ruining the moment and also desperately wanting to make sure everything's okay. Jack walks slowly back along the path we came. "I'll just be out here waiting," he calls over his shoulder.

Waiting. It strikes me that he's been waiting a lot for me. Waiting for me to figure out what the hell I'm doing at this school; waiting for me to catch up with him when I run; waiting for me to talk to Joni. I don't want him to have to wait for me anymore.

The phone rings and my mom answers right away. "Sweetie?"

"Is everything okay?" I ask. "Is Ella okay?"

"What? Oh, of course, everything's fine."

Then why are you asking me to call home on a Saturday night when I'm falling in love with Jack Wattson and all I want to do is kiss him? "So then what's up?" I ask, trying to keep annoyance out of my voice because I don't want to be disrespectful.

"Oh, it's just your father and I have been talking, and

I'm, um, *we're*, really missing you, and I wonder if sending you away was the right thing, and I just wanted to say maybe it's time for you to come home."

Come home? Now?

"Mom, I . . . ," I start. Cold air whooshes over me. Without Jack I'm suddenly freezing here sitting beneath the beautiful tree. "I need to stay here, Mom," I say slowly, my words careful but steady. "This isn't about you and Dad, because of course I miss you guys and Ella so much, but you were right to send me here. I'm becoming better. Stronger. More disciplined, even, like you hoped," I say with a little laugh.

My mom's quiet on her end. An animal calls in the distance. I crook the phone against my neck and wrap my arms around my shivering body.

"If that's how you feel," my mom says softly.

"It's how I feel," I say.

"Then I'm proud of you, sweetie," she says.

We say we love each other, and I promise to call her each night until her missing me gets a little easier. "I'm not forgetting where my real home is, Mom," I say. "My home is with you, and Dad and Ella."

We get off the phone, and I turn to see Jack. He steps out of the shadows and into the glow of the Christmas lights. "Everything okay?" he asks. There's a dark look on his face, even illuminated so beautifully like it is.

"Everything's fine," I say quickly, unsure of how to read the way he's looking at me.

"What did your parents say?" he asks. I can't put my

finger on it, but he almost seems suspicious. And why is he still standing so far away from me?

"My mom wants me to come home," I say. "She thinks it's where I belong, and she's probably felt that way the whole time, but my dad was kind of heading up this whole military school thing."

"So you're going home?"

"What? No, I didn't say that."

"But you want to? I heard you say it, Frankie, that your home is with your mom."

"Well, yeah, because it is. This isn't my home, obviously," I say, making a wide, sweeping gesture to indicate the Academy.

Color drains from Jack's face. "*Obviously?*" he repeats. "So then are you just pretending to care about the military and all of us here until you can escape back home?"

"No!" I say. "I just mean, my parents, my home that I was raised in . . . of course that's what I consider my *home*. My family *is* where I belong," I say. I know I'm making it worse, but I can't seem to stop talking or take it all back. And, anyway, why would I? It's all true!

Jack starts backing away, his broad frame silhouetted by the glow of the Christmas lights. "I told you I was worried you didn't really want to be here," he says, "and now, everything you're saying makes me think I was right."

"Jack, I'm trying my hardest to *stay* here, in case you haven't noticed. Doesn't that count for something?" I open my mouth to say *I love it here*, but I'm so taken aback by the sentiment, by the fact that it's truly how I feel, that I'm

244

momentarily paralyzed. *I love it here?* Oh my God: I love it here! "Please don't twist my words," I say, so nervous my voice sounds shaky. "I care so much about being here."

Jack's dark lashes catch the moonlight as he blinks, looking at me like he's trying to figure out what in the world just went down, and how this night could be swept out from beneath us so quickly.

"Please, just listen to me," I manage to say. I start moving toward him; I want him to fold his arms around me like he did moments ago. "Wait!" I say, but he doesn't. He takes off over the stone walkway, and I try to follow him but it's no use—I can't move fast enough in my heels. Jack turns, glancing at me one more time before curving around a dark building and disappearing from sight.

NINETEEN

I CAN BARELY FIT MY key in the lock with my tears blinding me. I finally get the door to my room open, surprised to see Joni sitting there with all the lights on. I just figured she'd still be at the dance.

"Are you okay?" Joni asks when she sees me. She appears to be studying, but then I realize she's editing one of Jack's articles for the school paper.

I start crying harder. I make it to my bed and sit, curling my knees to my chest. "No," I say, "I'm not." My shoulders shake as I sob. I'm worried Joni's not going to know what to do with my crying, like that first day I got to the Academy, but it's not like that anymore. She gets off her chair and comes to sit beside me. She doesn't put an arm around me or anything, but it feels so good to have her sitting there.

"What's wrong?" she asks, and for the first time I notice

her eyes are a little red. Mascara smears below the right one.

"Wait, are *you* okay?" I ask. "Why aren't you still at the dance?"

"It's a long story," Joni says. "How about you go first."

I let out a sigh. I don't know how to talk about this with her, because what if I try to explain why Jack was upset with me and she agrees with him? Still, I have to try. "Jack and I got in a fight because he heard me talking to my parents, and he thinks I want to leave the Academy, and that I'm just basically slumming it here and pretending to care about you guys."

Joni's eyes widen. "But you like the Academy," she says.

"I think you might have realized that before I did," I say.

Joni blows air out her lips. "It sounds like he's just scared you don't like him as much as he likes you."

"Joni, I *really* like him."

"Then you need to tell him, and *he* needs to listen to you."

A knock sounds at our door and my heart lifts. Maybe Jack snuck into our dorm to find me. I practically sprint across the floor and fling open the door, but it's not Jack, it's Ciara, and she's crying, too.

"What's wrong?" I ask, wrapping my arms around her shoulders. I don't understand how anyone can witness crying without immediately hugging the person.

Ciara slinks inside our room. I close the door, thinking she's there to talk to me about something. I stand there staring at her, waiting, but she's looking past me to Joni, who quickly turns away and stares at her computer. I can make out the way Joni's skin has flushed along her bare shoulders and arms, and that's the exact moment it hits me.

How could I have been so blind?

"Of course," I say softly.

Joni turns back to look at me, and her eyes confirm it. "I'm sorry," she says to Ciara.

"Me too," Ciara sniffs, and then she rushes over to hug Joni. "Can we tell Frankie, please?" Ciara asks into the sleeve of Joni's shirt.

"We can," Joni says, smiling at her.

Ciara collapses onto my bed. "Us," she says to me, then uses a skinny, cocktail-ring-adorned finger to point to Joni and herself. "We've been seeing each other all year."

I shake my head, bewildered. "That's so great!" I say. I glance from Joni to Ciara. "So why the heck does everyone look so sad?"

Ciara looks over at Joni, and I wait for Joni to explain.

"We got in an argument tonight," Joni says, "because Ciara's understandably tired of sneaking around, and I'm still not ready to come out." Her voice is flat like *that's just that*, like there's nothing to be done.

"Ah," I say, trying to seem wise, like I'm just so knowledgeable about this sort of thing. The truth is, there's nothing I can say. She's the only one who can decide what's right for her. At least she's told Jack and me.

I had forgotten about Jack for the tiniest second, but now my eyes fill up with tears with the thought of him carefully guarding Joni's secret. And even when I told him I was scared Joni liked him, he never betrayed her secret. And now he's somewhere without me, thinking I betrayed *him*.

"Wait, why are *you* crying now?" Ciara asks me.

"Life is so complicated!" I say, wiping my nose. "So is that where you've been when you're out so late?" I ask Joni. "With Ciara?"

Joni goes pink.

"That's so romantic," I say. I sniff back my tears. "I think sometimes breaking the rules is okay. Especially if it's for love."

I can tell Ciara is trying not to smile. Finally she says, "You are seriously so overdramatic, Frankie," but she says it so affectionately I can't help but smile at her. "Tell us what happened tonight and maybe we can help you fix it," she says.

I consider Ciara and Joni, wondering if Amanda knows they're together, or if she suspects it. I think about all the ways Amanda has tried to embarrass me, and how some of the ways have worked, and I just pray that never happens to my friends. Ciara and especially Joni have been kind to me, no matter how much of an outsider I was when I got here. And no matter how many times I failed, Joni has been the one to help me get up, and she and Jack have helped me get stronger. I don't ever want to lose them.

I take a breath, and then I tell Ciara and Joni everything.

TWENTY

Jack,
I'm really sorry about upsetting you last night. Can we meet and talk?

Okay, I know you must be mad at me. But please can we just see each other?

Hey. Have you gotten my messages? (Voice mails? Texts? Emails? The letter I folded into a paper airplane and tried to fly through your window?) I'm sorry about what happened last night. Please can we just talk about it and I can explain how I really feel?

Frankie

The next morning, the image of me facedown in the woodpile runs through my mind no matter how much I will it not to. Amanda must have taken it down—or at least, someone did—but it still hovers in my thoughts, and the feeling of failure from that day, plus all the other ones, like my first day of PT when I answered my phone and cried during combat training, the pool, the mile run, and so many others, make me more determined than ever to prove to Lt. Sturtevant, myself, and everyone else at the Academy that not only do I belong here, I *want* to be here. And just because Jack hasn't responded to my emails and I'm on the verge of tears every time I replay our conversation doesn't mean I can't give my all to this project. I'm not letting anything get in the way of proving myself—not even a guy I have major feelings for—and I'm not going to let myself get distracted from the importance of what I have to accomplish today, because I know I can make it here!

I have T minus eight hours to get my proposal into top shape, eight hours to show Sturtevant (and everyone else) that I can cut it at the Academy. I'm all revved up as I dig into my proposal, probably because I ran Jack's and my two-mile circuit this morning, and not just because I hoped to bump into him. I actually found myself wanting to run to clear my head.

Albany temperatures dropped again last night, and everyone seems to be hibernating and/or buried in school-work. (Joni told me she was sorry to leave but she had to study alone today because of some *difficile* French test she has tomorrow.)

By midmorning I'm double-checking my work and putting the finishing touches on my research on the connections between the military, wartime, and fashion, like:

1) Women who suddenly needed to work during WWI wore split skirts so they could move effortlessly between work and home, which was arguably the first step toward women wearing pants in regular life rather than just sporting events.

2) Blackout conditions during WWII created the need for luminous, bright buttons and accessories so pedestrians could be seen.

3) Wartime restrictions on raw materials forced the creation of man-made fibers we still use in fashion today, and a simple, cleaner line changed the silhouette during WWII. So-called Utility Fashion went on sale in 1942 in an effort to control both quality and price, and the new materials regulated by the government made the production of clothes more efficient and cost effective. Plus, it helped people without enough money to

purchase higher-quality clothes that would last longer.

4) Specific garments were created in wartime eras to aid safety and peace of mind, like the siren suit: a onesie-type outfit that could be pulled quickly over pajamas if a civilian needed to escape to an outdoor air raid shelter.

5) So-called glamour bands—head scarves used in factories to keep long hair away from the machinery, but also to add a splash of color to monotone factory uniforms—showed civilian desire to be both wartime-practical and fashionable.

I look over my work and pray I'm doing the right thing. It would be so much more foolproof to present a project more in line with Sturtevant's sensibilities! But I don't think I'm being stubborn for selfish reasons, like when I first got here. This feels a little different, more like determination.

I keep going.

I find more and more evidence of the way fashion changed to accommodate wartime and women's changing roles, and there's just so much good stuff—like a fashion series advertising proud-looking women, titled: *Practical Wear for War Work. Free Inside Pattern of Smart Shirt and Overall*, plus a WWII propaganda poster instructing women to *Go through your wardrobe: Make-do and Mend*, and I put all of it into my proposal and include a section detailing how I plan to bring a presentation like the one Sturtevant will see on paper to a live stage. I pretend like

I'm already an editor at a big magazine and do major art boards. Black-and-white photos of men and women from the 1910s, 1920s, and 1940s parade across my corkboards, along with images of rayon dresses, split skirts, and hand-bags designed to house gas masks during WWII, which I'm hoping will drive home the point that I fully grasp fashion was changing because it had to accommodate the reality of war, rather than for some reason Sturtevant might deem frivolous. There are decades-old articles and ads I paste to my boards, like a Sears, Roebuck ad for nautical fashion, and then my favorite article, titled: "Expect Few Nylons Until Late in 1947," which calls nylons *those things most dear to a woman's heart.* Isn't that just priceless?!

I'm nearly delirious from all the work when I finally put down my pen and shut my laptop. I've never worked for eight hours straight without a distraction on anything in my entire life. It's exhilarating.

At 1630, it's time to get ready for Sturtevant, and I decide to wear my uniform because admittedly I've grown to feel stronger in it. I zip up my Academy parka and leave the warmth of my dorm for the snow. Freezing air slaps my cheeks. I need one of those face-warmer things to survive Albany. I've seen a few kids wearing those around campus. They look like burglars, but warm ones.

I enter Flannery Hall, the brick building that houses Sturtevant's office. Glass cases showcasing various awards, plaques, and military medals of honor line the walls. A long wooden table that looks a hundred years old divides the front room. The last time I was here was that day Archie brought me to Sturtevant's office, when I got into trouble for sneaking out with Jack. It feels so long ago.

The door to Sturtevant's office is open, and she's sitting with Sgt. O'Neil. In archery this week, O'Neil waxed on about my grandfather's dedicated service to the military, so maybe he thinks the Academy only let me in because of his legacy, which is obviously actually true, and which means I have even more to prove.

When O'Neil and Sturtevant glance up to see me, I say, "I could come back another time" to Sturtevant, just in case they were in the middle of something.

Sturtevant and O'Neil salute, so I do, too, balancing my proposal in my left arm. I'm a little wobbly, and I feel my upside-down boat hat slip forward just a bit. I need to get better about pinning it right.

"Now is just fine, Private Brooks," Sturtevant says. She gestures to a wooden seat in front of her desk, and right next to Sgt. O'Neil. There's a new paperweight on her desk that was clearly made by a child: a clay snowman adorned with an emerald rhinestone. Does Sturtevant have children? Is she married? Why is it so bizarre to think about teachers living lives outside of school?

I sit. My proposal is pressed against my chest. It was so heavy to carry all the way over here, and I'm suddenly terrified to show it to them. What if they hate it?

"Um," I say.

"Enough of the ums and uhs, Brooks," O'Neil says

impatiently. "You're clever enough to speak in full sentences. Convey confidence rather than insecurity. That's an order."

"Yes, sir," I say, nodding. I try again. "This is a presentation I'd like to show you," I say, making my voice steady. "It demonstrates the interrelation of fashion and the military. It is also a pitch of why I'd like to present a fashion show focused on military fashion for my leadership project this year. As a side note, ticket sales from my project will go to Operation Paperback."

I don't wait for them to say anything—I'm too nervous. This is it—the moment my fate gets decided, the moment I get to earn my spot here, or be doomed with an expulsion.

I put my presentation carefully down on the table between them. I have four corkboards with photos and captions I made explaining the importance of each photo, so I separate the boards, and all four fit perfectly on Sturtevant's desk without knocking into her rifle snow globe or her military manuals.

Sturtevant clears her throat. I realize I'm just staring down at my corkboards. I look up to meet her eyes, and she says, "May we begin perusing your proposal?"

I nod. "Yes, ma'am," I say.

Sturtevant opens a case on her desk and retrieves her reading glasses, unfolding them carefully. She places them on her face, and each little moment starts to feels like forever, just like whenever anything important is happening. O'Neil hunches forward, and he and Sturtevant start reviewing the boards in total silence. Aren't they going to say something?

I watch as Sturtevant's eyes hover on a photo I labeled LAND GIRLS, showing trouser-wearing women from the land army in WWI. I swear O'Neil blushes when he sees my section on the emergence of one-piece bathing suits and the first modern bra. Sturtevant's eyes widen just a hair at the photo of Kim Kardashian from *Us Weekly* I pasted next to WWII-era star Deborah Kerr modeling wartime utility fashion in a March 1942 edition of *Picture Post*, and labeled it: *Did Deborah Kerr start the trend of celebrity-endorsed fashion we see today?* The article shows Kerr in three poses wearing a utility dress and coat, and it begins: *Look in your shops for Utility Clothes. They are a fashion revolution.* I think about the writer, a woman named Anne Scott-James, and I wonder if we're alike, writing about fashion nearly eight decades apart.

I can hardly bear watching them evaluate everything— so I glance away, spotting a tiny piece of paper taped on the corner of Sturtevant's desk. On it she's scrawled a quote attributed to Colin Powell: *Have a vision. Be demanding.*

I take a breath. *This* is my vision. I turn back and watch as they take in my work and I feel a little flutter of confidence, and then I say, "I find it fascinating that even amid the realities of war, fashion was still at the forefront of society's mind. You could argue that fashion changed during war, but it also flourished. Maybe that means something even bigger than this proposal, something about fashion itself, about how it's a part of us. It's there, throughout history, everywhere we look."

Sturtevant glances up. She considers me, and O'Neil nods. "That's well said, Private Brooks," she says slowly. Then they both look down at my boards again. "Brooks, why don't you tell us how you plan to see this through to fruition," Sturtevant says, still looking down at my work. I can't read the look on her face, but it has to be a good sign that she hasn't said no yet!

I clear my throat. "Well, first, I plan to gather participants, and lead them in a creation of my fashion show, the first ever fashion show in the history of Albany Military Academy, if my research is correct."

"I see," Sturtevant says, finally lifting her gaze. "And how do you plan to enlist participants? Do you have a plan for that?"

Participants. Right. "Yes, I do," I say, rummaging through the bag at my feet. I pull out the two flyers I made and pass them across the desk.

COME ONE, COME ALL!
TRY OUT FOR THE ACADEMYS FIRST-EVER
FASHION SHOW!

That's right! You can be a part of history! Albany Military Academy will be hosting its very first fashion show to raise money for Operation Paperback, a program that serves the United States military in myriad ways, like sending them books to read, or children's books to read to their children via webcam. Please bring your positive attitude and willingness to be styled in both military and military-inspired street fashion by me, Francis Abernathy Brooks (that's right! My initials spell FAB!) this Saturday, 6 p.m., Flannery Hall, room 121.

(PS EVERYONE is welcome! Even if you're probably not going to make War Games like me! ☺ xo Frankie. PPS These aren't even really auditions, because EVERYONE will make it! Totally not like War Games—seriously!)

Email me at Frances.Brooks@AMA.edu to sign up!

My confidence falters as they read over my flyer. What if they think I jumped the gun by making it?

"What's this, Brooks?" Sturtevant asks as she sees the next flyer. It's a special flyer I made for the back of bathroom doors; I used that famous wartime picture of Uncle Sam pointing his crooked index finger so he'd be pointing right at the person as they were peeing, and then I wrote: *Don't flush my leadership project dreams down the toilet! I want YOU for my fashion show!*

"Just some marketing materials I worked on," I say confidently, purposely not saying any *ums* and *uhs*.

Sturtevant looks up from the paper. She might actually be trying to conceal a smile. "It pleases me to see you be so thorough, Brooks," she says. Then she looks over my corkboards one more time, and says, "This is impressive, private," and my little flutter of confidence swells to a starburst. Even O'Neil meets my eyes and nods.

"And how do you plan to showcase military fashions other than the ones the current students own?"

"Well, I'd like to open the show with my grandfather's military uniform. My dad has it. And he already said I could borrow it, and that my grandpa would probably be psyched if he were still alive, because he was actually quite a fashionable man. My father says he thinks I inherited my unique personal style from him."

"I see," Sturtevant says.

I go on, "My presentation will also include a slide show of images of military uniforms I don't have access to, all from WWI and WWII. I'd like to focus on the world wars so that my coverage doesn't get too scattered. Then, after the slide show, I'll stage a live runway show of current military fashions and military-inspired street looks."

Sturtevant nods. She even looks a little impressed! She glances me over, and then says, "I'm going to grant you approval to do this project, Brooks. We'll need to work out a few logistics, obviously. But we should be able to find a space on campus for your fashion presentation at the end of the semester."

Fashion presentation. It sounds so official. I let out a little squeal—I can't help it! "Thank you so much," I say.

"I'll look forward to seeing it," says Sturtevant. "And I'll help you organize."

Sturtevant's going to help *me*—little old me! I practically explode with pride as she checks her watch. "You are dismissed," she says. "Please use the copier down the hall to make copies of your flyers, and I'll sign the bottom of each granting you permission to hang them in dorms and in the mess hall and wherever else you deem appropriate."

I smile. I can't believe this is happening. "Thank you so much," I say again.

"Academy apostrophe *S*," O'Neil says. I stare blankly back at him. "*Academy apostrophe S*," he says again. Is he speaking in military code? "On your flyer, Brooks!" he scolds. "You need an apostrophe after *Academy* before the *S* to show possession."

"Oh," I say, flustered. "Thank you."

"Correct grammar is a sign of fastidiousness and a bright mind," O'Neil says. To Sturtevant, he says, "I was an English major."

"So you've said," Sturtevant says. To me, she says, "Good day, Private."

TWENTY-ONE

LATER THAT NIGHT I'M WALKING along the sidewalk when I see Jack sitting on the wooden bench near my dorm.

"Jack?" I say softly. He's silhouetted in the darkness by the light coming from the lobby. I move closer and he stands from the bench, and the tiny hairs on the back of my neck wake up. He's standing there in his army-green coat with an unsure, embarrassed look on his face. Everything about him seems so different than at the dance, and I have the odd sensation that maybe I dreamed up the confident, handsome in his uniform, wildly dancing Jack who literally swept me off my feet and held my hand beneath Christmas lights.

"Hey," he says. I see him notice me wearing my uniform, but whatever he's thinking, he doesn't say out loud. He looks even more sheepish as he stuffs both hands deep into the pockets of his jeans. "Can we talk?"

I nod. We duck into my dorm together without saying anything. There's a long hallway that leads to a first-floor study room, and that's where I want to go. It's always empty.

Jack follows me, and I look at everything but him as we walk down the hall. The floor is a speckled brown marble, and the walls on either side of us are the color of wet sand. (Who picks a gross shade like that?)

There's a long mirror at the end of the hallway, and it reminds me of that first night when I saw myself in the mirror sneaking out with Jack. But I look different now, stronger and more sure of myself.

Jack and I swing right into the study room and close the door behind us. We sit on a cold iron bench next to a wall of windows looking out onto the quad, and a strange thing happens: I start feeling upset with him. Did I really do something bad enough to deserve a day of the silent treatment? He didn't even let me explain what I meant. I turn so that I'm facing him, but scoot back so we aren't too close.

"Why didn't you answer my messages from last night and today?" I blurt. I lean back on my butt and curl my knees to my chest. He looks a little stunned at the way I said it.

"I-I'm sorry," he says.

"You should be," I say.

He lets out a self-conscious laugh. "I was thinking I got to be the one who was upset," he says. I can tell he's trying to lighten the situation, but I'm not ready to give him that.

Someone shouts outside the window and I glance onto the quad just in time to see a short, stocky boy peg a snowball at a taller boy and miss. A few yards away from the snowball boys are a dozen students in uniform practicing a drill. A tall girl in the center holds a flag, and all the cadets march with such precision that I'm pretty sure they're the drill team. Joni told me she tried out two years in a row, but didn't make it. It was the first time I'd heard of her failing at something military.

I turn back to Jack. "We're supposed to be friends," I say softly, "and I was just trying to explain something, and you wouldn't even stick around long enough to listen."

Jack's cheeks go pink. "I'm sorry," he says again. "I didn't think about it like that, because I guess I couldn't think at all, because I just started telling myself you were leaving the Academy and going home, and that I was going to lose you."

I take in his sweet face, and all the worry on his features. "If you'd just let me explain myself . . ."

He raises an eyebrow.

"I'm not going anywhere," I say. "Not just because of you, but because I like it here, too, and it feels meaningful for me to be here, I want to do things here that make my parents and me proud, and maybe even make the Academy proud." I take a breath. I have to say it. "I also like you, Jack, *a lot*." Now it's my turn to blush. I'm nervous, but it feels amazing to have said that out loud.

"You do?" he asks. His voice is so incredulous I can't help but smile.

"Yeah," I say. "I do." I don't know how to make him understand just how much I like him, and I'm scared to let him know because putting myself out there romantically isn't exactly something I have a lot of practice with. But the big thing I've learned here besides discipline and strength is how important it is to be honest and true.

"Back at home I always fell back on this crush I had— on the guy I told you I kissed who had a girlfriend." I take a breath, feeling really emotional all of a sudden. "My friend Julia pointed out to me recently how I barely knew him. So I guess maybe I mostly just liked the idea of him. But now I'm here, and there's *you*, and the more we hang out and get to know each other, the more I like you, and I want to get to know you even better, and the dance, that whole night was perfect until . . ."

Outside the window, the drill team drummer plays his snare drum. It's that traditional military marching rhythm—*ba-da-dum-dum-dum . . . ba-da-dum-dum-dum! Duh-duh-duh-duh-duh-duh-duh-duh-dum-dum-dum!*—and somehow it makes our conversation seem even more urgent. There's this term I learned in Military Strategy: non-zero-sum game. It can mean lots of things, but in terms of a conversation, it can mean that both sides feel like they've been heard, that they've both gained something rather than one winning and one losing. There's something else I need to say to Jack, because I can't walk around on eggshells trying to be perfect for him or anybody else. "You have to try harder to trust me," I say, my voice unwavering. I feel nervous confronting him, but strong, too. "If you don't trust me, this isn't going to work."

Jack nods slowly like he knows what I mean, and then he says, "I'm sorry, Frankie. I promise you I'll work on it. Maybe I won't be perfect—but I promise you I'll try."

A quiet moment passes between us, and I realize this is about so much more than just us. "There are so many things I've done this year that I wasn't supposed to," I say. "I lost my parents' respect, and it felt so, so awful, and I want to prove to them I deserve their trust again, and I want to be a good friend to Joni, too, and a good friend to you. Maybe more."

"More," Jack says softly. "I like how that sounds."

"Me too," I say

We're quiet for a beat, our eyes on each other, waiting.

"So you said you want to get to know each other better?" Jack asks. He seems so nervous.

"I do," I say.

"And maybe if you like me when you get to know me better, you'll want me to be your boyfriend?"

My heart lurches. I try to think of something to say to hide how startled I am he just said that.

"Who said anything about being my boyfriend?" I tease.

"You're killing me," he says.

He covers my hand with his and it feels like electricity sparking where our skin touches. His eyes hold mine, his dark gaze so intense it makes me flush, and then he says, "Can I take you out Friday night?"

I swallow. "I can't sneak off campus, Jack," I say carefully.

"Not off campus—nowhere that could get us in trouble," Jack says.

"A date," I say.

"A date," he says.

"Yes," I say, that one word meaning more right now that any other time I've ever said it. "I'd like that."

"Good," Jack says. He stands and pulls me to my feet, his body strong and sure as he guides me closer to him. The warmth of him feels like everything I need. I think back to one of those first days with Jack when he showed up in the cafeteria wearing a hairnet, ready to help me. Right away it felt easy with him, right away it had been *good*. I lift my chin to see his dark eyes wide and bright. I smile, still in his arms, never wanting to leave this place. "I like you more than I've ever liked anybody, and I'm so scared of it getting ruined," I say.

A bugle sounds along with the snare drum, but neither of us looks toward the quad as the music filters through the glass to the space between us. We're locked on each other's eyes as the bugle plays on, soft but insistent, and then Jack leans into me until our lips are only a breath apart. His arms around me warm me from the inside out. "So we protect us," he says, voice low.

I arch onto my tiptoes. "We protect us," I whisper. I can see the curve of his mouth, his lips scarlet from the cold. His mouth presses mine, and his kiss tells me exactly how he feels. Warmth spreads through me and I can barely catch my breath. He's kissing me like it means something—*every-thing*—and I can feel us melting into each other; I can feel how much we both want this kiss.

His hands go into my hair, desperate and wild, and then they drop to my hips. A shiver runs through me as his body presses against me, and we kiss until I'm giddy with his nearness, heady with what it feels like to have my feelings returned by a guy, a *good* guy, someone who puts other people first, someone who thinks about things worth protecting, someone who wants to be brave so that others won't have to be scared. And it gets me thinking. What if the Academy was everything I didn't know I needed until I got it?

Jack's kiss deepens and there's no more thinking, no more wishing and wondering. There's just me, here, tonight, fashionably and proudly rooted to the halls of the Academy, and Jack, his warm, brave hands circling my waist and pulling me even closer.

TWENTY-TWO

WE'RE IN PT AT DAWN the next morning, and of course my imagination keeps replaying Jack's kiss, and it makes me so crazy fluttery I can barely stand still!

Last night after Jack left my dorm I had so much nervous energy I called my mom and told her a little about the dance, and then all about my upcoming fashion show. Now I feel on the verge of tears every time I think about our conversation, about how lucky I am that my parents are mine, how excited they were to be there when I do my fashion show, because they're *my mom and dad*.

Being this far away from my family has made me feel silly for all the times I complained about them suffocating Ella and me. And it makes me want to show them that I can use the focus and discipline I've learned here on creative projects like this show. It's weird. I always knew I was a little different back home. But Mount Pleasant is full of artists, and children of artists. It's the kind of place where it's totally fine to be artsy-fartsy. But it's so different here at the Academy that it's made me even surer of how I want my life to be when I leave this place.

"Attention!" Sturtevant screams for what might be the eightieth time this semester. She blows her whistle, which is overkill because of course by then we've all already gone silent. It's one of the many things I've grown to love about this place: you don't bend the rules and talk a little past the time when you're supposed to shut up. It's freeing, really. It's no longer uncool to do things exactly like you're supposed to.

Sturtevant, O'Neil, and two other TACs are standing beneath the basketball hoop. Only Sturtevant is grinning, but it's like a Cruella de Vil type of smile with her teeth bared. "Good morning, cadets," she says, starting to pace. "This is your final trial for War Games. The selection will be posted this morning after your TACs and I confer, and the cadets selected will begin a special process of evening training sessions to prepare for the games in May."

Evening training. I glance over at Jack. I guess this would mean we'd have to put our nighttime runs on hold. We're already up to three miles per night, and Jack is pretty sure we can get to ten by the end of the semester. He catches my glance and gives me a secret look that makes me feel just as buzzy and nervous as I felt last night. All I can think about is being alone with him tonight on our run and kissing him again. And the way he looks at me make me sure he's thinking the same thing.

"This morning's test takes much more than physical strength," Lt. Sturtevant says. "It takes intuition and instinct." The memory of Sturtevant's fist coming millimeters from my face that first day flashes through my brain. So much has changed. "Your final War Games trial will consist of partnered sprints, and you will aim to reach your fastest time *as a three-person team*. That means you must stay together; you are only as fast as your weakest member." She glances over all of us, giving a look that says: *this part is really important.* "If you sprint ahead more than twelve inches from any member of your team, your entire team will be disqualified." I take a breath and try to relax my muscles. I'm pretty sure she just means sprinting in a straight three-person line. "As you sprint for the length of the gymnasium, you must sense how fast your team can move without leaving a member behind," Sturtevant continues. "Pick your teammates wisely. It *matters*."

I'm sandwiched between Jack and Joni, and Amanda and Ciara. I look down at my feet. I can sense Amanda tightening her stance with Ciara, inching toward her and away from me. I get it. Even though my athletic skills and my endurance have greatly improved, I'm still far from the fastest sprinter.

"Partners?" Joni says to Jack.

He puts out his hand to low-five her.

"Um," I say, "I'm just going to . . ." but I can't even finish my sentence because I don't know what to say. I don't want to assume I'll be on Jack and Joni's team because he's my maybe-almost-boyfriend and she's my best friend here.

271

I want Jack and Joni to have their best chance at winning this, because making War Games means something to all of us, not just me. I can't believe that after all these months of training, today's the day we'll find out who made it.

My eyes meet Amanda's. They're green and hard and there isn't an ounce of sympathy in them. It's obvious she doesn't want me on her team. Ciara opens her mouth to say something but I beat her to it. "I'm gonna go find another group," I say, pointing vaguely toward the other side of the gym like I have a plan.

"No, you're not," Jack says.

I lift my gaze. Jack's dark eyes are just as hard with determination as Amanda's, but instead of coldness, there's something else.

"You're coming with us," he says. "You, me, Joni. Unbeatable."

Joni nods at me. "Unbeatable," she says. She grabs my hand and pulls me closer, right to her side, like that's where I belong.

Once everyone's settled into their groups, Sturtevant instructs us to do two warm-up laps and then lines us up along the back wall of the gym. She gives me a slight nod when she sees me standing with Jack and Joni. I watch as she calls forward the first group of teams and repeats her instructions. Then she blows her whistle, and the cadets take off like they're on fire. But only two of the first six groups are able to stay within one foot of one another. Two boys leave their third teammate almost a full four feet

272

behind before realizing that they've disqualified themselves. The other three groups are finding it so hard to stay within one foot of one another that they're practically stopping and starting for the entire length of the gym. Sturtevant shouts out last names: "Lucke! Peterson! Mazza! You're disqualified!"

I watch the next heat of six start. They're even worse. Only one group manages to stay together, but they're only able to do it by jogging, not sprinting.

Our turn is coming up, and I think about Military Strategy and all the myriad strategies to use to gain what you deem victory. I pull Jack and Joni close, and then lower my voice so only they can hear. "You guys know I'm not the fastest," I say. "So let me set the pace. I'll run in the middle of us, and I'll sprint with all I've got. You two stay right with me. Okay?"

"That's brilliant," Jack says, and Joni grins her approval.

Sturtevant signals for the next six groups to approach the start line. Amanda, Ciara, and their muscle-guy teammate move up, too. They're right next to us.

"On your marks!" Sturtevant shouts.

"Don't forget—it's my lead," I say softly.

"Go!"

I lunge forward with all my might. My chest seizes with adrenaline as I sprint toward the far wall. I can see Amanda and Ciara sprinting ahead with their teammate—but Jack and Joni are right in line with me; it's almost like our arms and legs are moving together, like we're one force moving through the air. I'm breathless, sprinting like I did that night with Jack through the dark hallway my first week here, giving it everything I have.

Amanda's still ahead, and I can just make out how good she and Ciara are at staying together. But then Ciara stumbles, and their teammate doesn't realize quickly enough that she's dropped behind. He surges at least three feet forward before Amanda grabs his arm. But by then, Sturtevant is already yelling: "Moore! Washington! Goldberg! Disqualified!"

It only makes me sprint faster. The group on our other side is slowing, and everyone else seems to be stopping and starting to stay together, but Jack, Joni, and I are flying. In the last ten yards we gain even more distance as our shoes squeak over the hardwood floor. We cross the finish line and Joni lets out a cry of victory. I whirl around. There's no one at the finish line yet. We won. And we stayed together. And—

"Brooks! Murphy! Wattson!"

I turn to see Sturtevant, standing stock-still, staring at us. I can't make out the expression on her face. Is she disqualifying us?

She blows her whistle and the gym goes quiet. Even the cadets who got disqualified halfway through the race stand at attention.

Sturtevant turns away from us to face the majority of the student body. "I hope you all witnessed that effort," she says plainly. "Because that was what I was asking for. Well done, cadets."

She turns to walk away, but then Jack says, "Excuse me, Lt. Sturtevant?"

Sturtevant spins on her heel to face him.

"It was Private Brooks," he says, his breath coming faster. "It was her plan."

Sturtevant nods quickly. "I thought so," she says, and my entire body buzzes with happiness. She knew it was me!

I did it. *We* did it. I turn to Jack and Joni to see both of their hands raised, waiting for me to high-five them. I do, realizing I've never high-fived anyone for an athletic accomplishment in my entire life.

"Well done, private," Jack says, the happiness in his voice like fresh air and true friendship. I reach up to his hand with mine and slip my fingers through his.

"Take ten, cadets!" Sturtevant calls out. She makes her way over to O'Neil and the other two TACs. There's a shuffle in the gym as the rest of the students start chattering excitedly. Everyone's so on edge, you can feel it running through the gym like a current. I can't believe we're about to find out who made it!

"That plan was killer," Joni says, and Jack nods his agreement. "I seriously think there's a chance you make War Games." She and Jack exchange a glance.

I try to act like it's no big deal, like it's not everything I've been wanting. I've been telling myself over and over not to get my hopes up, but it's useless.

Jack leans back on his heels. "I think Joni's right," he says. His voice is soft but his eyes are like fire as he stares at me. I know he wants this for me, too, and I go warm

275

beneath his gaze. His fiery stare, plus the thought of making War Games, makes me feel so awake and alive I can hardly bear it. "Maybe," I say with a smile, trying to think confidently: another thing the Academy has taught me. Because if you don't make big plans for yourself, then who will?

I catch my breath as Jack and Joni recite a play-by-play of what they think the TACs are talking about. At one point Sturtevant looks over at me, then starts talking heatedly with O'Neil and the other two TACs. I don't say it out loud, but I'm pretty sure Sturtevant's arguing on my behalf. I can't explain it, but I can feel it: there's something she sees in me that she thinks is worth nurturing. No matter how strict she is with me, I know that's at the root of it. It makes it easier to suffer through her discipline lectures when I remember that.

So much has happened since I got here and became a part of something bigger than me. I think about how hard the physical training is, and about how many papers I've had to write this semester, and how the Academy is going to drill responsibility and leadership into my fashion-wired brain no matter what. I think about what it's felt like to become Joni's friend, and then, of course, I think about Jack, and my heart squeezes with everything this place makes me feel.

Back home, no one paid too much attention (besides my parents) and it was comfortable—it made it easy to hide out and just do my own thing. But here I realize I have a responsibility to do the right thing—not just for me, but for all of us. The Academy taught me we're all in this together.

Joni, Jack, and I are quiet while Sturtevant, O'Neil, and two other TACs heatedly discuss our fates. What else is there to say?

"Attention, cadets!" Sturtevant calls out. "This piece of paper holds your War Games final rankings. Congratulations to the top fifty percent of cadets who have made the Academy's one hundred and tenth annual War Games."

I bring my heels together and my elbows just slightly behind my back, fists curled at my sides. I glance over at Jack and see how proud he looks standing at attention.

"You ready?" he asks me, his dark eyes clear and bright.

I glance up to the American flag silhouetted against a window, showing a crisp blue spring sky.

I straighten my shoulders and smile up at him. "I am."

ACKNOWLEDGMENTS

[TK]